A CHILL RAN DOWN HER SPINE . . .

. . . with the realization that she was looking at an empty coffin.

Was it for her? Were there other coffins in there? Final resting places for naïve women who had wandered into Wolfram Castle, never to be seen or heard from again?

A sob rose in her throat as the door of her hiding place opened and Drake stepped into the room.

"Elena. Elena!" He stroked her hair, hoping to calm her. "You are safe now."

She stared up at him, wide-eyed and fearful. "Is it . . . is it . . . for me?"

"What? No, of course not."

"Then . . . why?"

He ran a hand through his hair, wondering how to explain.

When he didn't immediately reply, her brow furrowed. "You're not sick, are you?"

He laughed softly as he sat down beside her. "No, I am not sick."

"Then why . . . ?"

"It has been in there for centuries. Are you not curious about what those men wanted?"

"I know what they wanted." She wrapped her arms around her middle. "Me."

Books by Amanda Ashley

BOUND BY BLOOD

BOUND BY NIGHT

DEAD PERFECT

DEAD SEXY

DESIRE AFTER DARK

EVERLASTING DESIRE

EVERLASTING KISS

IMMORTAL SINS

NIGHT'S KISS

NIGHT'S MASTER

NIGHT'S PLEASURE

NIGHT'S TOUCH

A WHISPER OF ETERNITY

Bound
By Night

AMANDA ASHLEY

ZEBRA BOOKS
KENSINGTON PUBLISHING CORP.

ZEBRA BOOKS are published by

Kensington Publishing Corp.
119 West 40th Street
New York, NY 10018

ISBN-13: 978-1-61129-945-8

Printed in the United States of America

To Kathy Jund
First, a reader
Now, a friend

"In Dreams"

When the cold of winter comes
starless night will cover day
In the veiling of the sun
we will walk
in bitter rain

But in dreams
I hear your name
And in dreams
we will meet
again

When the sea and mountains fall
and we come to end of days
in the dark I hear a call
I will go there
and back
again.

—CORY MELONI

Prologue

His favorite lair was in the remains of a castle that had been built only a few years before he had been turned. He came back every thirty years or so, whenever the noise and the smell and the busyness of modern life became more than he could bear. He much preferred the life he had once known, before the advent of cell phones and iPods, a time when life had been slower, simpler. There had been a beauty to those days long gone, a grace that was missing now. An innocence that could not be restored, and was sorely missed.

But Wolfram Castle remained, exactly the same as it had always been. It was an impressive structure, rectangular with round turrets at three corners and a high, arched entrance. Battlements edged the flat roof. A barbican surrounded the building. The single entrance, flanked by two towers, faced the rising sun. Stone steps, many of them broken, led to the imposing entrance. The outbuildings, save for a large stable in sore need of a new roof, had been destroyed long since.

The ground floor of the castle housed the kitchen and storerooms; the main hall occupied the first floor, along with several smaller rooms, including a garderobe and a bathing chamber, as well as quarters in the rear that had once housed the servants. The chambers on the upper floor had been used exclusively by the Wolfram family.

Drake had purchased the castle and the surrounding acreage from Thomas Wolfram, the last of the Wolfram line, over four hundred years ago. In this day of malls and superstores and housing tracts, holding on to the land had been no easy task, but a good lawyer, and a bit of supernatural magic, had ensured that the castle, the ground it sat on, and the meadow below, would be his as long as he lived.

Standing in the pouring rain, Drake ran his hand over one of the ancient walls. Even though the castle was inanimate, he felt a kinship with it, for they had both endured much in the course of their long existence.

He had survived angry villagers eager to burn him alive; the king's guards, who had desired his head on a pike; pious minions of the Church who had hoped to redeem his soul before they drove a sharp wooden stake through his heart; mercenaries who wanted to sell vials of his blood to the highest bidder.

The castle had been ravaged by fire and flood, pummeled by rain and hail, struck by lightning, buried in an avalanche, and yet both he and the castle remained, still strong and nearly indestructible.

On rare occasions, he had thought of tearing the place down and building something more contemporary, but it had been a favorite retreat of his for centuries. Destroying the castle would be like destroying a part of himself.

He grunted softly. Maybe ending his existence wouldn't be such a bad idea. Perhaps he would find peace in true death. He might even find forgiveness. At the least, he would find an end to his hellish thirst, to the loneliness that could never be assuaged by brief encounters with nameless women. An end to watching the rest of the world change and develop while he remained forever the same. Best of all, it would put an end to what was expected of him.

He shook all thought of self-destruction away. Suicide was a cowardly thing to do. Perhaps it was time to go to ground, to rest for a hundred years or so. When he awoke, the times would have changed. There would be new things to see, to learn, a whole new world to explore.

He gazed into the distance. Dark clouds hovered low in the sky, spitting rain and lightning. There was little to see in this part of the country save for the castle, and a small township at the foot of the mountain. A movie company had used the town as the backdrop for a horror film that had, to everyone's surprise, become a worldwide phenomenon. Since then, tourists had come from all over the world to take pictures and buy souvenirs and pretend, for a day or two, that they were part of that fictional world.

He shook his head. He had little interest in movies, but the tourists who wandered throughout Romania looking for Dracula made for easy pickings. The rain would keep most of them inside on a night like this, but there were always an adventurous few who were willing to brave the elements in search of excitement.

He smiled inwardly as the hunger rose up within him, and with it, the urge to hunt. Any tourists out looking for a thrill tonight would find more than they bargained for.

Chapter 1

Elena Knightsbridge paused outside the back door, her gaze drawn to the gray stone castle at the top of the hill. No one knew exactly how old the castle was, only that it has been passed down from one generation to another. No one had lived there for as long as Elena could remember. From time to time, developers had come, hoping to buy the land, tear down the castle, and build a Dracula-style theme park, but the land was held in perpetuity for the heirs of a man no one in town had ever seen.

There were those who said Wolfram Castle was haunted, that ghosts wandered the long dark halls. There were other tales as well, scary stories whispered in the dark of the night, of witches and warlocks, of demons and dragons.

There were other stories, too, of young women who had been lured into the castle in days gone by, never to be seen or heard from again. Elena's uncle, Tavian Dinescu, insisted that stories of devil worship and witchcraft were a bunch of nonsense, and that the girls who had supposedly disappeared had been employed at the castle as hired help. Whether any or all of the old stories were true or not, there was something about the castle that repelled visitors.

With a shake of her head, Elena bent over the wicker

laundry basket and began hanging the clothes on the line. A haunted castle was nothing compared to the hell her life had become since her parents were killed in a car accident seven years ago, when she was twelve, and she had been sent from Colorado to this nothing little town in Transylvania to live with her father's sister, Catalena, Catalena's husband, Tavian, and their daughter, Jenica, who was a few years older than Elena. Fortunately, communicating with her cousin hadn't been a problem, since Elena's parents had often spoken Romanian at home.

Life hadn't been too bad when her aunt was alive, but Catalena had passed away some years ago, and Jenica had recently run off with a boy from the next town.

Elena shuddered when she thought of her uncle, with his cropped brown hair, thick brown mustache, and close-set gray eyes.

Uncle Tavian was such a skinflint, he refused to buy a new dryer. Times were hard, he said. They didn't have money for silly things like dryers. He had money for whiskey, though. She supposed, if the washing machine broke, she would find herself pounding the laundry on the rocks in the river. Her workload had doubled since her aunt passed away and Jenica had eloped.

Caring for the house, doing the washing and the cooking and the mending, as well as the shopping left little time for anything else. The only bright spot was that her uncle, who was now the chief of police, was rarely home these days. Truly a blessing. He had made her uncomfortable for as long as she could remember. She hated the way he called her "my little cabbage," the way he smiled at her, the way he found excuses to touch her.

He had grown bolder since Jenica ran off with one of the neighbor boys. Her uncle's touches had become more intimate, and more frequent. It was all Elena could do not to cringe when he caressed her hair or stroked her cheek. His conversation was laced with double entendres. Lately, Elena wanted to hide whenever he was in the house. The way he looked at her, like a hungry wolf contemplating its next meal, made her skin crawl. One night, during dinner, he had reminded her that he was her uncle by marriage and not by blood.

Last night, she had awakened to find him standing by her bed, staring down at her. Though she had no experience with men, every instinct she possessed had warned her that she was in danger. She had kept very still, feigning sleep, until, after what seemed like hours, he tiptoed out of her bedroom.

Jenica had whispered about abuses by her father, confiding that, since her mother died, he had come into her room many times. She claimed that he had done things so vile she couldn't repeat them. Elena had been horrified to learn that her uncle had raped her cousin, not once, but many times. She'd always thought that kind of thing only happened to people you didn't know. But that was only part of it. Jenica had told her that, before Elena's arrival, he had often locked her in the cellar for days at a time.

Both girls were terrified of him. Elena hadn't been surprised when her cousin ran away from home. She herself had considered it on more than one occasion.

Returning to the house, Elena looked out the window, a shiver of unease snaking down her spine when she saw her uncle staggering up the street.

She needed to get away from here, but where could she go? Walking to Brasov was out of the question. It was many miles away, on the other side of the mountain. She had no car, no cash, no one she could turn to for help.

* * *

Elena was acutely aware of her uncle's repeated glances in her direction at dinner that night. His advances had become more blatant with every passing day. Though the table was large, he insisted she sit close beside him. She flinched when his arm brushed against hers, gagged at the smell of his whiskey-sour breath.

"How old are you now, Elena?" he asked.

"Almost twenty."

"Far past the time when a young woman should be wed. Do none of the young men in town appeal to you?"

"No, sir."

He nodded, looking pleased, and then thoughtful. "Perhaps you would prefer an older man? One with experience, if you know what I mean?"

She swallowed hard, her heart pounding. "No, sir." She recoiled from the look in his eyes as he leaned closer toward her.

"It's been five months since Jenica ran off. It isn't proper for the two of us to continue living together without a chaperone." He laughed, a mean, ugly sound. "People might get the wrong idea."

Elena clenched her hands in her lap, sorely afraid she knew what was coming, and dreading it.

"I think we should marry." He nodded, as though pleased with the idea. "I need an heir, someone to carry on the family name."

She stared at him, mute with horror at the idea of sharing his bed.

Smiling, he took hold of her arm and drew her closer. "You'd give me a son, wouldn't you?"

She tried to pull away, but he tightened his grip on her arm, his pudgy fingers digging into her skin to hold her fast. And then he leaned forward and kissed her.

Eyes wide with revulsion, she fought down the urge to vomit as his tongue plunged deep into her mouth.

"Perhaps tonight," he said, "I will take you down to the cellar."

The cellar. Sheer terror engulfed her. Jenica had told her about the cellar.

Tonight, she thought when he released her. Tonight she would make her escape. The castle on the hill was a good distance away. Old and run-down, with no electricity or modern conveniences, it would be the last place anyone would think to look for her—if she could just find the courage needed to go inside.

Better to face the ancient ghosts in Wolfram Castle, Elena thought as she got ready for bed that night, than to endure another moment in her uncle's presence.

It was well after midnight when she tiptoed into the kitchen, carefully avoiding the squeaky board in the floor. Since she hadn't been shopping in almost a week, there was little in the refrigerator, but waiting another day was out of the question. She dropped a few apples and a doughnut into a sack; then, holding her breath, she opened the back door as quietly as possible and slipped outside.

She paused a moment, suddenly unsure. Was she doing the right thing? How would she survive on her own? Maybe she should wait. If she was lucky, she might find someone to take her to Brasov. But she didn't have the luxury of waiting, not with Uncle Tavian talking about marriage. The idea of sharing his bed, of having his hands pawing her, his mouth on hers, lent wings to her feet and she ran away from the house and into the darkness.

It seemed as if the night closed in around her as she hurried up the hill toward Wolfram Castle. She was halfway there before it occurred to her to wonder if she would even be able to get inside. For all she knew, the place was locked up tighter than the bank in town.

A sudden, wayward wind lifted the hair from her shoulders and sent a flurry of dry leaves skittering across her path.

Dark clouds gathered overhead, shutting out both moon and stars.

The wind grew colder, stronger, causing the trees to moan as they swayed back and forth. The tall grass bent as if in supplication to the force of the wind as it howled across the land.

An omen? Elena wondered, shivering. She lowered her head and drew her coat closer around her shoulders as thunder rumbled overhead.

Continuing on, she realized the castle was a lot farther away than it looked. She paused several times to catch her breath, wondering if she would ever make it to the top of the hill.

The clouds released their burden just as she reached the castle door.

Taking a deep breath, she reached for the latch, blew out a sigh of relief when, with a creak loud enough to wake the dead, the heavy wooden door swung open.

Hurrying inside, she quickly closed the door, shutting out the wind and the rain, and then stood there, her heart pounding with the realization that it was pitch black inside and that she had forgotten to bring a flashlight. But at least she was away from her uncle.

With one hand outstretched, she moved across the floor, a soft cry of pain rising in her throat when she bumped into something. Exploring with her free hand, she discovered it was a high-backed sofa.

It was late and she was tired. She dropped her food sack on the floor, then stretched out on the sofa, her coat spread over her. No matter what tomorrow held, she was safe from her uncle's repulsive advances tonight.

* * *

Drake paused when he reached the castle door, his preternatural senses alerting him to the fact that there was a human female inside. A human who was either very brave, he thought with a wry grin, or very foolish. The castle possessed a dark aura that kept most people at bay. Few dared to come here in the light of day; no one came here after sunset. There was little need to lock the door; those who ventured inside never stayed long. And yet, the fact remained, there was a woman in the castle.

Materializing inside the great hall, Drake moved unerringly toward the high-backed damask sofa in front of the hearth, his nostrils filling with the combined scents of lavender soap, peppermint toothpaste, and salty perspiration tinged with fear.

And over all, the intoxicating scent of woman.

He stared down at the sleeping female. She was a comely lass, with suntanned skin, delicately arched black brows, and a mass of long ebony hair that fell in soft waves over the arm of the sofa and down her slight shoulders.

Pretty, yes, he mused with a frown. But who the devil was she and what the bloody hell was she doing here?

He considered tossing her out on her lovely arse.

He considered leaving her on the sofa.

In the end, he tossed her plain brown coat aside, then scooped her into his arms.

She stirred as he started up the winding stone staircase. Her eyelids fluttered open, revealing a pair of velvet brown eyes. Before she could scream, he trapped her gaze with his. Summoning his preternatural power, he lulled her back to sleep.

With a shake of his head, Drake continued up the stairs and into the lord's chamber. After removing her T-shirt, khaki shorts, and shoes, he tucked her under the thick blankets in the big four-poster bed. He glanced at the hearth and a fire sprang to life. He needed neither the light nor the warmth; he could see perfectly fine in the dark, was impervious to the cold. But there was a chance the woman would awaken during the night.

He gazed down at her for several long moments, admiring the unblemished smoothness of her skin, the sweep of long sooty lashes against her cheeks, the pale pink of her lips. Unable to resist, he lifted a lock of her hair. Thick and silky soft, it curled around his fingers as though each strand had a life of its own.

He felt the first stirrings of desire as he inhaled the fragrance of warm fresh blood flowing sweetly through her veins.

Sitting on the edge of the mattress, he gathered her into his arms, then lowered his head to the curve of her throat. He tasted her with his tongue and then with his teeth.

She was incredibly sweet.

Having satisfied his curiosity and his thirst, he returned to the main hall. After pouring himself a glass of wine, he stretched out on the sofa and gazed onto the hearth. In spite of the distance between himself and the girl, he could hear the steady beat of her heart. What had brought her here? And what was he going to do with her?

He considered the possibilities until dawn, then headed for the lair hidden behind one of the tapestries in the great hall.

He smiled as he drifted into oblivion. For the first time in centuries, he had something to look forward to when darkness again covered the land.

Chapter 2

Tavian Dinescu frowned when he entered the dining room. The table had not been laid. His breakfast tea was not at his place, nor was his newspaper. There was no fire in the hearth, no noise or scent of food coming from the kitchen.

And no Elena standing at the stove.

Where was that girl?

Thinking perhaps she had overslept, he went down the hall to her room and knocked lightly on the door. "Elena?"

When there was no answer, he rapped again, harder this time. And when there was still no reply, he opened the door and stepped into the room. The bed, neatly made, was empty.

Moving into the room, he went through the dresser drawers, peered into the closet. As far as he could tell, all of her clothes were there, so she couldn't have gone far, but the question remained: Where was she?

He checked the other rooms, then went outside, but she was nowhere to be found.

Rubbing a thoughtful hand over his jaw, he returned to the house. Had she run off with one of the local boys? That seemed unlikely. Just last night, he had asked if she had taken a liking to any of the young studs and her reply had been a resounding "no."

Hunger rumbled in his stomach. Not one to prepare his own meals, Tavian put on his coat and left the house. He would breakfast in town and then he would ask if anyone had seen Elena. Though he was affluent, she was not. She had nothing to call her own, only what he had given her.

Tavian was a man who knew what he wanted, and he wanted Elena for his bride. And so it would be. She was but a woman and his ward. Like it or not, she would do as he commanded or suffer the consequences.

Chapter 3

Cocooned in blankets, Elena woke slowly. She experienced a moment of panic when she rolled over and realized she was no longer lying on the sofa where she had fallen asleep.

Bolting upright, she rubbed the sleep from her eyes. Where was she? Had her uncle found her and carried her back home? But no. She had never been in a room like this before. Unlike her bedroom at home, this one was large and rectangular, the whitewashed stone walls bare save for one large painting of a black knight astride a prancing white horse. Heavy burgundy velvet draperies that matched the bedspread hung at the windows. Thick rugs covered the floor. A cheerful fire blazed in the hearth across from the bed.

Frowning, she brushed a lock of hair from her forehead. Was she still in the castle? And if so, who had put her to bed?

She blinked as a hazy memory surfaced. Or had she only imagined being carried up a winding staircase by a man with long, dark hair and mesmerizing blue eyes?

When her stomach growled, she slid her legs over the edge of the mattress and stood, only then realizing that whoever had carried her up the stairs had undressed her down to her underwear. She found her khaki shorts and T-shirt at the foot of the bed. Dressing quickly, she tugged a blanket around her shoulders to turn away the chill.

Barefooted, she tiptoed quietly across the floor, opened the heavy wooden door, then glanced left and right before stepping into the corridor. She paused a moment, listening, before she made her way cautiously down the stairs and stepped into a large, high-ceilinged room. The same one where she had fallen asleep?

She thought it must be the castle's main hall. Weak sunlight filtered down from the high, narrow, slitted windows. A cheery fire snapped and crackled in the huge stone hearth. A gray cat, quite the largest one she had ever seen, lay stretched out on the furry rug in front of the fireplace. It stared up at her through curious, bright yellow eyes, its long tail slowly swishing back and forth.

Elena regarded the animal apprehensively for several moments. She had been leery of the creatures ever since she was a little girl and her grandmother's tom had scratched her cheeks.

When she was certain the beast wasn't going to attack her, she walked toward the sofa, intent on rooting around in her sack for one of the apples and the doughnut she had brought with her, only to be sidetracked when she noticed a covered tray, a carafe of some kind—was it actually a medieval flagon?—and a goblet, all of which looked like they were made of gold, sitting on a large, rough-hewn trestle table against the far wall. There was a single plate, which also appeared to be made of gold.

Hurrying across the floor, she lifted the cover of the tray to find a loaf of freshly baked bread, several thick slices of roast beef and cheese, a bowl of strawberries, and two blueberry muffins, as well as packets of honey, sugar, and cream.

Elena worried her lower lip between her teeth. Was this repast meant for her? Who could have brought it? No one knew she was here, and there didn't seem to be anyone else in the castle. But surely the cat belonged to someone.

When her stomach growled again, she put her doubts away, dropped the blanket on the floor, and sat at the table. A rolled linen napkin held a gold-plated knife and fork. The flagon contained wine, stronger and sweeter than anything she had ever tasted.

Nibbling on one of the muffins, she wondered again who had provided the meal, and where that person was now. Maybe the castle really was haunted, she thought with a grin. Maybe a friendly ghost had generously provided the meal.

Or had it been the mysterious man who had carried her up the stairs? She wondered again if he had been real, or merely a figment of her imagination. Probably the latter, she thought, since she had never seen a man as tall and devastatingly handsome as that except in her dreams.

Her gaze darted around the room as she ate. Large tapestries hung on the walls. Most of them depicted hunting scenes—a wolf chasing a deer, a trio of men bringing down a wild boar, a pack of wild dogs running after a silver fox. The head of a large stag was mounted over an enormous stone fireplace. Wrought-iron wall sconces held fat candles covered with a fine layer of dust. Besides the high-backed sofa where she had fallen asleep, there were several other couches, chairs, tables, and benches randomly situated around the room.

She washed down the last of the meat and cheese with a second glass of wine and licked her lips. Sated, and warm inside and out, she propped her elbows on the table, cupped her chin in her hands, and closed her eyes. She wasn't used to drinking strong wine. It left her feeling relaxed and drowsy. She needed to think of what to do next. She had planned to stay here for a few days but that no longer seemed wise, not if the mysterious man was real rather than a figment of one of her daydreams. Did she dare linger until after dark? But if she left here, where would she go?

Growing sleepier by the minute, she stood up, then grabbed the back of the chair to keep her balance. Good grief, was she drunk? Carefully placing one foot in front of the other, she made her way back up to the bedroom and crawled under the covers.

She was asleep as soon as her head hit the pillow.

Elena woke with a start to find a man standing beside the bed. One look at his face and she knew he was the man who had carried her up the stairs—she would never forget those eyes. Just as she knew that taking refuge here had been a terrible, perhaps fatal, mistake. She had no doubt whatsoever that he was the owner of Wolfram Castle.

Tall and broad-shouldered, he wore a loose-fitting white shirt that was open at the throat, revealing a long, crooked scar that ran down the right side of his neck. Black jeans and well-polished boots completed his attire. His hair was thick and black, his brows straight above eyes as dark blue and restless as a stormy sky. His lips were finely shaped, with a hint of cruelty; his jaw firm and square and stubborn. But it was the almost tangible aura of danger emanating from him that made her mouth go dry. This was a man to be reckoned with. She could easily imagine him at the helm of a pirate ship, or leading a medieval army into battle.

She stared at him, too frightened to speak, but even had she found her voice, what could she say? She had entered his home uninvited, eaten food no doubt meant for him, slept in his bed. A rush of heat enflamed her cheeks. She was still in his bed.

"Who are you?" His voice was as deep and mesmerizing as his eyes.

Feeling as though he was looking right through her, she pulled the blanket closer, swallowed once, twice, as she tried to find her voice, then stammered, "E-Elena."

"What are you doing here?"

"I . . . I ran away." She clutched the covers tighter, intimidated by his unblinking gaze. "From my uncle."

"Who is your uncle?"

Elena hesitated, wondering if she should tell him the truth. But even as she considered lying, she felt the words being drawn out of her. "Tavian Dinescu."

"The chief of police?"

"Yes."

He crossed his arms over his chest, his eyes narrowing. "Why did you run away?"

"My uncle . . . he wants me to . . . to marry him." She blinked up at him in confusion. Why was she telling him these things? "And give him an heir."

Drake grunted softly. He had seen Dinescu—a big bull of a man if ever there was one, and old enough to be the girl's father. Little wonder she had run away. "Why did you come here?"

"I had nowhere else to go, and I . . . I thought the castle was empty. I didn't mean to eat your dinner, but I was so hungry, and it looked so much better than what I brought . . . and . . ." She realized she was babbling and closed her mouth.

Drake shoved his hands into the pockets of his jeans. "The food and wine were for you."

"But . . . I . . . Thank you, Mr. . . . ?"

"Just Drake." He grinned faintly. She had fed him. It had only been right that he offer her nourishment in return.

She sat up, clutching the blankets to her chest. "I'll be going now."

"No need."

She scrambled off the bed, panic engulfing her. Did he mean to keep her here against her will? Had she jumped out of the frying pan and into the fire? For all she knew, he could be a rapist or a mass murderer.

"I've been trouble enough," she said quickly, and started for the door, only to get her feet tangled in the blankets.

He caught her as she stumbled forward, one long arm curling around her waist, drawing her body against his.

Elena stared up at him, her heartbeat thundering in her ears. She had never been held so tightly before, never been in a man's arms like this. She was instantly aware of the hard length of his body pressed intimately against hers, of his big hand splayed over the small of her back, of just how tall and broad he was. She had no doubt he could break her in two with no trouble at all.

She gazed up into his eyes—eyes so dark a blue they were very nearly black. Fear mingled with uncertainty as he continued to hold her close, his hand sliding lazily up and down her spine. And then he lowered his head and covered her mouth with his.

This man's kiss was nothing like her uncle's. A delicious warmth spread through every inch of her, draining the strength from her legs, filling her with a sweet lethargy, and an unexpected yearning to sink into his embrace and never leave. She inhaled and his scent filled her nostrils. For a moment, she tried to place it, but it was an earthy, musky scent like nothing she had experienced before. Like everything else about him, it was compelling.

His lips moved over hers, slowly exploring their taste and texture, nibbling at the corners.

Feeling suddenly light-headed, Elena grasped his shoulders. A soft moan rose in her throat as she swayed against him. And then his tongue was sliding over her lips, probing gently. It sent a shaft of heat straight to the core of her being and she moaned again. She had intended it to be a cry of protest so he would release her. Instead, he drew her closer, his hand delving into her hair to cup the back of her head as he kissed her again, harder, deeper, until she wasn't aware of anything but his mouth on hers, the rapid beating of her heart, the heat spreading through her, pooling low in the depths of her being.

What was he doing to her? She had never felt like this before, never dreamed a man's kisses could be so intoxicating.

If he hadn't been holding her so tightly, she was certain she would have collapsed at his feet when he took his mouth from hers. Breathless, she could only stare up at him.

"Like I said, there is no need for you to go."

She blinked at him.

"You will be safe here."

Elena nodded. "Safe." She lifted her fingers to her lips as she watched him stride out the door, and wondered if she would ever feel safe again.

The next day, Elena awoke fully intending to leave the castle, but somehow she couldn't summon the will to do so. Sitting up, she noticed three dresses spread across the foot of the bed, along with four pairs of jeans, several T-shirts and sweaters in a rainbow of colors, a small pile of modest underwear, and six pairs of socks.

Leaning forward, she ran her hands over the dresses. She rarely wore anything but jeans, shorts, and T-shirts. She certainly didn't wear dresses made of silk, fancy or plain.

Rising, she picked one up and held it in front of her. It

was sky blue and as soft as . . . silk. It could only have come from Drake, but why would he buy her clothes? And shoes, she thought, noting a pair of sandals and a pair of running shoes on the floor beside her sneakers.

Suddenly curious to try on the blue silk, she took off the clothes she had slept in, pulled the dress over her head, and smoothed it over her hips. It fit as though it had been made for her, which begged the question, how had he known her size?

She pondered that for several minutes; then, eager to see how she looked in the blue silk, she glanced around the room, only then noticing there wasn't a mirror in sight.

She was wondering if she might find one elsewhere in the castle when the big gray cat padded into the room. It leaped effortlessly onto the bed, then sat there, head cocked to one side, watching her.

She had the oddest feeling that it was admiring her.

With a shake of her head, Elena changed into a pair of jeans and a purple T-shirt and went downstairs in search of something to eat. Another feast awaited her in the main hall—fresh fruit and a square of cheese, a loaf of bread still warm from the oven, a pot of honey butter and another of jelly, a flagon of wine. She poured herself a glass, wishing for coffee instead.

It had been in Elena's mind to leave the castle before nightfall, but it occurred to her that leaving would be foolish. In spite of his fearsome appearance, Drake didn't seem to mean her any harm. He had provided her with food, gifted her with a wardrobe . . . She frowned. Was she being naïve, thinking he didn't expect anything in return for his generosity? Would it be rude to ask what his motives were? Better rude than foolish, she decided. She could only think of one thing he would want from her, and she wasn't about to part with that, not for all the silk dresses in the county.

She gasped, startled, when the cat jumped up on the table. "Here, now," Elena said, making a shooing motion with her hand. "Get down."

The cat made no move to leave. Instead, it began washing its face.

"Impudent beast," she muttered. "Why aren't you out catching mice and rats or something?"

The cat didn't answer, of course, but stared at her through unblinking yellow eyes. And then, with a flick of its tail, it jumped lightly to the floor and left the room.

Elena was still sitting at the table, goblet in hand, trying to marshal her thoughts, when she heard a noise behind her. She glanced over her shoulder, thinking perhaps Drake had entered the room. Seeing no one in the doorway, she glanced down, and let out a shriek. A dead rat lay on the floor. Behind it, the cat sat watching her.

Startled, Elena dropped the goblet. It hit the floor with a loud crash.

Tail twitching, the cat stared up at her, a feline grin on its face.

"Get out of here!" Elena exclaimed. "And take that disgusting thing with you."

The cat looked at her for a moment, then snatched the rat up by its tail and padded out of the hall.

With a huff of annoyance, Elena picked the goblet up off the floor and set it on the table. There was something definitely strange about that cat.

She sat there a moment; then, driven by boredom and a growing sense of curiosity, she decided to explore the rest of the castle.

The kitchen was one flight down. Glancing around, she noted floor-to-ceiling cupboards along the back wall. A fireplace with a spit and an old-fashioned oven took up most of another wall. A large square table hewn of oak stood in the middle of the room. An open door led to a storeroom that held a number of bins and baskets, all of which were empty.

Leaving the kitchen, she climbed the stairs to the second floor. Walking down the corridor, she saw that there were other, smaller bedrooms besides the chamber she had slept in. For the lord of the keep's children, she supposed. There was no furniture in any of these rooms, no rugs on the floors, no pictures or tapestries on the walls. A window in the last room on the left provided an excellent view of the forest that stretched away behind the castle. A thin ribbon of blue was visible between a copse of trees. A river, perhaps? Or a lake.

Moving down the hall to the room she had slept in, Elena peered out one of the tall, leaded windows. From here, she could see the whole town spread far below. And there, on the narrow path leading up to the castle, she saw two men in uniform, men who worked for her uncle. A sudden shiver ran down her spine and she knew, knew without doubt, that they were coming here to look for her.

She needed a place to hide, but where?

Frantic, she gazed around the room. Useless to hide in the armoire or in the big trunk at the foot of the bed. Searchers were sure to look inside. The other bedrooms were empty. Nowhere to hide there.

She was fighting back tears of panic when Drake stepped into the room. "What is it that distresses you?" He glanced around, wondering if a spider or some other unwelcome creature had frightened her. But he saw no cause for alarm.

"My uncle!" She waved a hand toward the window. "He's sending his men up here to look for me. I just know it."

Drake crossed to the window. He stood there a moment, looking down, then turned to face her. "Come with me."

Heart pounding, Elena followed him down the stairs to the main floor. Was he going to turn her over to her uncle?

"I don't want to go back home," she said, hurrying to catch up with him. "Please, don't send me. . . ."

He drew back a corner of the tapestry that covered a portion of the west wall. "In here," he said.

Elena stared at the whitewashed wall. In where?

His hand moved over the rough stone. With a low rumble, a narrow opening appeared as if by magic.

Elena shook her head as she peered into the dark abyss. Surely he didn't expect her to go in there. Did he?

"Your uncle's men are here," Drake said.

The words had scarcely left his mouth when she heard the clang of a bell announcing someone was at the door.

Before she could protest, Drake gave her a push. Unable to recover her balance, Elena stumbled inside. She choked back a cry when the opening closed behind her, leaving her in total darkness. She told herself there was nothing to be afraid of. It would only be for a moment. Drake would send her uncle's men away and then he would come for her.

But the moments became minutes. How long was he going to leave her in there? What if he wasn't going to let her out again?

She told herself she was worrying needlessly. He was hiding her to protect her from her uncle.

She sat down on the floor, her knees drawn to her chest. "Nothing to fear," she murmured, hoping to reassure herself. "Nothing to fear."

Panic quickly overcame her determination to stay calm. It was suddenly hard to breathe. Was the room getting smaller? Darker? She had to get out of here. She scrambled to her feet. Where was the door? She had to find the door. In the pitch blackness, she couldn't see her hand in front of her face.

She had to find a way out. With her arms outstretched,

she moved forward until she found a wall, then inched along it, searching for the entrance.

A grunt of pain rose in her throat when she bumped into something. She ran her hands over the object. It was long and made of wood. A box of some kind. Was she in a storeroom? Her questing fingers continued their exploration and she found a seam in the wood. Lifting the lid, she paused a moment, then reached inside the box. An oblong box lined with satin.

A chill ran down her spine with the realization that it was an empty coffin.

Was it for her? Were there other coffins in there? Final resting places for naïve women who had wandered into Wolfram Castle, never to be seen or heard from again?

A sob rose in her throat as the door opened and Drake stepped into the room.

At first, Drake thought it was being in the dark for so long that had frightened Elena, and then he realized she was standing beside the open casket, a look of stark horror frozen on her face.

Rushing forward, he swept her into his arms, then carried her out of the room, pausing just long enough to activate the mechanism that closed the door. He elbowed past the tapestry, then carried her to the sofa in front of the hearth. When he was sure she was comfortable, he lit the fire.

"Elena. Elena!" He stroked her hair, hoping to calm her. "You are safe now."

She stared up at him, wide-eyed and fearful. "Is it . . . is it . . . for me?"

"What? No, of course not."

"Then . . . why?"

He ran a hand through his hair, wondering how to explain.

When he didn't immediately reply, her brow furrowed. "You're not sick, are you?"

He laughed softly as he sat down beside her. "No, I am not sick."

"Then why . . . ?"

"It has been in there for centuries. Are you not curious about what those men wanted?"

"I know what they wanted." She wrapped her arms around her middle. "Me."

Drake nodded.

"You're not going to take me back to him, are you?" she asked anxiously.

"No."

She knew a quick surge of relief, but it only lasted a moment. What was she going to do? She couldn't stay here indefinitely. To do so would mean going outside only after dark, when no one could see her, never walking along the river, never attending church again, or visiting with her friends. If she stayed, she would be no more than a prisoner in this castle. But at least she would be safe from her uncle.

And for now, that was reason enough to stay.

Chapter 4

"Well?" Tavian Dinescu glared at the two men standing on the other side of the desk. "Speak up!"

"She wasn't there," Vasili said, scuffling his feet.

"But it wasn't empty," Ivan added.

"What do you mean?" Dinescu demanded.

"There was a man," Ivan said. "Big fella. Scar down one side of his neck. Looked dangerous, if you ask me."

Dinescu frowned. He'd been unaware that anyone was currently living in the castle. "Who was it?"

"He didn't give his name," Vasili replied. "And I didn't ask."

Dinescu looked at Ivan. "What about you?"

Ivan shook his head. "Never seen him before. Hope I never see him again. There was something about him . . . something kind of spooky."

Dinescu looked at him disdainfully. "Spooky?"

Ivan shrugged.

Dinescu made a dismissive gesture with his hand. Had one of the heirs come to claim the place? It had been years since anyone had occupied the castle on the hill. How long had the fellow been there? No one had reported seeing anyone new in town. Perhaps he would look into it. As chief of police, he had every right to make sure that the person occupying Wolfram Castle had a right to be there. But he would look into that later. Right now, his main concern was finding his niece.

He glanced at Ivan and Vasili. "That'll be all."

Frowning, Dinescu watched the two men shuffle out of his office. Where the hell was Elena? His men had searched the entire town. He, himself, had questioned every man, woman, and child, but to no avail. No one had seen her.

He slammed his hand on the edge of the desk, an oath rising to his lips. Dammit. She couldn't have just vanished into thin air.

So, she had run away, in which case someone must have helped her, but who? Everyone else in the village was accounted for. Try as he might, he couldn't believe she had found the courage to run off on her own, yet there was no other answer. Where would she go? As far as he could tell, she hadn't taken anything with her, so she couldn't have gone far. He would find her, and when he did, he would make her pay.

Scowling, he paced back and forth, his anger growing. He had lusted after the girl since she was thirteen years old, patiently biding his time while he waited for her to grow up. He had discouraged the young men who had wanted to take her out. He frowned. Had she been meeting one of them behind his back? Someone from another town, perhaps? No, that was impossible.

Where had she gone?

He paused to stare out the front window. It had been a hard year for the townspeople. Tourism had been down due to a bad turn in the economy. Perhaps the offer of a sizable reward for information regarding her whereabouts would yield results.

Chapter 5

For Elena, the next few weeks passed like something in a fairy tale. For a girl who didn't believe in ghosts, goblins, or magic, she was beginning to think that Wolfram Castle was under some sort of enchantment. Or that she was.

Drake was definitely magical. Whenever he was near, she had to fight the urge to touch him, to go to him. When they were apart, she yearned for the sound of his voice. At night, he haunted her dreams. She told herself it was merely infatuation, that it would pass, that what she felt was gratitude because he was providing her with food and shelter.

The cat, which she had taken to calling Smoke, kept her company during the day. Elena had no idea where the mysterious Mr. Drake spent his days and when she asked, he merely shrugged and told her, firmly but politely, that it was none of her business.

With no one else to talk to, Elena often chatted with the cat. Strange as it seemed, there were times when she was absolutely certain that the creature understood every word she said. Odder still was the fact that the silly feline seemed to appear whenever she was feeling lonely. Even though she didn't like cats, she was grateful to have another living, breathing creature to keep her company in the drafty old castle.

When she complained to Drake that she needed something to do to occupy her time, he brought her a dozen of the latest paperback novels, a number of crossword puzzle books, drawing paper, pens, crayons, and markers.

When she complained she was growing tired of wine, he bought an ice chest and kept it stocked with cans of soda, iced tea, and lemonade, as well as fruit and milk. He also stocked the kitchen with snacks and other, nonperishable items.

Meals continued to appear morning and evening. When she asked where they came from, he told her he had an arrangement with one of the women in town.

Elena had never cared for cooking, but she loved baking and she spent a part of every day in the kitchen, learning how to bake in the ancient oven. Her first few endeavors ended up in the garbage, but eventually she learned to make a decent pie, and then turned her hand to cakes and cookies. And always, the ubiquitous cat looked on, a bored expression on its face.

Drake refused to eat anything she made, declaring that he preferred to take his meals in private, and that he had no taste for sweets.

He was gone every day and most of the nights, and felt no need to explain where he went. At first, being alone didn't bother her. She was an only child; back home in Colorado she had always been good at entertaining herself. But as the days passed, Elena began to long for more than just a cat for companionship. She wanted someone who would do more than just listen, someone with whom she could share thoughts and hopes and dreams. And so it was that she decided to stay up one night and wait for Drake's return.

She was staring into the flames in the hearth, the book

in her lap forgotten, when Drake suddenly appeared beside the sofa.

"I didn't hear you come in!" she exclaimed, one hand pressed to her rapidly beating heart.

"I thought you would be in bed." He removed his long black cloak and tossed it over the back of the sofa.

She stared up at him, struck anew by how tall and broad-shouldered he was. As usual, he wore black—boots, shirt, and pants. But it was his face that held her attention. He was incredibly beautiful for a man, with finely shaped lips, straight black brows, sculpted cheekbones. And those incredibly blue eyes. Looking at him made her want to touch him, to trace the curve of his lips, to sift her hand through his thick black hair, to explore the muscles flexing beneath his shirt.

He was looking at her oddly, one brow raised as if in amusement.

Elena curled her hands into fists and buried them in the folds of her skirt, her cheeks burning with embarrassment at her wayward thoughts. Beyond some exploratory kissing and necking in high school, she had never been intimate with a man, partly because her uncle had refused to let her date, and partly because she had seen what happened to one of her friends who ended up sixteen and pregnant. Elena had never wanted to have to decide whether to keep a baby born out of wedlock and try to raise it on her own, or to give it away and never see it again. Her friend Dorina had given her baby away and regretted it every day of her life.

Drake dropped onto the sofa across from her. Stretching out his long legs, he regarded her over his steepled fingers. "What are you doing up so late?"

"I was bored." Her gaze slid away from his. "And lonely."

Drake grunted softly. It hadn't occurred to him that she might be lonely. "Would you care to go for a walk?"

She looked at him, her eyes wide. "Do you mean it?"

"Of course."

She bounded to her feet, her heart racing with anticipation as she ran upstairs to change her shoes.

He was waiting for her by the front door when she returned. He opened it with a flourish and bowed her through.

Outside, she hesitated, not sure which way to go.

Drake made the decision for her. "This way."

He turned down a narrow, tree-lined path that led away from the castle toward the distant hills. It was a beautiful night. A new moon hung low in the sky. Stars glittered like millions of sparkling diamonds flung across the midnight sky by a careless hand. A faint breeze rustled the leaves of the oaks and chestnuts.

He was ever aware of the woman walking silently beside him, just as he was cognizant of her growing desire and the confusion it caused her. Young and untouched, she wasn't sure what to make of her feelings for him.

A shift in the wind carried the faint fragrance of her perfume. During the nights she had been with him, he had memorized the silky texture of her inky black hair, the softness of her petal pink lips, the delicate curve of her throat. But it was the scent of her blood that sang to him, a dulcet song that called to him like nothing else he had ever known. The taste of it lingered on his tongue long after he had sipped the crimson nectar that flowed warm and sweet through her veins.

He had tasted her several times in the nights she had been with him. Never more than a few sips at a time, to be sure, but a few sips of her blood was more satisfying than a pint of any other. With luck, he could keep her with him indefinitely.

He came to a halt when he reached the meadow nestled between a pair of low hills. The lake, located in the middle of the grassy expanse, gleamed like a sorcerer's dark glass in the moonlight.

"Oh!" Elena breathed, turning a slow circle. "It's lovely!"

Drake nodded.

"Does all this belong to you?"

"Indeed."

"Can we go down by the water?"

"If you wish."

With a smile, she hurried toward the lake, then paused as an owl swooped down out of the sky, coming to rest on a tree branch. In the light of the moon, she saw that it was a barn owl. They were beautiful birds, with their white, heart-shaped faces and golden buff-colored feathers. She took a step toward it, sighed with disappointment as it took wing, soaring effortlessly out of sight.

Continuing on, she made her way to the lake where a myriad of ferns and rushes grew along the shore. Night birds called to each other across the lake's expanse.

"It's so beautiful," Elena murmured. But it was more than beautiful. It was an enchanted place, filled with wonder. A magical place where anything might happen, where dreams might come true. Had she been a princess in a fairy tale, she would have met her handsome prince here, by the lake, and he would have carried her away to his castle.

She glanced quickly at Drake. He had a castle. Was he a prince in disguise? The thought made her smile.

Pausing at the lake's edge, she sank down on her knees and leaned forward, her fingers trailing lightly back and forth in the water, which felt refreshingly cool.

She was thinking how daring it would be to shed her clothes and underwear and slip into the cool, clear water, when Drake knelt beside her. The idea of swimming in the nude, with Drake looking on, brought a flood of heat to her cheeks.

"Shall we go for a swim?" he asked.

She looked at him sharply. Was he reading her mind? The thought of swimming while Drake looked on had been outrageous enough. But to go skinny-dipping with him . . . did she have the nerve?

"Together?" It was all she could do to force the word past her lips.

"Why not? It is dark and we are alone."

"But . . ." She felt her cheeks grow even hotter, if that was possible. All her life, she had been called a prude. Chicken. Scaredy cat. The most daring thing she could remember doing was sneaking out of the house and going to a movie with Jenica. Elena had thought it the height of daring to be out at night without her uncle.

Drake was watching her, one dark brow arched as he waited for her answer. Elena was about to say no when some rebellious part of her asked why she was hesitating. She was a big girl now. Besides, no one would ever know.

He grinned at her, a wicked gleam in his deep blue eyes. "I know you want to."

Goaded into action, she gathered her courage and gained her feet. Her courage wavered when she began to undress, and she turned her back to him.

Drake grinned as he pulled off his boots, then stood and shrugged out of his shirt.

Elena was careful to keep her gaze averted as he undressed, yet the same naughty imp that had urged her to agree to swim with Drake had her continually darting glances at him. His back and shoulders were broad and well muscled, his skin smooth and pale in the moonlight. His arms were long, corded with muscle that rippled as he moved.

When he unfastened his trousers, she dashed into the lake, keeping her back to the shore.

The water was cool but not cold and she struck out for the other side of the lake, reveling in the touch of the water on her bare flesh. She couldn't believe how different it was, how exhilarating it was, to swim in the nude.

She was halfway to the opposite bank when Drake swam up behind her. How had he caught her so quickly? She slid a glance in his direction, felt her insides quiver at the brush of his naked thigh against her own. A rush of heat suffused her, and with it a sudden need to touch him, to run her hands over his broad shoulders, to sift her fingers through his long black hair, to press her mouth to his.

Good grief! What was she thinking?

She gasped as his arm circled her waist. What was he doing? She couldn't reach the bottom. Thoughts of drowning flashed through her mind.

"Relax," he murmured. "I have you."

She noticed he wasn't treading water, so why weren't they sinking?

All thoughts of drowning fled her mind as he drew her body closer to his, crushing her breasts against his chest. Did he mean to ravish her, there, in the middle of the lake?

There was no mistaking the lust that burned in his dark eyes, or the evidence of his desire pressing against her belly. She had never been sexually active, but she wasn't totally ignorant, either. She had taken biology in high school and talked about it with her girlfriends. Sex had been their main topic of conversation. Who was doing it? Practically everyone. Where were they doing it? Practically everywhere, including the back of the school bus.

"Elena." His gaze moved over her, hot and hungry.

She stared at him, troubled by the insidious thought that he wanted more from her than sex, though she had no idea what that might be.

"Moonlight becomes you," he said quietly.

Her gaze slid away from his as she murmured, "Thank you."

A smile tugged at the corner of his lips as a flush rose in her cheeks. "Not used to sweet talk, are you?"

She stared at him, not knowing what to say. Her uncle had often complimented her, but instead of making her feel pretty or desirable, his flattering words had made her feel dirty somehow.

"You are of an age to be married," Drake remarked, his brow furrowing thoughtfully. "How is it that you are still unwed?"

"No one ever asked me."

"Except your uncle?" he guessed.

"Yes." She shuddered at the mere mention of him.

"If you were to marry someone else, your uncle would have no further claim on you."

"There is no one else."

"I take it none of the young men in the village appeal to you."

"It's a small town. There aren't many boys my age and . . ." She shook her head. "I don't care for any of them. I know you must be tired of having me here, an uninvited guest, but please, don't send me away."

Drake frowned. He had no intention of sending her away. She was a beautiful young woman. Her skin was smooth and clear, her limbs nicely rounded, her breasts full. Unless all the young men in the town were blind, it was hard to believe that none of them had offered for her hand, he thought. It was far more likely that her uncle, wanting her for himself, had turned all of her suitors away.

His gaze moved to her lips, which were full and pink and inviting. Too inviting to resist. He heard the sudden intake of her breath as she realized he was going to kiss her. But she didn't pull away when he lowered his head toward hers.

At the touch of his mouth, Elena went suddenly still. In a distant part of her mind, she admitted she had been longing for this since the first time he had kissed her. It was even better the second time. Just a kiss, she thought, until his tongue slid over the seam of her lips and coaxed her to open her mouth. Her uncle had kissed her like that and she had found it repulsive. But there was nothing repulsive about Drake's kiss. It burned through her like chain lightning, heating her from the inside out.

She moaned a soft protest when he took his mouth from hers, leaving her aching for more than just kisses.

Drake gazed down at her. He wasn't surprised by his body's reaction to her. He was a strong, virile male, and she was a very young, very desirable woman. It was only natural for him to want her, just as it was in his nature to hunger for her blood. So easy to take what he wanted, to ease his lust while he slaked his thirst.

So easy. Tempting as she was, he knew that if he took her in his current state of mind, she would never survive. Somewhat taken aback, he realized that for the first time in years he was more concerned with a mortal's happiness and well-being than with his own.

"We should go back," he said abruptly. Releasing her, he struck out for the shore without a backward glance.

Elena stared after him. What had just happened? One minute he was kissing her like there was no tomorrow. And the next, he was gone.

Drake was waiting for her on the bank when she waded out of the water. His gaze caressed her. Never, in all his existence, had he seen anything as breathtakingly lovely as Elena as she stood naked on the moon-dappled sand, her long black hair falling over her shoulders, her damp skin glistening like alabaster in the silver light of the moon. Her limbs were long and perfect, her waist incredibly small.

His gaze moved to the graceful curve of her neck, to the

pulse throbbing in the hollow of her throat. Need rose up within him, reminding him that he was a hunter and she his prey, and as much as a lion might love a lamb, there was little hope that the lamb would survive such a relationship.

Even though he had fed earlier, the need Elena aroused in him would not be denied. Drake dressed quickly, then waited impatiently for her to do the same. He escorted her back to the castle and saw her safely inside. Then he fled into the night without a word of farewell lest he take her in his arms and satisfy the thirst that burned hot and heavy within him.

Later that night, Elena lay in bed, staring up at the ceiling, her thoughts in turmoil. Why had Drake put her away from him so abruptly? Had she said something to anger him? Done something to displease him?

Troubling as his sudden leave-taking had been, it was the memory of his kiss that kept sleep at bay as she relived the incredible pleasure that had suffused her from head to heel when Drake's lips touched hers. It had been so much more than just a kiss.

She touched her fingertips to her lips, wondering how she could get Drake to kiss her again. Wondering, as heat flooded her cheeks, what it would be like to share his bed. Shameful creature that she was, she couldn't help imagining what it would be like to run her hands over that hard, male body, to feel his hands stroking hers. She knew she should be shocked to even think about such things, but after seeing Drake naked in the moonlight, after feeling the length of his body pressed intimately against her own, she couldn't think of anything else. Couldn't stop wanting him.

A bold idea came to her as she remembered something Drake had said earlier. She smiled, thinking it would solve all her problems, if she only had the nerve to propose it.

* * *

Elena was sitting on the rug in front of the hearth, thumbing through a magazine, when Drake entered the room. She looked up, surprised to see him so early. It was usually well after dark before he made an appearance, if he showed up at all. Could it be that, after last night, he was as anxious to be with her as she was to be with him? The mere idea made her heart skip a beat. In all the world, had there ever been a man who was as tall and dark, as sinfully handsome, as the one who now stood before her?

"Good evening, fair Elena," he murmured, smiling.

His voice flowed over her like silk, soft, sensuous.

"Good evening, Drake. I didn't expect to see you so soon."

"Shall I leave?"

"No! I mean, it's your home, after all."

"Indeed." He regarded her solemnly, one brow raised. "Is there something you wish to say?"

She blinked up at him. Did he know what she was thinking? But how could he? He couldn't read her mind. Such a thing was impossible.

He took a seat on the sofa, then gestured for her to join him. Suddenly nervous, she hesitated a moment before taking a place beside him. What had seemed like such a good idea late last night now seemed utterly ridiculous.

"You look upset," he remarked. "Is something amiss?"

"Yes. No." She twisted her fingers together to still their trembling.

"Something obviously has you upset," he remarked. "Why not tell me what it is? Perhaps I can help."

"Yes, you can," she said, the words spilling out in a rush. "I don't want to go back to my uncle, and I have nowhere else to go, and you live alone with no one to care for you, so I thought maybe, if it wasn't too horrid a thought, that you might marry me. Not a real marriage, of course. It would just be in name only. . . ." she said, her words slowing as her cheeks burned with embarrassment.

"You want to marry me?" Of all the things she might have said, a proposal had never entered his mind.

"Well, my marrying someone else to get away from my uncle was your idea, after all. I can cook and clean and wash your clothes, and . . ." She swallowed hard, her courage suddenly deserting her. "I won't be any trouble."

Lifting one brow, he muttered, "Somehow I doubt that."

At his words, she bowed her head, her shoulders slumped in defeat. It had been a stupid idea. "If you don't want to marry me, maybe you could lend me some money so I can take a bus to Brasov and find a job. I'll pay you back, somehow, I promise."

"Elena?"

She didn't answer, refused to meet his gaze. He was a grown man, older than she was, refined, educated. Why would he want a wife in name only when he could probably have any woman he wanted?

"Elena, look at me."

"No." She was too embarrassed to face him.

"Elena, I accept your proposal of marriage."

She lifted her head. "Do you mean it?"

"Indeed, I do."

For a moment, she could only stare at him. She hadn't really expected him to agree and now that he had, she wasn't sure how to respond. "I promise to do my best to keep your house clean, and to make you happy, except for . . ." Her voice trailed off as her gaze slid away from his.

"Never fear. I promise not to make any husbandly demands upon you unless you ask me to."

"Thank you, Drake."

"How soon do you wish to wed?"

"Oh, there's no rush," she said. "We can have a long

engagement." The longer, the better, she thought. After all, an engagement was almost as good as a marriage for keeping her uncle at bay.

"I think not."

"What's the hurry?"

"I have reasons of my own. Is tomorrow night too soon?"

She blinked up at him. "Tomorrow night?"

It was easy to see he had taken her by surprise. "Tomorrow night," Drake said, lightly kissing her on both cheeks. "Be ready at sundown."

Elena stared at him, unable to shake the feeling that he had somehow manipulated her into doing exactly what he wanted.

Chapter 6

Elena woke early after a restless night. Her dreams had been fitful, filled with shadowed images of Drake pursuing her through a long, twisting maze that had no end.

She spent a few minutes wondering what it meant, if it meant anything at all, then shrugged it off. Probably just a case of prewedding jitters manifesting themselves in a nightmare.

Sitting up, she stretched her arms over her head. It was her wedding day. Last night, marrying Drake had seemed like the answer to all her problems; now, she wasn't so sure. He was devastatingly handsome and physically appealing, and there was no denying that she was attracted to him but—she didn't really know anything about him. He was little more than a handsome stranger. And he didn't know any more about her than she knew about him. Why would he agree to marry a woman he had known such a short time? What did he hope to gain?

Shaking off her doubts, she went downstairs for something to eat. As usual, a tray awaited her. While drinking a glass of orange juice, a new thought occurred to her. She had nothing suitable to wear to a wedding. True, Drake had gifted her with a number of dresses, but even though they were silk, they weren't really elegant enough for a wedding. And she didn't have any heels. Or a veil. Or flowers.

Of course, none of those things were necessary. All that was needed for a wedding was a bride, a groom, and a priest.

And then she frowned. She had no idea where the ceremony would take place, no idea what her future husband's religion might be. For all she knew, he might not practice any religion at all. Her uncle professed to being Catholic, but in all the years she had lived with him, he had never accompanied the family to church, never attended Mass, not even at Christmas.

Elena glanced down as the cat rubbed against her ankles. "Where did you come from?" she asked, and received a loud "meow" in reply.

"I guess it's too late to worry about where we're getting married," Elena mused as she lifted the cat onto her lap and idly scratched its ears. "I can either marry my uncle, marry Drake, or run away again, although I don't know where I'd go from here. Do you?"

Smoke stared at her through unblinking yellow eyes.

"I just hope I'm not making a horrible mistake."

A low rumble rose in the cat's throat.

"I've never done anything so impulsive and yet, it feels right, somehow." She glanced around the hall. "Maybe there really is some kind of enchantment on this place. Oh, I know, that sounds silly, and yet, ever since I walked through the door that first night, I've felt like I belong here, you know? It's nonsense, of course. I don't believe in Fate."

The cat had no opinion on the subject. Instead, he rubbed his head against her breast.

She stroked the cat's fur for several minutes, her thoughts turned inward. "One good thing, when I'm a married woman, I won't have to stay hidden away in this old castle during the day. I'll be Mrs. Drake. . . ."

She shook her head ruefully. "I don't even know his last

name. But he's been kind to me, you know. I told him I wanted a marriage in name only, because, after all, I don't really know him, but—there's no denying he's very sexy, and I can't help wondering what it would be like to taste more than his kisses."

The cat looked up at her, its golden yellow eyes bright. If it hadn't been impossible, she would have sworn the animal was smiling at her. Or maybe laughing.

Elena was torn between wishing the sun would set and hoping it would never go down when there was a knock on the castle door. In all the time she had been here, Drake hadn't received any visitors. The only outsiders to come calling had been her uncle's men. Had they returned?

Hands clenched, she glanced around the room. What should she do? If she stayed quiet and didn't answer the door, maybe whoever it was would go away.

The knock came again. Harder. Louder. And then a voice. A woman's voice.

"Miss Knightsbridge? Hello? Is anyone home? It's Madame Raschelle."

Elena frowned. Who on earth was Madame Raschelle, and what was she doing here?

"The dressmaker," the woman clarified. "From Brasov. I have a delivery for Lord Drake."

Lord Drake? He hadn't said anything about being royalty. Curious, she went to open the door.

"Miss Knightsbridge?"

Elena nodded. Madame Raschelle was tall and lean. Her hair was bright red under a frilly bonnet that was the same shade of green as her eyes. Her russet-colored silk gown and colorful fringed shawl were like nothing Elena had ever seen before, except in period movies.

"May I come in?" Madame Raschelle asked, a note of amusement in her voice.

"What? Oh, yes, of course." Elena took a step back, allowing the other woman entrance, only then noticing that she had several large plastic garment bags draped over one arm, and a large handbag over the other.

"I've brought you a number of gowns to try on, my dear," Madame Raschelle said. She dropped the garment bags onto the trestle table, along with her bag.

"Gowns?"

"For the wedding."

"Oh, but I can't . . . I mean, I don't have any money to pay for . . ."

Madame Raschelle dismissed Elena's concern with a wave of one beringed hand. "Not to worry, my dear. Lord Drake has taken care of that."

"But . . ." Elena sighed. There was no use arguing with the dressmaker. She obviously had orders from the master of the castle.

Madame Raschelle removed her shawl, then began unzipping the bags, pulling out one dress after another, each more beautiful than the last. Rich silks and brocades, lush velvets, smooth satins, most of them in varying shades of white from ivory to cream. Two gowns stood out from the rest, one the color of a midsummer sky, the other a pale rose. In addition, there were a number of undergarments.

Elena could only stare at the amazing assortment. So many styles and fabrics. How could she ever be expected to choose just one gown when they were all so exquisite?

Madame Raschelle held up a velvet gown with a square neck and long fitted sleeves that ended in points. "This is one of my favorites," she said, smiling.

Elena ran her hand over the soft, cream-colored velvet. Lace edged the neckline. The skirt was gathered up on one side, revealing more lace. It reminded Elena of dresses worn in medieval times.

"Why don't you try it on?" the dressmaker suggested.

With a nod, Elena took the dress and hurried up the stairs to her chamber. She changed under the curious eyes of the cat, then glanced around, only then remembering that there was no mirror in the room. She frowned as she realized there were no mirrors in any of the rooms of the castle.

Lifting her skirts, she made her way down the stairs.

"So," Madame Raschelle asked, smiling. "Does it suit?"

"I need a mirror."

The dressmaker glanced around the room, then rummaged in her bag and produced a large hand mirror, which she offered to Elena.

"Oh," Elena murmured, "it is lovely, isn't it?"

"Quite. Perhaps you should try them all on?"

There was no need, Elena thought. She had already made up her mind. Still, who knew when she would ever have a chance like this again? Between the two of them, they carried all the garments up to Elena's room.

Trying on all the gowns was not only time-consuming, but a mistake. Elena had been certain the velvet was the gown she wanted, but there was a lovely silk adorned with pearls, a beautiful satin with an empire waist, an elegant ivory brocade fit for a queen. How was she ever to decide?

"Lord Drake instructed me to tell you that you might keep them all, if you so desired," Madame Raschelle remarked.

"All of them?" Elena had never seen such lavish attire, could scarce imagine their cost.

"He is a man of wealth and power," the dressmaker said. "He can well afford the price."

"But . . . all of them?" Aside from her wedding, when would she ever again have need of such finery? "Perhaps just the velvet. And the blue satin. And the rose silk. And the ivory brocade."

Madame Raschelle laughed heartily as she began hanging the gowns Elena had selected in the wardrobe.

"Of course, you will also need shoes." Reaching into her valise again, the dressmaker produced a pair of satin pumps and placed them on the floor.

She reached into her valise yet again and pulled out a long, thin box. Lifting the lid, she shook out a shoulder-length veil.

"Oh, it's lovely," Elena murmured, stroking the delicate lace.

"I knew you would like it. And now, the pièce de résistance," the woman said, and dipping into the valise once more she withdrew a long white nightgown that was so sheer, it was little more than a mere whisper of diaphanous cloth.

Elena stared at it, thinking it was as delicate as a spider web. A web for catching a man's interest.

"For the wedding night," the dressmaker said, a knowing twinkle in her eyes.

"But . . ." Elena bit down on her lower lip. Had Drake misunderstood her? Theirs was to be a marriage in name only.

Madame Raschelle smiled. "The nightgown was my idea. I added it to his order when I saw that he had neglected to think of it."

Elena forced a smile. She was relieved that the nightgown hadn't been Drake's idea. Wasn't she?

"I wish you every happiness, my dear," Madame Raschelle said. "If you have need of more gowns, you have but to let me know."

"Thank you," Elena said sincerely, though she doubted she would be calling on the dressmaker any time soon.

Elena accompanied the older woman to the front door, bid her good-bye, and then closed and locked the door behind the rather eccentric dressmaker.

She stood there a moment; then, realizing it would soon be sundown, she hurried back to her room to bathe and dress.

Drake stood in front of the fireplace, a glass of wine in one hand as he waited for his bride to appear. The priest from the next town sat in one of the chairs facing the fire, his hands folded in his lap, his benign expression belying the nervous tic in his left eye, the rapid beating of his heart.

Drake grunted softly. He had never seen the cleric until tonight, when he summoned him to the castle, yet it was obvious that the good Father possessed a strong inner sense that warned him of danger. Though Drake meant the man no harm, it was an instinct for survival that would serve the priest well if he but listened to it. The priest's cook and her husband stood nearby, called to serve as witnesses.

At the sound of footsteps, Drake glanced toward the staircase. For a moment, he stood frozen as he watched Elena descend the steps. She was exquisite. The cream-colored velvet gown clung lovingly to each curve, outlining a figure so perfect as to make other women weep. A delicate lace veil covered her face, giving her a ghostly appearance in the flickering light of the candles. Her hair fell over her shoulders like a fall of thick black silk.

He moved quickly toward her, eager to be near her, to touch her. To taste her. Reining in his rampant lust, he took her hand in his. Her skin was cool; he could feel her trembling. "How lovely you are," he murmured. "And how lucky I am."

She blushed prettily. "Thank you, Lord Drake," she replied, emphasizing the last two words.

He lifted one brow.

"Why didn't you tell me you had a title?"

"It is merely a title of respect," he said with a shrug. "Are you ready?"

"Yes."

Keeping hold of her hand, he led her into the hall where the priest waited. "Elena, this is Father Andrew. He will be performing the ceremony."

Elena smiled tentatively. "Good evening, Father."

Rising, the priest offered her his hand. "Good evening, my child."

Elena smiled at the man and woman who were to be their witnesses. She thought they both looked ill at ease. Certainly they didn't believe the rumors about ghosts in the castle?

Elena tried to concentrate on what the priest was saying, but she couldn't stop stealing glances at Drake. He was devastatingly handsome in a pair of black trousers, black boots, and a long black coat over a white silk shirt. When he looked at her, a thousand butterflies took wing in the pit of her stomach. Was it fear? Or excitement? Or perhaps a bit of both?

When he squeezed her hand, she realized Father Andrew was waiting for her response. She blinked at the priest. If she said yes, there was no turning back, no changing her mind. How could she marry a man she hardly knew?

Panicked, she looked up at Drake. The calm assurance in his eyes drove her uncertainty away. Lifting her chin, she murmured, "I do."

A rush of heat warmed her cheeks when the priest pronounced them man and wife. And then Drake was lifting her veil, taking her into his arms, lowering his head to kiss her, and everything else faded into the distance. There was only a pair of strong arms to hold her, a pair of firm lips playing over hers, his tongue teasing her own. She leaned into him, wanting to be closer. A soft moan rose in her throat as she slid her fingers up his nape to curl in his hair.

A cough reminded her they weren't alone. She moved away from Drake, her cheeks burning with embarrassment when she saw the priest and the witnesses staring at her, mouths agape.

Mortified, Elena turned her back to them.

Moments later, she heard the creak of the front door opening as Drake ushered the priest and the other two people out of the castle.

The sound of the door closing brought a sense of relief, and an unexpected rush of anxiety. She was Drake's wife now. If he chose not to honor his promise to leave her chaste, there was nothing she could do about it. It was a husband's right to make love to his wife and no one would condemn him for it. She was his now, for better or worse.

"You have not eaten, wife," he said when he returned.

"No."

He gestured at the trestle table in the hall. "Sit," he said, and left the room.

Already giving her orders, Elena thought with a flash of resentment, but she did as she was told, noting that the table was covered with a clean white cloth. Several vases filled with primroses and yellow daisies were grouped in the center, surrounded by a number of flickering red candles set in wrought-iron holders.

Drake returned moments later carrying a large covered tray. He placed it before her, then removed the lid with a flourish, revealing a roasted hen on a bed of rice, a small loaf of fresh bread, a pot of butter and another of honey. Lastly, there was a bottle of wine and two delicate crystal goblets.

"There's only one plate and one set of silverware." Elena looked up at him, a question in her eyes.

"Have you forgotten that I prefer to take my meals alone?"

"No. Why didn't you tell me you were rich?"

"You never asked."

"But . . . why do you live here, in this old castle? I mean, it's lovely, but there's no plumbing or electricity or . . . or anything."

"I have other holdings that are more modern," he said, "but every now and then, I like to come here for a while and meditate." Sitting in a chair across from hers, he filled the wineglasses, then offered her one. "A toast," he said, touching his goblet lightly to hers, "to my bride. I give you my oath that I will cherish and protect you for as long as you wish."

He watched as she lifted the glass to her lips, his gaze moving to her throat as she swallowed. Sipping from his own glass, he could not help wishing that it was his wife's sweet nectar flowing smoothly over his tongue.

Elena kept her gaze on her plate as she ate her dinner. Nevertheless, she was acutely aware of her husband watching her every move. Perhaps that was what made her so careless as she cut a piece of chicken. She gave a little cry of dismay when the knife slipped in her hand. Blood welled from the shallow cut, dripping down the blade onto her plate.

Drake's nostrils flared as the scent of warm, fresh blood filled the air. Reaching across the table, he took Elena's hand in his, lifted it to his lips, and licked the blood from the wound. Sweet, he mused, sweeter by far than the finest wine.

Elena gasped, startled by his action, and by the sensual heat that curled in the center of her being when his mouth closed around her finger. She had licked her own blood before. Who hadn't? It was a normal thing to do when one received a small cut—a scratch from a thorn or some other minor injury. But to have someone else do it was oddly erotic and slightly repulsive at the same time.

After a last lick, Drake tore a strip from her napkin and wrapped it around her finger.

Murmuring her thanks, Elena stared at him. What kind of man had she married?

It was a question that continued to plague Elena later that night when she went to bed. Lying there, she relived the evening.

After dinner, she had removed her veil, and then she and Drake had danced to music provided by an old-fashioned music box. Elena had never considered herself to be much of a dancer, had never really enjoyed it very much, but all that changed when she was in Drake's arms. His very nearness caused her whole body to hum with pleasure as they waltzed around the room. She followed his lead as if she had been doing it for years.

"I never knew dancing was so much fun," she had remarked with a shy smile.

"Neither did I, until tonight, wife."

"You're very light on your feet for such a big man."

He arched one brow. "Do you find that odd?"

"Well, um, yes. I remember watching my uncle dance with my aunt when I was a little girl. He lumbered around the floor like a great clumsy bear."

"And did he roar, as well?"

"Only when he was angry," she had replied with a grin. "And he was angry most of the time."

Laughing, Drake spun her around and around until she clung to him, breathless. And then he kissed her, ever so lightly.

Later, they had taken a walk under the stars. Standing in the shadows, with their arms around each other, she had marveled at the wonder of the stars that twinkled like tiny diamonds carelessly tossed across the vast black expanse of the heavens. He had pointed out the constellations.

There was Andromeda, the princess; Cassiopeia, the queen; Draco, the dragon, and Leo Minor.

Elena's heart had skipped a beat when he drew her into his arms, there, in the drifting shadows of the night. She gazed up at him, bewitched by his nearness. Even though she couldn't see his face clearly, his eyes gleamed with an odd reddish glow in the moon's light. She could feel the tension in his arms as he pulled her closer. As he lowered his head to hers. As he claimed a kiss.

Her eyelids fluttered down as his mouth closed over hers. At his touch, the strength seemed to drain out of her legs, and she grasped hold of his biceps to steady herself; the muscles in his arms felt like iron beneath her fingertips.

His kiss went on and on and she leaned into him, hoping he would never take his mouth from hers.

She smothered a small cry of protest when he broke the kiss. She pressed her fingertips to her lips. She had no right to ask for more, shouldn't want more, not when she had insisted on a marriage in name only. Perhaps that had been a mistake.

Now, lying in bed, she stared up at the ceiling, confused by her yearning for a man she hardly knew. What was there about him that intrigued her so? That made her long for more than his kisses? Why did he refuse to dine with her? Where did he go during the day?

She was drifting, on the brink of sleep, when he slid into bed beside her.

Startled to full wakefulness, she sat up, the covers clutched to her breasts. "What are you doing?"

"That should be obvious," he replied.

"Yes, but . . . we . . . you . . ."

"I am your husband. You are my wife. I promised not to consummate our marriage. I never promised not to share your bed, which is, after all, my bed."

She stared at him. Even though the room was dark, she

could see that he was shirtless. Was he completely naked under the covers?

"Go to sleep, wife," he said, and turned his back toward her.

She sat there a moment, her heart pounding. This was something she had not bargained for. Slowly, she slid under the covers, careful to avoid touching him. Turning onto her side, she closed her eyes and took several deep breaths.

Was he really naked?

She fought the temptation to ease her foot across the short space between them and satisfy her curiosity. Oh, this was never going to work. How did he expect her to sleep when he was lying there beside her—maybe stark naked—and taking up most of the bed?

She flopped over onto her stomach, opened her eyes just a bit, and glared at the back of his head. His hair was long and thick and black and straight. Ever so slowly, she eased one hand out from under the covers, and like a soldier sneaking across a battlefield, she inched her fingers toward a lock of his hair. It was remarkably soft. She jerked her hand away when he rolled over to face her. His eyes glinted in the darkness.

"What are you doing, wife?"

She swallowed hard. "Nothing."

"Turnabout is fair play."

"I don't know what you mean," she replied indignantly.

"Do you not?"

She stared at him, mute, as his fingers sifted through her hair.

"Anything else you would like to touch?" he asked.

With a shake of her head, she put her back to him again. Oh, but he was the most aggravating man!

Smiling inwardly, Drake closed his eyes and let himself disappear into the dark sleep of his kind.

* * *

Elena was surprised to find herself alone in bed when she awoke in the morning. Not exactly alone, she thought. The cat lay curled up on Drake's pillow.

She lingered there for some time, contemplating the night past, recalling Drake's kisses, the sensual heat that had flared between them. In spite of her insistence that they not make love, she couldn't stop wondering what it would be like to let him have his way with her. Would it be wonderful? Or degrading? She supposed it all depended on who you talked to. There had been girls in school who claimed to enjoy it, girls who did it just to be popular, and girls who did it once and said it was disgusting. Maybe a girl's point of view depended on the guy's expertise.

Sighing, Elena stroked the cat's head. At the first touch of her fingers on the animal's fur, her mind flooded with images of herself and Drake lying in each other's arms, making love.

With a start, Elena jerked her hand away.

The cat purred loudly, its golden yellow eyes unblinking. And then it pushed its head under her hand.

"Go away!" Elena gave the cat a shove. "Go on! Get out of here!"

With lazy grace, the cat hopped off the bed and padded silently out of the room.

Elena stared after the beast. What on earth had just happened?

Later, after breakfast, Elena decided she had been cooped up inside long enough. An earlier exploration of the castle had revealed a small door in the kitchen that led to a large garden surrounded by a high stone wall. The door creaked loudly, making her wonder how long it had been since anyone but herself had opened it.

Crossing the threshold, she stepped outside, then lifted her face to the sun. Its warmth felt wonderful on her skin and she stood there for several minutes, absorbing the warmth of the light, the chirping of the birds, the faint breeze that stirred the leaves of the trees.

A glance around showed the garden to be badly over-grown. A few primroses fought for survival in a forest of weeds. A small round fountain and a wrought-iron bench were almost completely hidden under a mass of tangled vines.

Her only experience with gardening was growing toma-toes and carrots in a small garden in her uncle's backyard, but she found work gloves and a pair of shears in a wooden shed and went to work with a vengeance. She worked steadily for two hours before taking a break. Stepping back, she removed the gloves and wiped the perspiration from her brow as she eyed her handiwork. With most of the weeds removed, she saw that a few daisies and daf-fodils bordered the primroses.

She regarded the weeds piled to one side. She would have to dispose of them, but not just now.

She sat in the shade of one of the trees for twenty min-utes, then attacked the vines that shrouded the fountain and the bench. The vines proved to have very small, very sharp thorns. She let out a little yelp of pain when one of the nasty little spines scraped her arm, drawing blood.

As if attracted by the scent of it, Smoke appeared with a loud meow.

"What do you want?" Elena asked irritably. Sitting on the newly cleared bench, she pulled a tissue from the pocket of her jeans, but before she could wipe the blood away, the cat lapped at the thin line of crimson on her arm.

Horrified, Elena sprang to her feet. She was about to

lash out at the animal when she realized that the pain was gone, the shallow cut was no longer bleeding, and the skin was, in fact, knitting together even as she watched.

She stared down at the big gray cat, who stared back at her. What kind of creature was it? Surely this was no ordinary cat.

Telling herself she was thirsty, she hurried into the kitchen, shutting the cat outside.

She paused a moment, her back to the door, the image of the cat licking her blood melding with a similar image of Drake doing the same thing.

Shaken, she went to the ice chest for a bottle of water, then made her way up the stairs to the main hall. With a shake of her head, she sank down on the sofa in front of the hearth, felt an odd foreboding when the cat padded into the room.

Jumping up on the back of the sofa, the cat purred loudly, then sat down and began to wash its paws.

Elena shivered as a chill ran down her spine. She had shut the cat up in the garden only moments ago. How had it gotten into the castle?

Chapter 7

Knowing that Drake would appear with the coming of nightfall, Elena felt a growing sense of excitement as the shadows grew long. She was anxious to tell him about the odd behavior of the cat, curious to hear what Drake's reaction would be.

But as she thought it over, she began to wonder if she had imagined the whole incident. After all, how could a cat's tongue heal a scrape on her arm? But something had happened, because there were no scratches on her arm, nothing to show where the thorns had nicked her skin. There should have been something there—a red line, a scab. Something. But her skin was smooth and clear.

She was still pondering how the animal had managed to get inside the castle when Smoke jumped off the sofa and ran out of the room.

With a shake of her head, Elena went down the stairs to the kitchen to prepare her evening meal, something simple tonight. Just a tuna sandwich, a bowl of tomato soup, and a glass of milk.

She was washing the dishes when Drake strolled into the kitchen, his own steps as silent as those of the cat.

"Good evening, my lady wife," he murmured.

"My lord," she replied with a smile. Living here, in the castle, it was easy to believe he was indeed the lord of all he surveyed.

Her heart fluttered with excitement as he drew her into his arms. He was so tall, so broad, so overpowering, just looking at him filled her with a warm longing to touch him and taste him, to feel his hands caressing her.

"So, wife, what would you like to do this evening?"

"Whatever you wish, husband," she replied, her voice breathless with anticipation.

His gaze moved over her, his eyes hot. "Surely you know how I would wish to spend the evening."

Heart pounding, mind racing, she stared up at him, mute. As enticing as he was, she was not yet ready to surrender her virtue.

Drake chuckled softly. "Fear not, sweet wife," he chided. "I do not intend to ravish you against your will, though you are a sore temptation. So," he said, slipping his hands into his pockets, "would you care to go for a drive?"

"Oh, yes," she said quickly. "Very much."

Drake smiled at her. "My carriage awaits."

His carriage turned out to be a sleek black Porsche convertible. Drake opened the door for her, then went around the car and slid behind the wheel.

"Where are we going?" Elena asked as he turned the key and the engine purred to life.

"Nowhere in particular," Drake replied. "Is there somewhere you wish to go?"

"No."

It was a lovely night for a drive. He put the top down, giving her a clear view of the sky. The air was warm, fragrant with the scent of night-blooming flowers. But it was the scent of the man beside her that held Elena spellbound.

His profile was sharp and clear in the faint light of the dash. He glanced over at her now and again, and each time, the look in his eyes made her heart skip a beat.

She searched for something to say to break the taut silence between them. The incident with the cat came readily to mind, but in the here and now, it no longer seemed real. Or important.

The road they followed meandered through a moon-dappled forest and then along the edge of a cliff that plummeted straight down.

"Do not worry, wife," he drawled. "I have driven down this road many times."

Comforting words, she thought, but if the car went over the side, only an angel would be able to save her from being broken to pieces on the rocks below.

She studied him surreptitiously as they drove along the narrow road. She couldn't see much of his face in the light of the dash, but she couldn't stop staring at him. There was something about him, something that drew her gaze again and again. It was an aura of power that clung to him, she realized, a sense of strength that was more than physical. But how was that possible? He was just a man like any other. Wasn't he? And yet, there was an air about him, an old-world courtliness in the way he spoke, in some of the words he used.

"Where do you go during the day?" she asked, somewhat abruptly. "Why is it I never see you until after dark?"

"I have matters of business to attend to," he replied curtly. "Matters that do not concern you."

"But . . ." She bit down on her lower lip. She reminded herself that she had no right to ask, that being his wife in name only didn't entitle her to pry into his secrets. And she had a feeling there were many things he was keeping from her. Was one of them a mistress? Was that where he went during the day? And if so, she had no one to blame but herself. Not that she cared, of course. He could have a hundred women hidden away.

Elena ran her fingers over the crease in her jeans. She would prefer a hundred mistresses over one, she thought. With a hundred, it was unlikely he would be overly fond of any of them. But if there was just one, that implied caring, perhaps even a sense of sharing and belonging.

She was startled to realize that the mere idea of Drake being with another woman, sleeping with another woman, was too painful to contemplate.

"You're very quiet, wife," he remarked. "Have you fallen asleep?"

"No, of course not. I was just enjoying the night."

"It is lovely," he said. "Quiet. Intimate. So few mortals take the time to appreciate its beauty."

"Mortals?" she asked with a frown. "What an odd thing to say."

"Yes," he said, laughing softly. "I suppose it is." He stopped the car and switched off the engine.

She felt a rush of anticipation when he slid his arm around her shoulders. His eyes looked fathomless in the moonlight. A sigh escaped her lips when he leaned toward her.

"A kiss?" His fingertips stroked her cheek and slid down the side of her neck. "Will you give me a kiss from your sweet lips, wife?"

She nodded, her heart pounding as he lowered his head to hers. His kiss was infinitely gentle, his lips as light as down on her own. And yet, for all its gentleness, the touch of his mouth on hers sizzled through her like summer lightning. She felt the heat of it, the power of it, all the way to her toes.

She knew a moment of regret when he drew away. It

was on the tip of her tongue to ask him to kiss her again. Instead, she folded her hands tightly in her lap.

"Will I ever be able to go into town? I'm getting tired of spending all my time in the castle."

"Is that why you were out in the garden this afternoon?"

"How did you know about that?"

He turned to look at her, his teeth flashing in a smile. "I know everything that happens in my domain."

His domain, she mused with a frown. What an odd way to put it.

"Make any changes to the house or grounds you wish," he said. "If you need anything, you have but to let me know."

"Thank you."

"As for going into town, you are free to do so. I will set up accounts for you in all the shops. Do you know how to drive?"

"Yes, but . . . what about my uncle?"

"I will speak to him tomorrow night."

The tone of his voice left no doubt in her mind that her uncle would do whatsoever Drake asked, though it was hard to imagine Tavian Dinescu bending his will to that of another. The idea pleased her beyond words. Her uncle had had his own way for far too long.

"I should have informed him of our marriage before now. My only excuse," Drake said, smiling at her, "is that I've been too besotted with my bride to think of anything else."

"You're teasing me."

"Not at all. Your beauty puts the moon and the stars to shame."

His words brought a rush of heat to her cheeks. She didn't know if he meant them, but they pleased her just the same.

She could feel him watching her. Was he hoping she would ask for more than kisses? Foolish question. Of course he was. He had made no secret of the fact that he wanted to make love to her.

After a moment, Drake switched on the ignition. "Would you care to go into the city tomorrow night?" he asked after turning the Porsche toward home.

She looked at him, her eyes alight. "I'd love that! I've never been anywhere."

"Then it will be my pleasure to take you."

Elena could think of nothing but the upcoming trip on the way back to the castle. Her uncle had often gone into the city, but he had never invited Jenica or Elena to accompany him. Elena had often wondered why he insisted on going alone. Jenica had been of the opinion that he kept a mistress there. Elena had been shocked by her cousin's suggestion.

"You're frowning," Drake remarked as he parked the car in front of the castle. "Is something wrong? Have you changed your mind about going to the city?"

"What? Oh, no! I was just thinking. . . ." She paused a moment before asking, "Will we stay overnight?"

"If you wish." Alighting from the car, he opened the passenger door, then handed Elena out of the Porsche. He held her close for several moments, savoring her nearness, her warmth, before releasing her. "Go inside, it's getting cold." He gave her a kiss on the cheek. "I'll be along in a few minutes."

He watched her climb the stairs. A thought unlocked the castle door for her. Another lit the fire in the hearth to warm her. A third brought the candles in her bedchamber to life to turn away the darkness.

He was raising the top on the car when a sudden ripple in the air told him he was no longer alone.

Chapter 8

Breathing out an irritated sigh, Drake turned to face his visitor. "Stefan."

"Drake. It has been a long time."

"Not nearly long enough."

"You know why I am here."

Drake shoved his hands into his pants' pockets. "I can guess."

"You were to have returned to the Fortress a year ago. You cannot avoid him forever. The longer you make him wait, the angrier he will become."

"I have no desire to return to Rodin's Coven, not now, not ever."

"You are the chosen one, brother."

An oath escaped Drake's lips. "Let him choose Vardin!"

"Is that what you want me to tell Rodin?" Stefan asked, his voice brittle with fear.

"Yes. How many times do I have to say it?"

"Our sire will not be pleased."

Drake snorted softly. "When have I ever done anything to please him?"

"There is a woman in the castle," Stefan remarked,

changing the subject. "Does she have anything to do with your decision?"

"She has nothing to do with it," Drake said. The lie rolled easily off his tongue.

"Then bring her with you."

Drake smiled as he savored the effect his next words would have. "We are on our honeymoon."

Stefan stared at him, his deep gray eyes wide. "You married a mortal? Have you taken leave of your senses? You know such a thing is forbidden."

"Yet another reason to stay where I am."

Stefan's expression turned morose. "You know if you do not obey Rodin's summons, I will be the one to suffer for it."

Drake rocked back on his heels. How like his sire to threaten Drake's favorite brother in order to get his own way.

"Rodin never did play fair," Drake muttered. "Go back and tell him I will be there at the appointed time."

Stefan bowed his head in a gesture of gratitude and respect. Rodin's temper was well known. Drake was the only one of his sons who had ever willfully defied him.

"Stefan? A favor?"

A faint smile tugged at the other man's lips. "I will not mention the marriage."

"When you return to the Coven, the sword in my room is yours."

Stefan grinned. He had long coveted the ancient weapon. A wave of his hand, and he was gone.

Keeping a tight rein on his anger, Drake covered the Porsche. He had known this day would come, had dreaded it for centuries, and now it was here. Like it or not, he would have to return to Rodin's Coven. He would have to take his place on the Council. He would be expected to stay at the Fortress with his sire for as long as Rodin wished it.

Drake lingered in the shadows, his resentment twisting like angry snakes in his gut. He would not seek the warmth of his bride's bed this night, and it was all Rodin's fault.

Yet one more thing to hold against the man who had sired him.

Chapter 9

In the morning, Elena woke feeling strangely let down. Even though she had insisted on a marriage in name only, she had hoped that Drake would join her in bed last night, that he would take her in his arms. Even though she wished to remain a virgin, she yearned for his kisses, for the touch of his hand in her hair, for the sound of his voice whispering that she was beautiful, desirable. He had said he would come to her. Why had he changed his mind?

A loud "meow" announced Smoke's presence before the cat jumped onto the bed, turned around twice, and curled beside her.

"So," Elena said, stroking the cat's head, "where is his lordship this morning?"

Another "meow" was her only answer.

For a few moments, Elena was content to lie abed and let her mind wander while petting the cat. When she had entered the castle last night, the door had been unlocked. There had been a fire in the hearth that hadn't been there when she'd left. Someone had lit the candles in her bedroom. Who? Was there someone else living in the castle, someone she had yet to meet?

No sense lying there wondering about it. Smoke couldn't give her any answers. She had a feeling she wouldn't get any answers out of Drake, either.

With a sigh, Elena pushed the big gray tom away. The cat hissed softly, then curled up at the foot of the bed.

"Sleep all day if you want, you lazy beast," Elena said, throwing back the covers. "But I'm hungry."

Rising, Elena pulled on her robe and descended the stairs. As usual, she found her breakfast waiting for her. Taking a seat at the trestle table, she pulled the tray toward her and lifted the lid, uncovering a meal of hard-boiled eggs, fruit, cheese, and a chocolate doughnut, along with a pot of tea. Taking a bite of the doughnut, she instantly forgave Drake for leaving her to her lonely bed the night before.

When she unwrapped the silverware, she found a note, which read:

> *Elena, my sweet, the city awaits.*
> *Be ready at sundown.*
> *Your loving husband.*

She ran her fingers over his bold signature. Your loving husband. If only it were true.

Shortly after sundown, Drake rapped on Tavian Dinescu's front door. It was opened moments later by Dinescu himself.

"Yes?" Dinescu said gruffly. "How may I help you?"

Drake sketched a bow. "I've come to introduce myself," he said formally. "I am Lord Drake of Wolfram Castle."

Dinescu straightened slightly, impressed by Drake's

demeanor and title in spite of himself. "Please, won't you come in?"

"No, thank you. I merely came to inform you that I have taken your niece, Elena, as my bride."

Dinescu stared at him, mouth agape.

"I came here to set your mind at ease. She is quite well, and wishes to thank you for the years you supported her."

Dinescu found his voice at last. "I'm glad to know she's all right, but—Lord Wolfram, is it? Didn't she tell you she was engaged to me?"

"I am aware you offered to marry her," Drake replied with a wry grin. "However, since she is now my wife, I think we can assume that her answer was no."

Dinescu's eyes narrowed as an angry splash of red climbed up his throat and spread into his cheeks.

Gathering his preternatural power around him, Drake murmured, "Do not pursue the matter. I can assure you it will not end well if you do."

Dinescu took a step backward under the weight of Drake's steady gaze. Hands clenched tightly at his sides, he hissed, "What are you?"

"Your niece's husband," Drake replied mildly. "Good evening to you, sir." Turning on his heel, Drake slid behind the wheel of the Porsche, keenly aware of Tavian Dinescu's malevolent gaze on his back.

Elena stood in front of the wardrobe, trying to decide what to wear. The gowns from Madame Raschelle were too fancy, jeans and a T-shirt not fancy enough. She settled on the light blue silk that Drake had given her.

Ears twitching, Smoke sat on the foot of the bed, watching through avid yellow eyes as she changed into clean underwear, then slipped the dress over her head. She packed a pair of jeans and a T-shirt and a change of underwear in a small valise Drake had left for her, along with her nightgown and robe, her comb and brush and pins for her hair.

She was putting on her shoes when, with a flick of its tail, the cat jumped off the bed and left the room.

A moment later, Drake appeared in the doorway. Clad in gray trousers, a white shirt open at the collar, and a long black broadcloth coat, he looked every inch the lord of the manor.

She felt her cheeks grow warm under his blatant regard. "Good evening, my lord husband," she murmured, mimicking the formal language he always used with her.

"Good evening, my lady wife. Do you still wish to visit the city?"

"Yes, very much. Unless you've changed your mind."

"Not at all." He tucked her valise under his arm, then held out his hand. "Let us be on our way."

"How long will it take to get there?" Elena asked. They had been driving for perhaps an hour. Drake had said little in that time. To be fair, she hadn't said much, either.

"Another hour," he replied with a glance in her direction. "Are you warm enough?"

"Yes." Enena watched the miles slip by. "Your cat is very strange," she remarked a short time later. "Sometimes I think he understands every word I say."

"I do not own a cat."

"You don't? Then who owns that big gray tom? He seems quite at home in the castle." And in my bed, she thought ruefully.

"No one owns him," Drake said. "He comes and goes as he pleases."

"He brought me a dead rat the other day."

Drake laughed softly. "Indeed?"

"It's not funny! It was disgusting."

"He has never brought a rat into the castle before."

"It was probably my fault," she admitted. "I told him to go out and earn his keep."

"You know what they say," Drake said, grinning at her. "Be wary what you ask for lest you get it."

She glared at him, then burst out laughing. A warm glow suffused her when his laughter mingled with hers.

She was still smiling when the faint glow of streetlights came into view.

Drake pulled up in front of a large hotel with an old-fashioned ambiance. After turning off the engine, he got out of the car, then came around to open her door for her. Taking her by the hand, he ushered her into the hotel. After securing a room, he asked if she was ready to dine, and when she said yes, he escorted her into the hotel's elegant restaurant.

It was quite the loveliest place she had ever seen. The lighting was subdued, the walls papered with an elegant rose and cream stripe. The tables were laid with rose-colored damask threaded with gold, gleaming silverware, and crystal goblets. She looked at Drake, her brows raised, when all he ordered for dinner was a glass of red wine.

"Don't tell me you've already eaten?" Elena said, disappointment in her tone. "I know you like to eat alone, but I thought you might make an exception tonight."

"Sorry, sweet wife, but do not let my abstinence spoil your supper. I am told the cuisine here is quite good."

The roast, country potatoes, green beans, and bread looked good, smelled wonderful, and tasted even better, but when she offered Drake a bite of roast dipped in gravy, he refused.

"I don't understand why you won't eat with me," she said with a pout. "Are you embarrassed by your table manners or something?"

"Yes," he said with a wry grin. "Something like that."

She made a face at him. "I don't believe you." He was so polished in every other regard. His clothing was always impeccable, his speech refined. She decided then and there that, one way or another, she would discover what he was hiding.

After dinner, he took her walking down Republicii Street, which was lined with quaint storefronts reminiscent of days gone by. Most of the smaller shops were closed for the evening, but a few of the larger ones remained open. They passed stores that sold clothes, books, souvenirs, jewelry, electrical appliances, and even art, as well as cafés and restaurants. No cars were allowed here, which made it ideal for an after-dinner stroll.

Elena was treated to more evidence of Drake's generosity when he insisted on buying her another new dress—this one the color of a ripe plum. He also bought her a pink sweater, a pair of shoes, and a fur-lined jacket, and instructed the clerk to send it all to the hotel.

"Is there anything else you would like?" he asked as they continued down the street.

"I need a mirror. I can't believe you don't have any in the castle."

She couldn't be sure, but she thought she heard him swear softly. And then he smiled at her. "Of course."

He bought her a full-length, antique, stand-up mirror framed in polished mahogany. When she protested, insisting it was too costly, he silenced her by saying, "Consider it my wedding gift."

She could hardly argue with that.

After leaving the shop, he asked if she was tired. Elena shook her head. She felt as if she could walk for miles. It felt good to stretch her legs, to feel the breeze on her face. To feel Drake's hand holding hers.

They crossed the street at the corner and walked back toward the hotel. Elena paused to peer in the window of an old-fashioned tea shop, charmed by the unusual teapots and cups, the old-fashioned tins of tea. Moving on, they passed a bridal shop, several restaurants, and an ice-cream parlor.

A narrow alley took them away from the city. There were no lights here. Elena clung to Drake's arm, visions of muggers racing to the forefront of her mind.

"What are we doing here?" she asked, glancing nervously from side to side.

Drake quietly cursed himself. What was he thinking, bringing her here? His only excuse was the scent of prey being carried to him on an errant breeze. It quickened his hunger, made his fangs ache with need. But he couldn't hunt now, not with Elena on his arm.

An abrupt turn and he headed back toward the hotel.

"But I'm not ready to go to bed," she protested as he escorted her up to their room. "I'd like some dessert and a cup of coffee."

"I need to go out."

"Where are you going at this hour?" she asked, glancing at her watch. "Why can't I come with you?"

The lie came quickly to his lips. "I'm going to one of the clubs."

"What kind of club?" she asked suspiciously.

"A casino."

"Why can't I go? I've never been to a casino."

"Stay here and behave yourself. I won't be gone long." He dropped a kiss on the top of her head and left the room, closing the door behind him.

Elena stared after him. He was lying, but why? Was the truth so horrible? Before she could change her mind, she followed him down the stairs, determined to find out where he was going.

She hadn't expected it to be so easy to follow him, had

been certain that, within minutes, he would discover she was behind him and send her back to the hotel. But he appeared to be lost in thought as he walked quickly down the street, his hands shoved into his pockets. She trailed behind him, her gaze darting right and left. What was she doing, following him down dark streets in a strange city? Sometimes it seemed as if he wasn't real. His black attire made it easy to believe he was a part of the night, like the darkness and the shadows and the mare's tail clouds drifting across the moon.

Ahead, Drake turned right, into a park. What was he going to do there at this time of night? Was he meeting someone? But who? A woman? The thought of Drake with another woman hurt more than she would have believed possible. Still, she had no one to blame but herself. She had told him she wanted a marriage in name only, certain, at the time, that she meant it. But that had been before the wedding. And even though it was just a sham, she was his wife and he was her husband.

She ducked out of sight behind a tree when two disreputable-looking men strolled out of the shadows and approached Drake. She heard the taller of the two strangers demand his wallet and when he refused, the tall man and his companion both pulled knives hidden under their shirts. Moonlight glinted on the blades as the muggers lunged forward, their weapons driving toward Drake's chest.

Only Drake wasn't there. Miraculously, or so it appeared to Elena, he materialized behind the men, his hands curling around their necks, slamming their heads together with a sickening thud. The knives fell from their hands, clattering to the walkway as Drake dropped the bodies to the ground. She couldn't tell if the muggers were unconscious, or dead, but there was no mistaking the dark stains that spread out on the cement.

Frozen in place, Elena could only stare as Drake bent over one of the men. It took her several moments to realize what he was doing and even then she couldn't believe what she was seeing. She must have made a sound because he whirled about, his long black hair whipping about his face, his narrowed gaze piercing the darkness, zeroing in on where she stood.

Terrified, she stared at the blood dripping from his teeth—no, not teeth. Fangs. His eyes, once a deep, dark blue, had gone a hideous crimson red. Fear coiled like a viper in her belly and she braced a shaky hand against the tree beside her, her heart in her throat as the world spun out of focus. Black spots danced across her vision. With a fearful cry, she fell into the darkness that enveloped her like a cocoon and dragged her down, down, into oblivion.

Cussing softly, Drake summoned his preternatural power. Darting forward, he caught Elena in his arms before she hit the ground. What the hell was she doing here? He swore again. No mortal on earth knew what he was. He brushed a lock of hair from her forehead. What was he to do with her now? The answer came quickly to his mind—according to the laws of his kind, he should either wipe his memory from her mind, or take her life. Neither option appealed to him.

Turning away from the two bodies, he cradled Elena to his chest and transported the two of them to her room at Wolfram Castle. Holding her tight with one arm, he pulled down the covers on the bed, then lowered her onto the mattress. He undressed her down to her bra and panties, then pulled the blankets up to her chin. She was beautiful, so beautiful. Her hair flowed across the pillow like skeins of black silk. Her skin was smooth and clear and warm. So warm. So touchable.

He stroked the curve of her cheek. What was he going to do with her? He couldn't kill her. He would give up his own life before he sacrificed hers, a very real possibility once Rodin learned that Drake had taken a mortal bride, and that she knew the truth of what he was.

He rarely thought of Rodin, hadn't seen his sire in over three hundred years. He fervently wished he could put it off for another three centuries, but there was no chance of that now. An invitation to the Fortress was not an idle request. It was a command, one Drake dared not ignore.

Elena stirred, drawing his attention once again. Rodin wouldn't expect him for another few weeks. Drake blew out an exasperated sigh. Perhaps, by then, he could come up with a valid reason for breaking one of their strictest laws. His only hope to preserve his own life and that of his bride was to somehow mollify his sire.

He didn't want to think of the consequences should he fail.

Chapter 10

Elena awoke feeling groggy and disoriented and then, as the events of the previous night sprang to the front of her mind, she bolted out of bed. Only then did she realize she was no longer at the hotel but back in her room at the castle. How had she gotten here? And where was Drake?

It didn't matter. Nothing mattered but getting out of there just as fast as her feet would take her. The man she had married, the man she was falling in love with, was a . . . a . . . She couldn't make herself say the word. It was impossible. Good grief, what if she had let him make love to her?

She pressed a hand to her heart; then, as a new thought rose to the fore, she lifted an exploratory hand to her throat. Had he bitten her? Was she going to become what he was? Fear sat like a lump of ice in her belly. Was that why he had married her? So he could turn her into the same kind of monster he was?

She had lived in the land of Dracula for almost half of her life. Most of the tourists who came to Transylvania wanted to see Dracula's castle, which was, in reality, Bran Castle, located on the border between Transylvania and

Wallachia. The castle had been used by Vlad the Impaler, said to be the inspiration for Stoker's fictional vampire.

Suddenly chilled, she wrapped her arms around her middle. She had grown up on the myths and legends that surrounded vampires, but it had never occurred to her that Drake might be one of the Undead. Of course, no one believed such creatures actually existed. Sure, vampire books and movies were popular, and had been for years, but they were works of fiction, not reality.

But Drake was real, a man of flesh and blood. *Vampire.* She shuddered. It explained so much—why she never saw him during the day, the casket in the hidden chamber, the fact that he didn't eat or drink. Odd, that the memory of his kisses didn't repel her.

"Elena, get a grip!"

She had to get out of there before it was too late. Before he rose from the coffin hidden in the wall behind the tapestry in the main hall.

Her mouth went dry as she pictured him lying on the smooth white satin, his arms folded across his chest, his body cold and unmoving.

She pulled on a pair of jeans and a sweater, clumsy in her haste, then sat on the edge of the bed to put on her socks and shoes, only then noticing that the valise she had taken to Brasov the night before was on the floor beside the bed, and that the mirror Drake had bought her stood in the corner. She stared at it a moment, remembering how happy she had been only a few hours ago, but there was no time to dwell on that now.

Grabbing her handbag, another gift from Drake, she hurried down the stairs, her only thought to get out of the castle before nightfall. She was safe until then. If only he had a phone so she could call for a cab. Not that she had any money to pay for one. He had given her many gifts but never any cash. Maybe she could find the keys to the

Porsche. She spent a few minutes searching for them downstairs, and then upstairs, but to no avail.

Conscious of time passing, she ran down the stairs again.

When she reached the front door, Smoke was sitting in front of it. The cat stared up at her, its head cocked to one side.

Murmuring, "Good-bye, kitty," Elena put her hand on the latch and pulled, but nothing happened. She tugged on the latch with both hands, but the door refused to budge. She frowned. The crossbar wasn't in place. The door wasn't locked. Why wouldn't it open?

Heart pounding, Elena spun around and ran downstairs to the kitchen, only to find that the back door wouldn't open, either. What was going on? It wasn't locked. Why wouldn't the darn thing open? And what if it had? She willed herself to stop and think. Even if she could get into the garden, what good would it do her? There was no exit, no way over the high wall.

She had to get away, but how? The windows in the main hall were too high, too narrow. The doors wouldn't open. She was trapped inside the castle. With a vampire.

Feeling as though her feet were made of lead, she returned to the main hall and sank down on one of the sofas, hugging her handbag to her chest. What was he going to do to her? Images of Drake bending over the neck of one of the muggers flashed through her mind. Was that to be her fate, as well? Was that why he had let her stay here? Why he had agreed to marry her?

Smoke hopped up beside her, a low purr rumbling in his throat as he nudged her hand.

"Stupid beast," she muttered, and then, with a sigh, she dropped her handbag on the floor and stroked the cat's head. Smoke purred loudly, the noise soothing somehow. As she continued to pet the cat, her panic was swallowed up by a sense of well-being. She was safe here. There was nothing to be afraid of. If Drake had intended to kill her, he would likely have done so by now.

Suddenly weary, Elena stretched out on the sofa and Smoke curled up beside her. The cat's purring, softer now, lulled her to sleep.

The sun was setting when Elena awoke. She bolted upright. He would be here soon. What should she do? What would he do? She was alone in the castle with a monster. Even the cat had abandoned her.

Springing to her feet, Elena ran to the front door. Maybe it would open this time. It *had* to open now, before it was too late.

Eternally too late.

But time had already run out.

She didn't have to turn around to know that Drake was there. Though he made no sound, she could feel his presence looming behind her like a dark cloud. She swallowed hard, her hands clenching and unclenching at her sides. There was a moment out of time, as if someone had suddenly removed blinders from her eyes and her heart, and she knew him for what he was, almost as if she could see into his very soul. How had she not sensed his preternatural power before? She felt it now. It crawled over her skin, making the fine hairs on her arms stand at attention.

"Good evening, wife," he said quietly.

She couldn't speak, couldn't form the words to ask the questions that pounded in her mind, demanding answers.

"Have you nothing to say?" he asked in that same quiet tone. "No questions to ask me?"

Her silence, combined with her continued refusal to look at him, aroused his anger. She could feel the weight of it pressing down on her like a giant hand.

"Elena, look at me." It wasn't a request but a command.

Afraid to provoke him further, afraid of what she would

see, she slowly turned to face him, her gaze not quite meeting his. She had expected to find the monster staring back at her, but it was just Drake.

"You have nothing to fear from me, wife."

She licked her lips, but remained silent. Dozens of questions clamored in her mind: How long had he been a vampire? When and how had it happened? Was he the only one? How many other men—and women—had he killed? How often did he have to . . .

She shut the door on that train of thought, and all the others. Asking questions, hearing his answers, would make it all too real.

"Elena." He took a step toward her, but stopped when she recoiled. "Dammit, woman, I am not going to hurt you."

"How can I believe you?" She shook her head, as if to dispel the memory of what had happened the night before. "I saw what you did. I saw your eyes . . . they were"—she wrapped her arms around her waist—"they were red, and you looked like . . ."

"Go on," he said, his face and voice devoid of emotion. "How did I look?"

"Like death," she whispered. "You looked like death."

"I never wanted you to see me like that."

"Please, I just want to go home."

"You are my wife. This is your home now."

"No! We never consummated our marriage. Please, just let me go back home. I won't tell anyone what you are, I promise." Who would believe her?

"Is that what you really want?" Drake asked, his anger surfacing. "To go back and marry that fat old man? To have his hands on you?"

She forced the word through clenched teeth. "Yes." The lie tasted bitter on her tongue.

"Now who is lying? You want me, Elena. You have wanted me from the first night, and we both know it."

"No!" She shook her head again, more vigorously this time, as if that would make her denial true.

Drake took a deep breath, and changed tack. "Have I mistreated you? Hurt you in any way? Done anything to make you fear me?"

"You lied to me." She blinked rapidly in an effort to hold back her tears. She didn't want to go back to her uncle, but how could she stay here? With a vampire?

"I never lied to you."

"You let me believe you were human," she retorted. "I'd call that a lie, wouldn't you?"

"A sin of omission, perhaps," he allowed grudgingly. "But I had no choice. Telling mortals what we are is forbidden. I could not have told you the truth even had I wished it."

She stared at him in astonishment. "There are more of you?"

He nodded.

"How many more?" The idea that there could be other vampires living here . . . She felt a burst of hysterical laughter bubble up in her throat. Where else would vampires live but Transylvania? The laughter died in her throat. There were more of them. How was that possible? How on earth was any of this possible?

"I am the only one here," Drake said, "but there are others. Perhaps half a million of us worldwide."

It wasn't a vast number, given the world's population of over six billion people. Still . . .

"If that's true, why doesn't anyone know? If there are vampires running around drinking blood . . ." She paced back and forth a moment, trying to clear her head. "Sooner or later, someone would find out. Wouldn't they?" When he hesitated, she said, "The truth, Drake. I want the truth."

"The knowledge of our existence is erased from the mind of anyone who discovers it."

"Erased?"

"Wiped away. Obliterated."

"How? How can you do that?" The bitter taste of bile rose in the back of her throat as her imagination conjured visions of Drake cutting away a part of her brain.

When she swayed on her feet, Drake took her by the hand. "You need to sit down," he said. Guiding her to one of the sofas, he eased her down on the cushions, then went to the carafe on the table and filled a glass with water. "Here, drink this."

She accepted the glass with a hand that shook visibly.

Drake watched her, his arms folded over his chest, wondering if she was going to faint.

She drained the glass, then looked up at him. "How?" she asked again.

"Nothing as bizarre as what you are thinking," he assured her. "It is done by a form of hypnosis. Quite painless."

"Are you going to do that to me?"

"No." It was true, for the moment.

"What are you going to do to me?"

He lifted one brow. "Do?"

She touched the side of her neck, her gaze on his face.

"Ah, that." He sat beside her, an oath escaping his lips when she flinched.

"Are you going to . . . to . . . drink from me?"

"I already have."

She blinked at him. "I don't believe you. I would have known . . . wouldn't I?"

"I took only a taste now and then, while you slept."

Her eyes widened. "Am I going to become a vampire?"

"No."

She sank back against the sofa cushions, relief evident in every line of her body. "How did you become a vampire?"

"I did not 'become' a vampire." He looked at Elena. She was shivering. He glanced at the hearth. A thought touched the banked coals, bringing the fire to vibrant life. "Vampire." The word rolled easily off his tongue. "It is what I am. What I have always been."

Chapter 11

Elena stared at Drake, some of her fear receding as she considered what he had said. "But . . . I thought . . ." She had never heard of anyone being born a vampire. In books and movies, the only way to become one of the Undead was with a blood exchange. She shook her head. "I don't understand."

"We are not the monsters of myth and legend, but they do exist, although they are now few in number."

"Have you ever met one?"

"Yes, years ago."

"Do they live the way your people do?"

"No. We are enemies."

"Why?"

"The Others are a more violent, more barbarous race. They tend to kill their prey and often each other. They have no clan loyalty, no sense of family or honor, no care for anyone but themselves. Centuries ago, the Others declared war on humanity. They killed men, women, and children without reason or mercy, threatening to expose us all. My father summoned the Master Vampires of the other Covens and they destroyed all of the Others they could find. It was a long and bloody battle, but it accomplished its purpose.

The Others who survived changed their ways. They did not stop killing but they became more discreet."

"More discreet?"

"They stopped leaving bodies in the street. They started preying on those who would not be missed—transients and the like. But the war continued. Each Coven vowed to continue to fight them, and to destroy any that they find."

"Oh." She blew out a sigh. "I'm glad I never met one of those. But tell me more about you, about your people."

"We are a very old race, once hunted to near extinction by zealots and warrior-priests because we need blood to survive. We were accused of witchcraft, or of consorting with Satan, because, once we reach adulthood, the aging process slows as the need for blood becomes stronger." Though he spoke to her, his gaze was on the flames. "Some give in to the burning need for blood immediately. Some fight it, but the pain of resisting is excruciating. Sooner or later, we all surrender to what is, for us, a basic need for survival. Once we have ingested human blood, three things occur—we are no longer capable of digesting mortal food, we can no longer abide the sun's light, and we stop aging. The first year after we give in to the urge to drink, we must drink often. To resist can be fatal."

It was a fantastic story, Elena thought, something one might read in an ancient book of fairy tales. She looked at him closely as a new thought popped into her head. "How old were you when you stopped aging?"

"Nearly thirty."

She frowned, wondering how long he had fought the compulsion to drink blood.

"Vampires are considered mature at twenty."

She marveled at his self-control. He had resisted the urge to feed for almost ten years. It was a long time to endure the kind of pain he had described, to fight against something that was a basic need. "How old are you?"

"Five centuries as of last month."

The number was staggering. What would it be like to live that long? To never age? Never see the sun? Never consume anything but blood—no, that wasn't true. He drank wine. How was that possible? Curious, she put the question to him.

"I can drink small amounts with no ill effects," he replied, "as long as I feed beforehand."

"What's it like, to live such a long time?"

"It can be challenging. After a few hundred years, you have done everything, seen everything there is to see. For those who dislike change, the world can be a frightening place. Like mortals, our kind respond to the vicissitudes of life in a variety of ways. Some embrace them, some reject them, some choose to seek their own destruction. There are those who simply grow weary of living. They go to the Fortress and bury themselves in the ground."

Buried alive? She choked back her nausea. She had always been afraid of small, dark places, couldn't imagine anyone willingly entombing themselves in the ground.

Seeing the revulsion on her face, he said, "For us, it is a way to rest, to rejuvenate ourselves when we have lost the will to live."

"Have you ever done that?"

"No." His gaze caressed her face. "I must admit, I was considering it, until I met you."

"So, the vampires of fiction are just that, fiction?"

"Not exactly."

"Then what, exactly?"

"The vampires of legend, Nosferatu, also exist, but in very small numbers. I have never met one."

"Where did they come from?"

"Some believe a fallen angel found one of our kind

thousands of years ago. The vampire was dying of injuries inflicted by another of our kind when the angel found him. With his last breath, the vampire bit the angel. The angel died. The vampire was reborn as Nosferatu."

It was too much, Elena thought. Vampires who were made. Vampires who were born that way. It was all too bizarre to consider, too impossible to be real. She pressed her hands to her temples. She could feel a headache coming on, no doubt caused by the fact that Drake's revelations had turned her world inside out and upside down.

"Elena, look at me."

Though reluctant, she did as bidden.

His gaze captured hers as he placed his hands gently over her own. She stared into his eyes, deep, dark, fathomless eyes that seemed to draw her in until she saw nothing else. Gradually, the throbbing in her head disappeared. The tension drained out of her body, leaving her feeling warm and tranquil.

What was he doing to her? Was he hypnotizing her? Erasing her memory? Maybe that would be for the best.

"Relax, wife, the only thing I have done is erase the pain in your head."

Suddenly weary, she leaned against him. It was too much to absorb—what he was, what he had told her. It was all simply too fantastic to believe. Maybe she was dreaming. Yes, dreaming. Sighing, she closed her eyes. When she awoke tomorrow, life would be normal again.

Drake stroked Elena's hair, her cheek, the curve of her neck. He had violated vampire law twice now, first in telling her who and what he was, and then by not wiping the knowledge from her mind. He refused to consider taking her life. The rules of the Coven didn't seem important when she was near. The beat of her heart was music to his ears, the scent of her skin more fragrant than the primroses that grew in the garden, the heat of her body a welcome warmth against his own cool flesh.

After five hundred years as a vampire, there was little left in the mortal world that surprised him, but sitting there, with Elena sleeping beside him, he discovered that he cared more deeply than he had imagined for the woman who was his wife in name only. Even more astonishing was the realization that he wanted her love more than he had ever wanted anything in his life.

With a shake of his head, he stared into the fire, certain that he had a better chance of gaining heaven than winning the fair Elena's love.

Eyes closed, Elena turned over on her stomach and tried to go back to sleep. After last night, she was reluctant to face a new day, although a glance at her watch told her that the day was already half gone. Plagued by scary dreams, she had awakened several times during the night. Each time, Drake had been there beside her, his voice lulling her back to sleep. Odd, that finding him in her bed hadn't frightened her, considering all she had learned.

With a sigh of exasperation, she flopped over onto her back. A quick glance showed that she was alone in bed. Well, not exactly alone. Smoke lay on Drake's pillow, regarding her through half-closed eyes.

Elena turned onto her side, her chin pillowed on her hand. "So, cat, whatever am I to do? How can I stay here with him, knowing what he is? How can I ever trust him?"

The cat blinked at her, then yawned, revealing very white, very sharp teeth.

Elena stared at the cat, and the memory of how Drake's fangs had looked when he'd bent over one of the robbers rose in her mind. His teeth, too, had been very sharp and very white.

She shook the image away. All felines—and vampires, she supposed—came equipped with very sharp, very white teeth.

After slipping out of bed, she washed her face and hands, brushed her hair and her teeth, then pulled on her khaki shorts and a T-shirt and went downstairs. She was too upset to eat. Instead, she paced the great hall and then, on impulse, she went to the front door, which still refused to open.

She uttered every swear word she knew, but it didn't make her feel any better, and the darn thing still didn't open.

Turning away, she practically tripped over the cat. "Must you always be underfoot?" she muttered irritably.

"Meow."

Sidestepping around the cat, Elena made her way to the kitchen's back door. Maybe it would open today. Working in the garden might help to calm her nerves, help her to think of what to do next.

She wasn't surprised when the door still refused to open.

"This is so unfair!" She shook the handle with both hands, and then, her frustration rising, she kicked the door. "I feel like I'm suffocating in here!"

"Meow."

"Oh, go away."

But the cat didn't go away. Slipping between her legs, the big gray tom lifted one paw and gave the door a push.

And it swung open.

With another meow, the cat darted outside.

Elena stared after the remarkable creature for several minutes. Truly, it was a most unusual cat. Drake admitted to being a vampire. Was he a warlock, as well? Everyone knew witches often kept cats as familiars. But he had said he didn't own a cat. She frowned. Maybe it was just semantics. Or maybe, she thought with a rueful grin, the cat owned Drake.

With a shake of her head, Elena stepped over the threshold. She didn't care if the cat possessed some kind of feline mojo or not. All that mattered was that she was outside.

She took a deep breath of the clean, fresh air as she glanced at the high walls that surrounded the castle. There must be a gate. Maybe she had missed it the first time she'd looked. Starting at the corner nearest the house, she made a slow exploration of the wall, but there was no gate, no trellis, no way out. If only she had a ladder.

With a shrug, Elena found the gloves she had worn before and set to work on another patch of weeds. She tried to keep her mind blank as she knelt in the dirt, but, perhaps inevitably, Drake intruded on her thoughts. He was a vampire. It was impossible but true. Try as she might, Elena couldn't decide how she felt about him now, although, in truth, she had never been certain what to think of him. He was unlike any man she had ever met. Of course, she hadn't met very many men, especially men who were five hundred years old.

She wasn't surprised when the cat appeared. Sitting in the shade of an old oak tree, it watched her with a faintly bored expression.

"Too bad you can't make yourself useful," Elena muttered. "This would go a lot faster if I had some help."

With a flick of his tail, the cat curled up and closed its eyes.

An hour or so later, Elena decided she needed a rest. Rising, she stretched her back and shoulders. The exercise had done her good. Feeling suddenly hungry, she peeled off her gloves and dropped them on the iron bench.

Smoke trailed her into the house.

Elena glared at the cat. "You are such a pest. Can't you find something else to do besides follow me around?"

A loud "meow" was her only answer.

In the kitchen, Elena washed and dried her hands. As always, Drake had provided her with a tasty meal. Whatever faults he might have, he always made sure she had plenty to eat. Sometimes he left her prepared meals; sometimes just the ingredients.

Munching on a slice of bread smothered in butter and honey, she wondered if he ever missed real food—meat and potatoes, fresh peas and corn, hamburgers and hot dogs, potato salad, freshly baked bread warm from the oven, cakes and cookies, pie and ice cream, grapes and strawberries, malts and sodas and all the other good things to eat and drink that she took for granted.

She lingered at the table, her thoughts drifting. She wondered how long Drake was going to keep her here. Now that she knew what he was, would he ever let her out of the castle again? Take her to the city again?

She lifted a hand to her throat. He had admitted to tasting her. Was that why he kept her here? How much was "a taste"? How could she sleep through such a thing?

So many unanswered questions. She pushed them out of her mind. She would think about all that later. Right now, she was going back outside.

Rising, she headed for the garden, the cat at her heels.

Muttering, "Silly beast," Elena made her way toward the iron bench. Grabbing her gloves, she pulled them on while she regarded the ground she had cleared earlier. It looked barren now.

Returning to the shed, she found a shovel and began to dig up one of the rosebushes, intending to replant it in the newly turned plot of ground.

She dug a wide hole around the bush, then reached down and gently pulled the roots out of the earth. A bit of blue-and-white striped cloth was tangled in the roots. Taking hold of the cloth, she gave it a yank. . . .

And screamed when a desiccated hand appeared, tangled in the material.

Elena stared at the skeletal hand and at the small blue stone ring on one finger for several seconds, then dropped to her knees, retching. Jenica had been wearing a dress made from that very same cloth the last time Elena had seen her.

Smoke padded up beside her. The cat took one look at the contents of the hole, hissed softly, and ran into the castle.

Moments later, Drake appeared at her side. "Elena, what is it?"

She looked up at him, sobbing, then pointed at the grisly find. "It's . . . it's . . . Jenica. . . ."

Lifting Elena to her feet, Drake drew her into his arms. He didn't have to look into the hole to know what was there. The stench of death and decay was sharp in his nostrils. "Are you sure it is her?"

"She . . . when she ran away . . . she was . . . was wearing a dress made out of that same cloth. Uncle Tavian," she said, hiccuping, "he bought her the dress for her birthday. And the ring . . . it was a gift from her mother."

"Come inside and sit down."

She looked up at him through tear-filled eyes. "Who would do such a thing?"

"Come inside," he repeated, leading her toward the back door. "I'll unearth the rest of the remains. We need to make sure it is your cousin."

After settling Elena on the sofa and covering her with a blanket, Drake returned to the garden. In his five hundred years, he had seen death in all its forms and he studied Jenica's corpse dispassionately. An examination of the body showed she had died of a broken neck. He frowned as he detected Dinescu's scent on the body. It proved nothing, of course. She had lived in the man's house.

Squatting on his heels, he recalled reading in the local paper that there had been speculation that Jenica Dinescu had eloped with one of the neighbor boys. He remembered Jenica as being a quiet, frightened child, too timid to run away from home. Odd that Elena had never mentioned that her cousin had eloped. Drake grunted thoughtfully. Was the boy also buried here?

Rising, Drake brushed the dirt from his hands as he debated what to do with the body. There weren't a lot of options. He could rebury it here, wrap it in a blanket and take it to Dinescu to gauge his reaction, or drop it off at the local undertaker.

Drake shook his head. As callous as it sounded, it mattered little to him who had killed the girl. Except for Elena's well-being, he rarely took any interest in what went on in human affairs. At the moment, he had far more important things on his mind—like how he was going to explain to his sire why he had violated one of the Coven's most basic laws.

One thing was for certain, he couldn't leave Jenica's body lying out in the open while he made up his mind. Using his preternatural strength, he quickly dug a hole six feet deep, wrapped the corpse in a length of burlap he found in the shed, and reburied the body. He would let Elena decide what to do with the grisly find after they returned from the Fortress.

Elena looked up when Drake entered the room. "Was it . . . ?"

"I am afraid so."

"Why would anyone want to hurt Jenica?" Elena dabbed at her eyes with a handkerchief.

He shrugged. "Who can say why people do what they do?"

Elena stared at him, ashamed of what she was thinking.

He lived in the castle. He was a vampire. Vampires drank human blood. . . .

"You think I did this?"

"I . . ." A guilty flush stained her cheeks.

"I did not kill her."

"I'm sorry for thinking that you—"

He brushed her apology aside with a wave of his hand. "Considering what you know about me, I cannot blame you."

"We need to find whoever did this! He could live in our town. We have to stop him before he kills someone else."

"We will. But not now."

"Not now?" She stared at him in disbelief. "If not now, when?"

"I have something I must attend to, something that cannot be postponed any longer."

"I don't believe what I'm hearing! What can be more important than finding out who murdered my cousin?"

"Explaining to my sire why I disobeyed the law of the Coven and married a mortal."

Chapter 12

"Coven?" Elena stared at Drake. "I don't understand."

"My sire wants to see me. I cannot refuse."

"What does that have to do with your marrying me?"

"It is forbidden for us to marry mortals."

"Why?"

"Relatively speaking, we are small in number. Only the oldest males can father children, and then only for a short time. Thus, my father has arranged a marriage for me."

Elena stared at him in disbelief. "You married me when you were engaged to someone else?"

"Yes, in a manner of speaking."

"Who is she?"

"I do not know." He sat beside her, one arm stretched along the back of the sofa. "All I know is that her name is Katiya and she is fertile."

"He expects you to marry someone you've never met?"

Drake nodded.

"Then why did you agree to marry me?"

"Because you asked me."

Elena shook her head. "What's the real reason?"

"Because you are beautiful." He stroked her cheek. "And because I have no wish to wed and bed a woman of my father's choosing. I am hoping that the woman he has chosen for me will be offended when she learns I have wed a mortal and that her parents will dissolve the betrothal."

"Can't you just refuse to marry her?"

"No." His gaze moved over her face. "I have a favor to ask of you."

"What kind of favor?" she asked suspiciously.

"I promised you I would not consummate our marriage against your will, but if my father finds out that our marriage is only a charade, he will insist that we end it."

"And if I refuse to . . . consummate?"

"I will take you back to your uncle before I leave," he said calmly. It was an empty threat. He would cut off his right arm before he sent her back to Dinescu.

"That's blackmail!"

"Indeed, it is. But we need be intimate only once." He winked at her. "Unless you wish otherwise."

She glared at him. Did he truly expect her to sleep with him when he was engaged to another woman? She had thought he was being kind when he'd agreed to marry her. She should have known better. Should have known he had his own selfish reasons. It was her own fault. Secretly, she had hoped he cared for her a little. What a fool she had been.

"If you will do this for me, I will find out who killed your cousin when we return. And if you no longer wish to be my wife, I will give you this castle and the means to support yourself for the rest of your life."

Elena gazed into his eyes. If she refused, would he take her by force? She bit down on her lower lip. He was a vampire. As attractive as he was, as much as she yearned for his touch, how could she agree to let him make love to her?

He had shared her bed, slept at her side. But now he was asking for more than that. Much more. How could she give herself to a man who didn't love her? A man who wasn't a man at all?

"Elena?"

"I can't decide now." She clasped her hands together, then shook her head. "I need time to . . . to think about it," she said, her voice little more than a whisper.

Rising, he took her hand and kissed her palm. "Then I will leave you to it, my lady wife."

Elena stared after him. If he gave her all of eternity to make up her mind, she doubted it would be time enough.

A thought took Drake out of the castle. Standing on the steps, he shoved his hands into the pockets of his jeans, his mind turning, as always, to his bride. He had thought of little but Elena since that first night when he discovered her asleep on the sofa in front of the hearth. Elena. He had agreed to give her time to make her decision when, in truth, he had already made it for her. Even if Rodin decided to destroy him for breaking the law of the Coven, his sire wouldn't take his anger out on a helpless female. At worst, Rodin would wipe any and all memories of vampires, especially Drake, from Elena's mind and send her back home.

He cocked his head to the side as his preternatural hearing picked up the sounds of Elena climbing the stairs, going into her room, pacing the floor. He considered waiting until she was asleep, then hypnotizing her so that she would give him the answer he wanted. He hoped it wouldn't come to that, but if it did, so be it. He would do whatever was necessary.

He left her alone until she was asleep, and then he materialized inside the bedroom. After undressing, he slid under the covers, slipped his arm around her shoulders, and drew her close, reveling in the warmth of her slender body, the silky feel of her hair trailing over his shoulder.

Murmuring, "Good night, wife," he kissed her cheek, then ran his tongue along the side of her throat, teasing himself with the taste of her skin, the scent of her blood. A small sip satisfied his thirst and he closed his eyes, thinking how pleasant it was to drift into the dark sleep with the taste of Elena on his tongue.

Elena woke with a sigh. Eyes still closed, she stretched her arms out to her sides. And realized, with a start, that she wasn't alone in bed. A glance to the left showed Drake lying on his back beside her. What was he doing here? On those nights when he had shared her bed, he had always been gone in the morning. Maybe he was dead. Really dead. Was that possible?

Sitting up, she poked his shoulder. "Drake?"

"Yes, wife?"

"Nothing. What are you doing here?"

"It is my bed."

"I know, but you've never been here in the morning. I assumed you spent the day in your"—she took a deep breath—"in your coffin."

He wrinkled his nose. "I do not like it there. It is very confining."

She stared at him, thinking this was the most bizarre conversation she had ever had. "So, why are you here today?"

"I need your decision."

"You said I had time to think it over."

"I am afraid time is up."

"So soon? You just told me about this last night."

"We are expected at the Fortress tomorrow night." He looked up at her. She was staring at him, her eyes wide.

"Sorry, wife, but I will need your decision this evening." He sat up, the sheet pooling in his lap. "You have all day to think it over." Cupping her face in his hands, he kissed her lightly. "I hope you make the right decision." He kissed her again, longer this time, then slid out of bed.

And disappeared.

Elena stared at the place where he had been standing only a moment before. How had he vanished so quickly? And where on earth had he gone?

And what was she going to do?

She had no appetite for breakfast, no interest in reading. And certainly no interest in working in the garden. Just thinking about it made her shudder. Why would anyone murder Jenica? Her cousin had been a sweet-natured young woman, understandably a little timid and withdrawn. There had been times when Elena had wished Jenica would help out with the housework instead of cowering in her room.

Elena fell back on her pillow and stared up at the ceiling. How had she ever gotten into this mess? To consummate or not, that was the question.

She frowned as the cat jumped onto the bed and curled up on Drake's pillow.

"I really don't have any choice, do I?" Elena muttered. "I can either let Drake claim his husbandly rights, or I can . . ." She really had no other choice.

Smoke's ears twitched, as if he was thinking it over, and then he answered with a loud "meow."

Elena absently stroked the cat's head. Bedding Drake probably wouldn't be so bad. He had been kind to her. He was incredibly handsome and yes, sexy. She had reveled in his kisses. She had yearned for more. In fact, he would be very nearly perfect—if only he wasn't a vampire! How was she supposed to get past that? If he had been human, the decision would have been so much easier.

Eventually, hunger drove her downstairs to the kitchen. She made a ham and cheese sandwich and ate without really tasting it, her thoughts on what would happen when the sun went down and Drake appeared. Her biggest hope was that he would be gentle with her.

Smoke, who had followed her into the kitchen, hopped up on the table and meowed loudly. To Elena, the sound was oddly reassuring.

She sat at the table, deep in thought, long after she finished eating. Now that she had made the decision to do as Drake wanted, she wished to get it over with as soon as possible. She had once heard a lady comedian doing a monologue about sex. One of the things she advised women to do when having sex was close their eyes and think of something else. Yeah, right. How on earth was she supposed to think about anything else at a time like that? Especially when it was her first time?

Elena returned to the main hall, the cat at her heels. When she curled up on one of the sofas, Smoke stretched out beside her, his paw batting her hand until she gave in and stroked his head. It was relaxing, lying there with the cat purring softly at her side.

She woke with a start when the cat hopped off the sofa and left the room.

A glance at the window showed the sun was setting. And then Drake was striding toward her, and the time for decision making was over.

Elena sat up, her gaze moving over him. He wore black jeans and a long-sleeved white shirt open at the collar, the perfect foil for his long black hair and midnight blue eyes.

"Good evening, wife."

She swallowed hard. "Drake."

"I trust you have made your choice?"

"Do I really have one?" she asked with some asperity.

He smiled at her, a wicked gleam in his eyes. "One always has a choice."

"I'd like to get this over with as quickly as possible."

"You say that like you think it will be distasteful."

"Maybe it will," she replied flippantly. "I've never made love to a vampire."

"Or anyone else," he reminded her.

She stuck her tongue out at him. "How do vampires make love?"

"The same as everyone else," he said with an amused grin. "Why not wait until the foul deed is over before you judge me? You might find it enjoyable."

"And if I don't?"

"Then I will never lay a hand on you again."

"Why should I believe you? You promised you wouldn't demand your husbandly rights, yet you are about to ravish me."

He laughed again. "Fair Elena, I am demanding nothing of you. Only asking. Would you like it better if I begged?" And so saying, he dropped to one knee in front of her. "Please, my lady wife, I need you to do this for me."

With a sigh, Elena rose from the sofa. Taking his hands in hers, she urged him to his feet. Her heart was pounding like a drum at a rock concert when she led the way up the stairs to her bedchamber. Never had the climb seemed longer, or her bed smaller, than it did as she stepped into the room.

Once there, she came to a halt. The next move was his.

"Elena." He gazed deep into her eyes. "Trust me, wife. I will not hurt you."

She nodded. She had to believe him. It was too late to turn back now.

She shivered when he tugged her T-shirt over her head. His fingers were cool against her skin, his tongue warm as he laved the side of her neck. That quickly, she wanted him, wanted to know the secrets only he could reveal, discover the mysteries and differences between a man and a woman.

She trembled as he removed her jeans, her bra and panties, but couldn't deny the feminine thrill of satisfaction she felt when he looked at her.

"You are truly beautiful." His words confirmed the admiration she read in his eyes.

She slid under the covers when he began to undress. Her first instinct was to look away, but that seemed foolish. She had seen his naked backside. . . . She swallowed a rush of panic. But not the front.

Her gaze moved over him from head to foot, quickly the first time, and then more slowly. He was beautiful, with eyes the blue of a midnight sky and long black hair that fell past a pair of broad shoulders. His arms and legs were well muscled, his body lean and firm, his stomach hard and flat. And he had an arousal that would have done a stallion proud.

He smiled at her, his expression one of utter male arrogance as he slid under the covers beside her and drew her close, aligning her body with his so that there was nothing between them.

He aroused her slowly, his hands playing lightly over her quivering body, his tongue delving into her mouth, dueling with hers as he tasted her sweetness. He could have compelled her to respond to him. He could have forced her into submission, but it wasn't necessary. She came alive in his arms, eagerly returning his kisses. He had expected her to be shy, hesitant, but she was young and untouched and curious. He had thought to gentle her to his will as one might gentle a filly who had not yet learned the touch of her master's hand. But, again, it wasn't necessary. She was willing and eager to learn, to touch and to taste, to explore the hard planes and angles of his body.

They came together like two lost souls who had been searching for each other for years, and perhaps they had. His climax came with hers, and it was unlike anything he had ever known. His only regret was that the moment passed so quickly.

Elena lay in Drake's arms, her head pillowed on his shoulder, and wondered why any woman would find making love a chore. She had heard some of her aunt's friends complain about the sexual side of marriage, but Elena could scarcely wait to make love to Drake again. She smiled inwardly. Of course, other women didn't have Drake in their beds. If they did, she was certain they wouldn't be complaining. He had been a tender lover, patient, gentle, willing to give her all the time she needed to feel comfortable with him, letting her explore the length and breadth of him to her heart's content. His body was so wonderfully different from her own. She would have been happy to stay in his arms forever.

Gradually, her heartbeat slowed and her skin cooled, but not her desire. She wanted to touch him and be touched in return, to feel his breath on her face, to taste his kisses.

"Husband?"

"Yes, wife?"

She bit down on her lower lip, then huffed a sigh. They were married. It shouldn't be so difficult to ask for what she wanted. What if he rejected her? What if he didn't? "Can we . . . I mean, would it be all right if we . . . ?"

"Go on," he coaxed.

She cleared her throat. "Well, you promised never to lay a hand on me again if I didn't like it."

He nodded.

"Well, what if I liked it?" she asked boldly. "Can we do it again? Unless you'd rather not," she added quickly.

Drake laughed softly as he rose over her, his dark eyes alight with amusement. "My dear wife, I should be more than happy to indulge your every wish."

Chapter 13

In the morning, Elena woke with a song in her heart, a smile on her face, and aches in places that had never ached before, but it was a wonderful kind of pain. A wave of tenderness swept through her when she saw Drake sleeping beside her. He was an amazing lover. She hated to think what she would have missed if she had refused to consummate their marriage. How dreadful it would have been, to go through life never knowing how amazing making love could be. Remembering how disappointed some of her girlfriends had been after having made love to their boyfriends, Elena could only surmise that not every man was as skilled at the art of lovemaking as her husband.

Was it because he was a vampire? She frowned. And then she laughed. If being a vampire enhanced a man's lovemaking, every woman in the world would be clamoring for her man to join the ranks of the Undead!

Rolling onto her side, Elena studied her husband's face. His brows were nicely shaped, his lashes thick and rather long, his cheekbones high and pronounced, his lips . . . ah, those lips. A rush of warmth engulfed her when she remembered the intimate places his mouth had been last night.

A giggle rose in her throat. Would he make love to her like that again tonight? How could she wait until then? If she touched his shoulder, would he awaken and take her in his arms?

Why had it been necessary for them to make love? Not that she was sorry, but it would have been easy enough for her to lie to his sire and claim they had consummated their marriage. Who would know otherwise?

A breath whispered past Drake's lips and then he smiled. "Rodin would know," he murmured.

"I thought you were asleep!" Elena stared at him. "How did you know what I was thinking?"

"You were thinking so hard, it was impossible not to hear you."

Even though his eyes were still closed, she made a face at him. Was there anything he couldn't do? He came and went like the wind, he could read her mind. And he was the most amazingly attractive and virile man she had ever met.

"Thank you, wife."

"Oh!" she exclaimed in exasperation. "Am I to have no secrets from you at all?"

A wry smile twisted his lips. "Probably not."

She glared at him. There had to be a way to keep him from reading her mind. She tapped her fingertips on the mattress. There had to be a way. . . . Grinning, she began to mentally recite the recipe for chocolate chip cookies. And then, still thinking about flour and sugar and vanilla, she leaned over and kissed him full on the lips.

He opened his eyes with a start, then burst out laughing. "Very clever, wife."

"Thank you," she said smugly, and then shrieked when he rolled her onto her back and straddled her thighs.

"Do you know what I am thinking?" he asked, a mischievous twinkle in his dark eyes.

"I can *see* what *you're* thinking," she retorted with a quick, downward glance. "But it's daytime," she added primly.

"What has that to do with anything?" he asked.

"Well . . . the sun is up . . . and . . . and it's daylight. . . ." she stammered. "Shouldn't we wait until dark?"

"Daytime, nighttime, any time you desire, my darling wife."

It had never occurred to her that people engaged in such intimate relations in the broad light of day. Besides . . . "How can you be awake when the sun is up?"

"How can I think of sleep with you lying there beneath me?"

"So you can be awake during the day?"

"For short periods of time, as long as I stay out of the sun."

She stored that away for future reference.

Leaning down, he kissed her forehead, her cheeks, the tip of her nose, the corners of her mouth. "Should I stop?"

Feeling delightfully wicked, Elena clasped her hands behind his neck and drew him closer. "Read my mind," she murmured, and pressed her lips to his.

It was late afternoon before Elena slipped on her robe and left the room. Drake was sleeping soundly. Had he been an ordinary man, she would have thought him weary after a morning of lovemaking, but he was a vampire, with the stamina of twenty men. It wasn't exhaustion, but the sleep of his kind, that held him in its grasp.

In the kitchen, she heated water, then filled a small wooden tub. After removing her robe, she stepped into the water and scrubbed herself clean. She should be upset, she thought, frightened that the man she had married was a vampire. Instead, she felt like singing. What was wrong with her? Had a night and a morning of exquisite sex deprived her of her sanity? She felt herself smiling again as she thought of the hours she had spent in Drake's arms, the sweet love words he had whispered in her ear.

Drying off, she slipped into her robe again, then looked around for something to eat. She settled for a bowl of fruit and a cup of tea.

Sitting at the table, waiting for the tea to cool, she found herself thinking of Drake and wondering how soon they could make love again.

Drake woke with the setting of the sun, unable to dispel a sense of doom as he prepared to return to the Fortress. He had avoided thinking about returning home for centuries. He had always been an outcast, never quite fitting in with the others of his kind. And now there was Elena. He never should have married her, never entangled her in his life, but it was too late now. She was a part of him. The best part.

After dressing, Drake left the castle to feed. Knowing he would need all his strength to face his sire, he fed often and deeply. It would have been quicker, easier, to simply drain one human, but to do so meant the mortal's death. Only thoughts of Elena kept him from taking a life now.

When he returned to the castle, he found his bride in the main room, a vision in a knee-length dress of lavender silk that showed off her feminine curves to perfection. The neckline was square, the sleeves short and puffy. Her smile of welcome warmed his heart.

"Good evening, wife," he murmured, taking her into his arms. "How lovely you look."

"Thank you." She gazed up at him, a question in her eyes. "You're late this evening."

Nodding, he stroked her cheek, thinking it was as soft and silky as the dress she wore.

She tilted her head to the side. "Did you go out?"

"Yes. I needed to feed before we meet my sire."

The mention of Rodin sent a shiver of unease through her. Try as she might, she couldn't convince herself that Drake's father would be happy to see her, especially when he learned that his son could no longer marry the woman who had been chosen for him.

"You didn't tell me how Rodin would know if we had made love or not," she remarked.

"He would only have to read your mind."

"Can all vampires do that?"

He nodded. "We can read human minds, but not those of our own kind."

"So, all the vampires I meet will be able to read my mind?" That was a troubling prospect. It would be most embarrassing, having them all know what she was thinking, especially when all she could think about was making love to Drake and how anxious she was to be in his arms, and in his bed, again.

He smiled at her. "Soon," he promised. "But now, we must go."

Hoping to put the moment off, she said, "I haven't packed anything."

"No need." He gazed into her eyes. "Whatever happens, there is no reason for you to be afraid. My sire will not harm you. It is not Rodin's way to make war on women."

"War!" she exclaimed. "Are you going there to fight him?"

"No. At least not in the way you mean."

"How long will it take us to get there?"

"No time at all." He wrapped his arms around her. "Just hang on to me. You might experience a little dizziness or nausea, but it will soon pass."

Elena frowned at him, but she didn't have time to ask the questions forming in her mind. There was a strange sensation of moving rapidly through a thick gray haze, an odd buzzing in her ears, followed by a brief queasiness in the pit of her stomach. When the world righted itself again, she was standing in the middle of a large room like none she had ever seen before.

In front of her, two large chairs, ornately carved from black wood, stood side by side on a raised dais. A glance around the room showed a horseshoe-shaped table behind her. A quick count told her there were thirteen chairs at the table. Twelve of them were occupied by men—all of whom had long black hair, pale skin, dark eyes, and serious expressions. They looked so much alike, she was certain they must all be related.

She noted that the walls appeared to be white marble veined with gold and black; a thick gold carpet covered the floor; an enormous fireplace, also made of marble, took up one whole wall to the left of the dais. Heavy gold chandeliers hung from the vaulted ceilings, but it was the glow of hundreds of candles that illumined the room.

But it wasn't the décor of the room that held Elena's attention. Rather, it was the man and woman who occupied the chairs on the dais. The woman was quite simply the most beautiful creature Elena had ever seen. She wore a long black velvet dress that displayed a modest amount of cleavage. The dark fabric made her pale skin glow like alabaster. Waist-length, pale blond hair fell over her bare shoulders. Her eyes were a dark, vibrant green. She wore no adornments of any kind save for a bloodred rose in her hair.

The man stood. He, too, was dressed all in black. Tall and broad-shouldered, with inky black hair and deep blue eyes, he looked enough like Drake to be his twin. He did not look happy to see the two of them.

"Drake." His voice was deep, laced with an air of command. He made a sharp gesture with his hand, a silent order to approach.

Drake squeezed Elena's hand. "Stay here. Whatever happens, do not interfere. And do not lie to him," he murmured, and strode toward the dais, his head held high.

To her surprise, he knelt on one knee in front of the other man. "Sire."

So, she thought, this was Drake's father. Was the woman his mother?

Rodin made a broad gesture with his hand, and all the men seated at the table rose and left the chamber. The sound of the door closing behind them echoed like a death knell in Elena's ears.

"Drake. It has been a long time," Rodin remarked, his tone heavy with censure.

"Not long enough."

"You know why I have called you here."

Drake nodded curtly. "And you know I have no wish to take my place on the Council. Or to wed a woman of your choosing."

"Unfortunately, the decisions are not yours to make." Rodin lifted his gaze to Elena. "Who is this mortal and why have you brought her here, uninvited?"

Taking a deep breath, Drake said, "This is Elena. My wife."

Outrage flashed in Rodin's eyes.

The woman on the dais leaned forward, a gasp issuing from her lips. If possible, her face grew even more pale.

"I did not think you would go so far to defy me," Rodin said, his voice cold.

"I was not thinking of you when I took her for my bride."

"It is obvious you were not thinking at all! To marry a mortal is forbidden. You know that as well as I."

Drake shrugged. "You know the old saying," he retorted. "Laws are made to be broken."

"Those who willfully defy the laws of the Coven invite destruction."

Still kneeling, Drake flung his arms out to his sides. "Do your worst."

"No!" The woman on the dais rose to her feet, tension evident in every line of her body. "I will not have it!"

"Be silent! I will not let him go unpunished."

The woman relaxed visibly. "Of course not, my lord."

Rodin didn't say anything, but suddenly, there were four burly men in the room. They surrounded Drake. He made no move to resist when two of them pulled him to his feet and dragged him away. The other two men followed behind.

Elena stared after Drake, overcome with a sudden fear that she would never see him again. She yearned to run after him, but every instinct she possessed warned her to stay where she was.

Taking a deep breath, she turned to face Rodin and the woman. If Rodin treated his son like that, what would he do to her, an uninvited, unwelcome stranger?

Rodin regarded the female standing before him. It was easy to see why Drake had chosen her. She was young and pretty, with a slender figure and vibrant brown eyes. He sensed a streak of valor in her that she did not realize she possessed. It amused him to think that her courage might be put to the test before the night was out.

Drawing himself up to his full height, he said, "I am Rodin and this is my wife, Liliana."

"I'm Elena Knightsbridge," she said, only then realizing she didn't know Drake's last name. Perhaps he didn't have one.

"Has Drake told you of us, what we are?" Rodin asked.

Elena hesitated; then, remembering Drake's admonition to tell the truth, she nodded.

"You wed him knowing what he is?"

"No. I did not learn that until later."

"What has he told you?"

"Very little."

"Do you know why I summoned him here?"

"Yes."

"Your presence complicates matters. My son is betrothed to another. Their marriage was to take place when the moon is new."

Not knowing how to respond, Elena remained mute.

Liliana took a step forward, her gaze fixed on Elena's face. "Are you in love with Drake?"

"Yes," she said, and knew in that moment that it was true. Somewhere along the way, she had fallen in love with him.

"And does he love you?" Liliana asked, her brow furrowed.

"I don't know."

"Love!" Rodin said, sneering. "An overrated emotion, to be sure. It has nothing to do with Drake's responsibility to the Coven."

Elena cleared her throat. "I would think that our marriage would negate his betrothal to another."

"Our race is very old," Rodin said, resuming his seat. "Our men are strong and virile, as you undoubtedly know. However, in spite of their lusty nature, they are unable to procreate until they have survived for five centuries. And because our women far outnumber the men, it is forbidden for males who attain that age to waste their seed on mortal women. Such unions do not produce offspring."

Elena stared at him. She had not given any thought to having children, had just assumed it would happen sooner or later. Now, realizing it would never happen filled her with an unexpected sadness.

"The breeding season for our women is short," Rodin

continued. "The woman chosen for Drake is young and fertile."

Elena clenched her hands. Drake had told her that Rodin wouldn't hurt her, but she was beginning to have her doubts.

"Rodin," Liliana said quietly, "I believe you are scaring our guest."

He grunted softly. "I must think about this. Take her to dinner."

Elena felt a sinking sensation in the pit of her stomach. Was she going to *be* dinner?

"Come with me," Liliana said imperiously.

Filled with trepidation, Elena followed Liliana out of the room, down a wide candlelit hallway lined with portraits, and into a large dining hall. The walls were stark white, devoid of decoration. Dozens of young men and women sat at long trestle tables that were laden with bowls and platters and baskets filled with more food than Elena had ever seen. The women all wore long gray dresses; the men wore gray vests and pants.

The occupants all turned to look at Elena when she entered the room.

Liliana guided her to an empty seat at the last table near the back of the room. "Please, sit down. I will bring you a tray."

Murmuring, "Thank you," Elena sat down, acutely conscious of the stares being sent her way. Some of the occupants appeared merely curious, but a few regarded her with obvious malevolence. She thought it odd that, for so many people, there was no conversation at all.

Liliana returned a short time later. She set a tray before Elena that held more food than she could have eaten in a week.

"I did not know what you liked," Liliana explained,

taking the seat across from her, "so I brought you a little of everything. Please, eat."

Smiling faintly, Elena picked up the fork, surprised to find the utensils were made of stainless steel and not gold-plated, like the utensils at Wolfram Castle. She took a bite of an individual-sized casserole topped with mashed potatoes.

"Is it to your liking?" Liliana asked.

Elena nodded. "May I ask you something?"

"Of course."

"Are all these people vampires?"

Liliana smiled indulgently. "No. They are sheep."

"Excuse me?"

"The Fortress houses a number of vampires, both old and young," Liliana replied, as if that explained everything.

"I don't understand."

"The Fortress is our primary lair. Our people come here when they feel the need of solitude, or time to heal. Others come to rest, or to mate. There is no hunting allowed within two hundred miles. As the Master of the Fortress and the leader of our people, Rodin is duty-bound to provide sustenance for those who take shelter here."

Elena paused, fork in midair. "Sustenance?" She stared at Liliana in horror. "These people are food?"

"Do not look so shocked, my dear. We do not kill them."

"But you feed on them?" Elena dropped her fork. It clattered loudly on the table, drawing more curious gazes from the other diners.

Liliana made a broad gesture with her hand. "As you can see, they are well cared for."

"Are they free to leave here?"

Liliana sat up straighter, her expression suddenly hostile. "Please, finish your meal."

"I'm not hungry. I want to see Drake."

"I am afraid that is not possible at this time."

"Why not? Where is he? What have you done to him?" Merciful heavens, had they killed him?

"He is being punished for his disobedience."

Relief coursed through her. And then anger. "I'm his wife!" she exclaimed, rising. "I demand to see him. Now."

It was obvious, from the set of Liliana's jaw and the look in her eyes, that she wasn't accustomed to being addressed in that tone of voice, especially with others looking on. She took several deep breaths and then rose gracefully to her feet. "Very well. Come with me."

Feeling suddenly apprehensive, Elena followed Liliana up a narrow flight of stairs. She had expected to find a room of some kind when they reached the landing, but it only led to another flight of stairs and then another until they reached a squat wooden door. There was no visible latch on the door, yet it opened at the touch of Liliana's hand.

Elena peered into the room, which was lit only by a narrow shaft of moonlight shining through a slit in the roof.

"Drake? Elena wishes to see you. Call me when she is ready to leave," Liliana said, and pushed Elena into the room.

Elena stumbled forward into the darkness to be caught up in a pair of welcoming arms.

"Elena, what are you doing here?"

"Drake! Oh, Drake!" She collapsed against him, her face buried in the hollow of his shoulder. "We have to get out of here."

He brushed a lock of hair from her forehead, then kissed her lightly. "I cannot go."

"Why not?" She looked up at him, wishing she could see his face. "Why can't we leave the same way we got here?"

"I am bound."

"I don't understand."

He lifted one leg and she heard the rattle of chains.

"Shackles," he explained. "Only Rodin can free me." He caressed her cheek. "I never should have brought you here. Never brought you into my life."

"They feed on people."

"He told you that?"

"I saw it. I saw them. The . . . the sheep."

Taking off his coat, Drake spread it on the hard cement. "Come, sit down," he urged, and sat beside her, his arm sliding around her shoulders to draw her close.

"Did you do that? Feed on those helpless people?"

"Years ago," he admitted quietly. "When I was very young."

"Your mother said they don't kill them. Is that true?"

"Partly. Accidents happen when we are changing. Sometimes there is a loss of control." There were those in the outside world who preferred to kill their prey. There was no law against it, as long as there were no bodies drained of blood left behind. Vampires who went rogue and became a danger to the Coven were destroyed. But he saw no need to tell Elena that, not now.

"Where do they come from?" she asked hesitantly. "The sheep?"

Drake's gaze slid away from hers. This was another part of his existence he had hoped to keep hidden from her. "We raise them. They have never known any other life."

Elena listened in mounting horror as he told her how the people she had seen in the dining hall were the descendants of three couples that Rodin had captured hundreds of years ago.

"As I said, they are rarely mistreated. They are well fed. They are taught to read and write by their parents. Here, in the Fortress, they are given books to read and other things to occupy their time. Some of them work in the kitchens. Others in the laundry. They live in dormitories in the basement—boys in one, girls in another—until they are old enough to mate, and then a select few are allowed rooms of their own."

"But they're prisoners. It's wrong to keep people locked up for food, to breed them like . . . like . . ."

"Sheep?"

"Yes! How can you be a party to such a thing? It's barbaric!"

"I never said I approved. It is one of the reasons I do not stay here. The reason I left in the first place."

Elena frowned. If they raised the people for food . . . "Where are the children? The babies?"

"They are housed elsewhere until they are grown."

"With their parents?"

"Yes, until they are sixteen, and then they come here."

"But, the children? Are they always locked up? Do they ever get to go outside and play in the fresh air?"

"Elena . . ."

Her answer was there, in the tone of his voice.

Elena stared up at the sliver of sky visible through the roof, her heart aching for the people who were kept here against their will, for the children who would never know the freedom to run and play outdoors. These people deserved to be free, to live their own lives, to come and go as they pleased. She couldn't begin to imagine how they must feel. And yet, Drake had said they had never known any other life. She thought of the homeless people her uncle had told her about when she complained that she wanted a new dress. He had told her to be thankful for what she had, that there were children who lived on the streets in the big cities who had to beg for their bread, men who had to steal to feed their families.

She shook her head. As terrible as that might be, she thought she would rather starve than spend her life in this place, to have no other purpose than to provide sustenance for vampires.

Drake's arm tightened around her shoulders. "I cannot change it, Elena," he said. "It has been our way for centuries. Were it not for the ready supply of blood that is here, Rodin's people would be forced to prey upon those in the outside world."

"Are there places like this wherever your people live?"

"Yes. Every country throughout the world has a similar Fortress, and each one is ruled by a Master Vampire."

"And your father ordered you here to mate with another vampire?"

"Yes. And to take my place on the Council, something I have resisted for three hundred years."

"That empty chair. It's for you, isn't it?"

"Yes."

"I noticed that the men all bear a striking resemblance to your father."

"They are my brothers."

"All of them?"

"Yes, though we do not all have the same mother."

"What does the Council do?"

"They judge those who have broken our laws, and execute them, if necessary."

Elena went cold inside. Were they going to execute Drake for marrying her? Surely not! Surely the members of the Council wouldn't pass a sentence of death on their own brother. She felt as if she couldn't breathe, as if she had tumbled into a nightmare from which there was no escape.

"Is that what you wish?" Drake asked, stroking her hair.

"What?"

"To escape? To be free of me?"

She chewed on her thumbnail. Did she want that? Did she want to leave Drake and never see him again? Go back to her old life with her uncle? If she left Drake, he would be free to marry the woman Rodin had chosen for him and there would be no need for him to suffer anymore. She shook her head. How could she leave him? "I don't know."

"If it is your desire, Rodin will erase your memories of this place and everything that happened since the night we met. It will be as if none of it ever happened."

"And if I stay?"

"You would be wiser to go."

She tried to see his face in the darkness. "Is that what you want?"

"I am only thinking of what is best for you."

"Do you want me to go?"

"No. You are the only thing in my life that matters. But there is no place for you here. And even if there were, you would not be happy living among us, knowing what is going on." He took a deep breath and released it in a heavy sigh. "If Rodin offers you the chance to leave, you should take it."

It wasn't a decision Elena was ready to make, so she changed the subject. "Is this where you come to feed?"

"No. I hunted in the city." He laughed softly. "It is another of my sins."

"Why didn't you come here? Where is this place?"

"The Fortress is located high in the Southern Carpathian Mountains. A veil hides it from mortal eyes, though there are those, mostly people with paranormal powers of one kind or another, who have penetrated the veil from time to time."

She started to ask what happened to those people, then decided she didn't want to know.

"Do all the Fortresses keep people to feed on?"

"No. Most of our kind prey on the general populace of whatever country they call home."

"Are all the vampires united?" That was a scary thought.

He shook his head. "There are always those who lust for power. Rodin has had to defend his territory on numerous occasions. There are rumors that the ruler of the Hungarian Fortress wants to take over Rodin's domain."

Elena frowned. How could vampires go to war with each other without the mortal world being aware of it? In this age of cell phones and digital cameras, it seemed impossible.

"Master Vampires fight one on one," Drake said, answering her unspoken question. "Winner take all."

"What does that mean, winner take all?"

"The victor takes the loser's Fortress and everything that goes with it. All those who lived there are forced to leave and seek shelter elsewhere."

"And they always leave, without a fight?"

"Master Vampires possess an enormous amount of power. There are not many who have the courage or the strength to challenge them."

"So, do all the vampires in your father's command or whatever you call it live in the Fortress?"

"No. Usually only those of his own blood, and those who are in need of healing or rest stay here, although all the Carpathian vampires are welcome to visit. You are cold," he said, drawing her body closer to his. "You should go below."

She clutched his arm. "I don't want to leave you." Who knew when, or if, she would be allowed to see him again? Smothering a yawn with her hand, she laid her head against his shoulder and closed her eyes, her mind reeling with the events of the day, the things she had learned.

Sensing her distress, Drake let his mind brush hers, willing her to relax. A moment later, she was asleep.

Lifting her into his arms, Drake cradled her to his chest. He stroked her hair, caressed her cheek. In spite of the darkness, he could see her clearly. He had been certain that, given a choice to stay or go, she would leave this place. He had spoken truly when he'd told her it would be wiser for her to leave. He had no idea how long Rodin would keep him locked up, wouldn't put it past his sire to threaten Elena's life in order to get Drake to end his marriage so that he might wed and bed Katiya. And even though Drake was certain Rodin wouldn't harm Elena, he wasn't willing to risk her safety or her life to prove it.

"Ah, sweet wife, what am I to do with you?" he murmured, although the greater question might be, what would become of her if Rodin refused to let her go?

He glanced up as a chill wind eddied through the crack in the roof. Come morning, the light of the sun would penetrate that narrow slit. The fire of it, the feel of it dancing over his skin, would be excruciating beyond anything he had ever known.

There wasn't much in this life he feared, but being trapped in the sun, dying inch by slow inch . . . He shuddered at the thought.

How long would Rodin keep him locked in this accursed place? A day? Two?

How long would it take for the sun to burn away his flesh and steal his strength until nothing remained but a pile of charred ashes?

Chapter 14

Elena woke slowly, a sense of dread making her reluctant to open her eyes. She heard whispered voices, the shuffling of many feet.

Squinting through half-opened lids, she saw a dozen faces staring down at her. Startled, she jackknifed into a sitting position, her gaze flitting wildly around the room. A moment's disorientation quickly turned to panic. Where was she? Before the question was fully formed, she knew.

She was in one of the dormitories.

With the sheep.

"You're new, aren't you?" asked a girl with curly brown hair and slanted brown eyes.

Elena nodded.

"It's time for morning meal," the girl said.

"I'm not hungry."

"You must eat. It is the rule," the girl said with an airy wave of her hand. "Come along."

Elena shook her head. How had she gotten here? The last thing she remembered was falling asleep in Drake's arms.

"You'll be punished if you don't eat." A look of fear shadowed the girl's eyes when a bell rang. "We must hurry! We'll be late!"

Spurred by the trepidation in the girl's eyes, Elena sprang out of bed. She didn't know what kind of punishment vampires meted out, but she was certain it was something awful.

She followed the line of women down a high-ceilinged corridor. As soon as they crossed the threshold of the dining hall, all conversation ceased.

Elena took a seat near the back. She didn't belong here. There had to be a mistake. She glanced anxiously around the room, searching for Liliana, before realizing that the vampires were most likely resting at this time of the day.

Four large men patrolled the dining hall. Elena studied them, trying to determine whether they were human or vampire. Common sense told her they were human, but they were curiously lifeless, their movements almost puppetlike. They spoke in monotones, their eyes blank, their faces showing no emotion whatsoever.

Although she had declared she wasn't hungry, Elena ate everything she was served, surprised at how good it was. And then she grimaced. Of course, it only made sense that the vampires would take good care of their food supply.

When breakfast was over, two of the hulking men herded the women downstairs into a large rectangular-shaped room with stark white walls and a stone floor. A large hearth provided warmth.

Once the women were all inside, the doors were closed and locked. The girl who had spoken to Elena earlier told her that the men had their own place to spend the day.

There were books in the room, easels and paints, yarn and thread and a half dozen looms, a potter's wheel, several chess sets, iPods with ear phones, as well as a large-screen TV and what looked like every movie ever made. Elena frowned. The TV was the first sign she had seen that there was electricity in the Fortress.

The women spread out quickly, each finding a task or a pastime to her liking.

Feeling as though she were caught in a horrible nightmare, Elena watched the women. They all seemed happy, perfectly content to be locked away in this dreadful place. She overheard snatches of conversation—two girls talking about men they hoped to mate with, one girl whispering to another that she thought she was with child, several other young women talking about which vampires they hoped would come for them that night.

"I'm hoping for Cullin," a pretty brunette said with a sigh. "He's so handsome and his bite is so tender."

"You can have Cullin, Marta. I want Dallin," a tiny redhead said, a quiver in her voice. "He only takes a little and then he's gone."

"Dallin and Elnora, sitting in a tree . . ." Marta chanted, and burst into giggles.

"I don't care who it is," remarked another with a toss of her head. "As long as it isn't Vardin."

All the women within hearing distance nodded in agreement.

Eventually, boredom had Elena picking up a copy of *Jane Eyre*. She carried it to an overstuffed chair in the corner and sat down, one leg curled beneath her. She tried to read, but somehow, the fictional problems of Jane and Mr. Rochester paled when compared to the very real problems that beset her. Elena wasn't being kept in an attic, but in a very real prison. There were similarities, of course. Mr. Rochester couldn't marry Jane because he already had a wife. Drake couldn't marry the woman his father had chosen for him for the same reason. He already had a wife. Mr. Rochester's wife, who was quite insane, perished in a fire. If she had to stay here much longer, Elena thought she, too, might go insane.

With a sigh, she put the book aside. She couldn't concentrate on the words, couldn't think of anything but

Drake, locked up in a high tower room. She couldn't shake the feeling that he was in pain, that he needed her. How long would Rodin keep his son locked up? She pressed a hand to her mouth to stifle a gasp as a new thought pushed its way into her mind. There was a hole in the tower roof. Surely Rodin wouldn't leave Drake up there during the day, helpless to avoid the sun's light.

Worried for Drake's welfare, she lost track of time.

She looked up when a woman entered the room. She wasn't a vampire, but a female version of the men who had guarded the dining room. Elena watched nervously as the woman gazed around the room, then strode purposefully toward her.

"You," the woman said sharply. "Come with me."

When Elena didn't comply immediately, the woman grasped her roughly by the arm and yanked her to her feet.

Elena followed the woman down the corridor and into a small room.

"Undress," the woman ordered. Reaching into a cupboard, she withdrew a long gray dress. "Put that on." She dropped a pair of black shoes on top of the dress. "Quickly now."

When it became evident the woman wasn't going to give her any privacy, Elena turned her back on her and quickly changed into the gray dress, and as she did so, she was overcome with the feeling that she had just lost her individuality.

Moments later, she was back in the recreation room, indistinguishable from the rest of the sheep.

Drake pressed back against the wall of his prison. It kept him out of the sun's direct light, but he couldn't escape the scorching heat. It enveloped him like an invisible shroud, burning through his clothing to the flesh beneath, adding to the pain of the heavy silver leg iron that shackled his ankle to the wall. But for the chains that bound him he could have dissolved into mist and escaped.

He groaned deep in his throat. He could feel his flesh blistering inside and out. Not wanting Elena to see him like this, or to suffer the heat of the day with him, he had called Liliana to take Elena away last night, after she had fallen asleep.

Elena. Where was she now? Closing his eyes, he tried to concentrate on her whereabouts, but the intense pain clouded his mind, making coherent thought impossible.

He spent several minutes uselessly cursing his sire, then lapsed into silence. He had known Rodin would be angry, but he had never expected anything like this.

The pain intensified his thirst. He felt his fangs run out in response. As the hours passed, pain turned into agony. He felt his body shrinking in on itself, felt his veins constricting. The weight of his clothing became agonizing against his tender flesh.

A hoarse cry tore at his throat as a ray of sun found him and he scuttled to the other side of the tower, his arms covering his head in an effort to escape the withering heat.

Cringing in pain, he summoned Elena's image. Beautiful Elena, with hair like fine black silk and skin as soft as down. Elena, who cared for him in spite of what he was . . . or had her affection turned to hate now that she knew the truth about him, about his people?

"Elena." He forced her name through cracked, dry lips.

If he begged, would Rodin let him see her one last time?

The day dragged on. Elena took up the book again, pretending to read. She was aware of the curious gazes of the other women, but they seemed to sense she wished to be left alone, or maybe they were simply leery of a stranger in their midst.

Just when she thought the day would never end, the

door opened and Liliana stepped into the room. Without a word, all of the women rose and filed toward the doorway. Elena hung back so that she was the last in line. When she reached Liliana, she stopped.

"Where is Drake?" Elena asked anxiously. "I want to see him."

"I am sorry. That is not possible just now. Please, go to last meal with the others."

"I want to see my husband," Elena said, stressing the last word.

A humorless smile played over the vampire's lips. "You will see him at Rodin's pleasure and not before."

"Why not now? Please, I must see him."

"If you wish to see Drake again, you will do as you are told." Without waiting for an answer, the vampire left the room.

Fighting back tears, Elena went into the dining hall and took a seat. Several human girls served the meal. Tonight, a pair of male vampires patrolled the aisles dividing the men from the women.

Elena forced herself to eat, afraid that refusing would keep her from seeing Drake.

The meal was almost over when the door opened and a dozen or so vampires—both male and female—entered the room. Elena stared at them. They were all beautiful. Male or female, they moved from table to table with a languid grace no human could ever match. Most of the men wore black, but not the women. Clad in brightly colored clothing or lounging outfits, they looked like a flock of exotic birds.

One by one, the vampires called out a name, and the man or woman called left his or her seat and followed the vampire out the door.

"Elena Knightsbridge."

It took her a moment to realize her name had been

called. There had to be a mistake, she thought frantically. She wasn't one of the sheep! She was Drake's wife.

"Elena Knightsbridge, come to me."

To her horror, she found herself rising as if she had no mind of her own, moving toward the vampire who had summoned her. He resembled Drake in that he was tall and had long black hair and blue eyes. But that was where the resemblance ended. There was a cruel twist to this man's mouth, a coldness in his pale blue eyes.

"Poor thing," one of the women murmured as Elena passed by. "To get Vardin her first time."

Elena shivered when he looked at her. There was nothing of warmth when he smiled at her, no gentleness in his grip when his hand closed over her arm. This was a man who enjoyed inflicting pain, she had no doubt of it.

She couldn't stop shaking as he led her down three flights of stairs, then shoved her into a room that looked as though it had been decorated for a king—from the overly large bed draped with cloth-of-gold to the striped silk that covered the walls. An overstuffed chair covered in red velvet, a desk, and a large, beautifully carved wardrobe were spaced around the room. Aubusson carpets covered the floor; hanging candelabras provided illumination.

"Please," he said with exaggerated politeness. "Sit down." It was a demand, not an invitation.

She perched on the edge of the chair, her hands clenched in her lap. A sense of doom settled over her when the door closed, seemingly of its own accord.

The vampire came toward her like a hungry cat stalking its prey. He stood over her, his eyes going red, his fangs gleaming as he lowered his head to her neck.

Panic swept over her as his hand closed over her shoulder. She wanted to fight him, wanted to scream for him to leave her alone, but sheer terror at what he might do if she opposed him held her frozen in place.

"No." The word escaped her lips. "Please. There's been a mistake. I'm not one of . . . of the sheep."

But he didn't listen.

Didn't stop.

Didn't care.

There was no pleasure in his bite as he bent her back over his arm, only an excruciating pain that sizzled down the length of her neck like the sharp bite of a serpent, and then burned its way through every nerve and cell in her body.

She screamed with the pain of it as her body began to tremble uncontrollably. When he bit her again, the world spun out of focus. She was falling, slipping helplessly into a black abyss that felt like death. Sobbing, she whispered a single word.

"Drake."

He came awake with a start, the echo of Elena's terrified cry ringing in his ears. Ignoring the pain that burned through him with every breath, he pulled against the chain that shackled him to the wall. He struggled to free himself even though he knew it was useless. His preternatural strength had been leeched away by the silver that bound him, by the relentless sunlight that had scorched his flesh.

His whole body throbbed in agony. Blood oozed from where the silver had rubbed his skin raw. Sweat stung his eyes. His tortured body screamed for nourishment to relieve the pain and the thirst.

"Elena." Her name whispered past dry, cracked lips. "Elena, forgive me."

Chapter 15

Elena couldn't sleep that night. Every time she closed her eyes, she saw the vampire's hellish gaze, felt his fangs savaging her throat again and again. She huddled under the covers, shoulders shaking, eyes burning with tears. Where was Drake? Why wouldn't they let her see him? She needed him, needed him desperately. She was lost and alone in a nightmare from which there was no escape.

Gradually, exhaustion claimed her and she fell into a restless sleep, only to wake some time later, a scream on her lips.

"Hush, now, you'll be all right."

Elena opened her eyes. In the dim light, she saw one of the women kneeling beside her bed. "S-sorry," Elena said, sniffing back her tears.

"No need to apologize. We all have nightmares now and then. I am Northa."

"Elena."

"What are you doing here? You are not one of us."

Elena hesitated a moment, wondering if she should tell the truth, and then shrugged. "Drake is my husband."

Northa's eyes grew wide with astonishment. "You married Rodin's eldest son?"

At this announcement, someone lit a nearby candle and several other women clustered around Elena's cot, their expressions filled with curiosity.

Elena nodded.

"It is said that of all Rodin's sons, Drake is his favorite."

"I find that hard to believe," Elena said, remembering how angry Rodin had been.

"We only know what little we hear," Marta said. "It is rumored among us that Drake left the Fortress over three hundred years ago and in all that time, he has never come back."

A girl with straight brown hair and gray eyes nodded. "Cullin told me that his brother has never been one of them, that he never approved of his father keeping us here against our will." She made a vague gesture with one hand. "I don't understand what he means, against our will. If we didn't stay here, where would we go?"

"There's a whole world out there," Elena said. "You could have a place of your own, get married, have children."

"Some of us will be allowed to mate and have children," Northa said.

"And those children will be food for the vampires!" Elena exclaimed.

Northa shrugged. "It is how it has always been."

"But you're prisoners!" Elena looked at the women gathered around her. "Don't you want to be free?"

"What is free?" Marta asked.

"I'm free," Elena said. "I chose to marry Drake. We have a house of our own. No one tells us what to do or when to do it. We can come and go as we please."

A girl with short black hair snorted with disdain. "You look like us," she said, tugging on the sleeve of Elena's nightgown, which was like the gowns all the other women wore. "You feed the vampires. How are you any different?"

"I don't belong here."

"But here you are," the dark-haired girl said with an air of finality. "And once you are here, you can never leave."

Those words, and the finality with which the dark-haired girl had spoken them, haunted Elena in the recreation room the next day. It might be true for the sheep, that there was no escape, but it couldn't be true for her. She didn't belong here. Would never belong here. She refused to believe she would never leave this horrible place. She had to cling to the hope that she would soon be with Drake again, that they could return to Wolfram Castle, because hope was all she had.

Now and then, one or another of the women would ask her what it was like outside the Fortress. What did the outside world look like? Had she ever seen a tree? A flower? Felt the sun on her face? The sheep knew about these things. They read books, saw movies and pictures, but they had never touched a living tree, smelled a flower, walked barefoot in the grass.

When she found herself drowning in despair, she clung to Liliana's promise that she would see Drake again. She prayed it would be soon.

The day dragged on. She tried to read but couldn't concentrate on the words. More than anything, she wanted to go outside, to feel the sun on her face, to go for a walk. To spend some time alone. How did the women stand it, always being together, never having any privacy, never having a few minutes to themselves? She wondered why the vampires refused to let their captives go outside. Didn't they trust the guards to protect them? Or were the vampires afraid the guards would run away if given the chance?

After what seemed like forever, it was time for last meal. She was trembling when she entered the dining hall. Too nervous to eat, she kept glancing at the door, praying that Vardin would not call for her again.

When he appeared in the doorway, she could scarcely breathe. More frightened than she would have believed possible, she kept her head down, hoping he wouldn't see her. Her heart pounded so loudly she could hardly hear anything else.

But she heard his voice echoing loudly in her mind, felt herself rising, moving toward him on legs that trembled, following him down the stairs and into his apartment.

And then the door was closing and Vardin was standing over her, his eyes glowing a bright, hellish red, his fangs gleaming in the candlelight.

Elena came awake to the sound of someone calling her name. For a moment, she imagined it was Vardin leaning over her, lightly shaking her shoulder. She swallowed the scream rising in her throat when she opened her eyes and saw Rodin standing beside her bed.

"Get up," he said sternly.

"Where's Drake? Is he all right? I want to see him. I need to see him. Please, I'll do anything, just let me see him."

"Then do as I say."

Rising, her heart filled with trepidation, she followed Rodin out of the dormitory and up the stairs to the tower room.

Outside the door, a candle in a wall sconce came to life, seemingly of its own accord. Rodin plucked the taper from the holder, then opened the tower door and stepped inside.

Elena followed him, a soft cry of denial falling from her lips when she saw Drake curled up against the far wall.

Murmuring his name, she ran to kneel beside him. "Drake? Oh, Drake."

"Go away."

"No. What have they done to you?" His hands were swollen and blistered.

"Elena," he said hoarsely, "get out of here. I do not want you to remember me like this."

"I'm not leaving." She glanced over her shoulder. "How could you do this to him? What kind of monster are you?"

"He is my son," Rodin replied coldly. "He has violated our laws. The usual punishment is death. But I have decided to be lenient, for his mother's sake."

"Lenient!" She screamed the word at him. "You call this lenient?" Tears filled her eyes when she looked at Drake again. Gently, she stroked his hair.

He flinched at her touch and she realized his scalp was also burned.

She looked up at Rodin again. "Do something. He's suffering."

Rodin nodded. "It would not be punishment if he were not."

"I want to be alone with him."

"I will allow you five minutes."

"How very generous of you." It took all the willpower she possessed to keep the sarcasm out of her voice.

Rodin inclined his head. He placed the candle in a crack in the floor, then left the tower, closing the door behind him.

"Drake, you need blood," Elena said urgently. "Hurry, we only have a few minutes. Take mine."

"No." He shook his head. "Go away."

"Stop being so stubborn. We don't have time to argue."

Raising his head, he looked at her, only then noticing that she wore the same plain white nightgown the sheep wore. "Why do you not hate me for bringing you here?"

"It's not your fault. You didn't know this would happen."

"I promised he would treat you well." His nostrils flared. "Vardin." The name hissed past his lips. "I will kill him for this."

"I'm fine." She forced the lie past her lips. "Please, my husband, take what you need."

He shook his head. "I dare not," he said. "If I begin"—he shook his head again—"I am afraid I would not be able to stop."

"Please, Drake," she begged softly. "I can't bear to see you suffering like this."

"It will pass, in time."

She stared at him. His beautiful face was blistered almost beyond recognition. She yearned to take him in her arms, to hold him close and comfort him, but touching him would only cause him more pain.

Leaning forward, she kissed him ever so lightly. "I love you."

"Foolish girl."

"Tell me," she begged. "Tell me you love me, even if it's a lie. Tell me we'll be together again soon and that nothing will ever part us."

He cupped her cheek in his hand. "I love you," he said fervently. "Whatever the future holds, never doubt that I will always love you."

"And we'll be together again, promise me."

"We will be together again, wife," he said, brushing the tears from her cheeks. "I swear it."

She forced a smile. She knew he was lying, but for now, it was all she had.

"Rodin is coming," Drake said.

Leaning forward, he kissed her again, an achingly tender brush of his scorched lips across hers. A fleeting caress that she knew meant good-bye.

And then Rodin was there, dragging her to her feet, leading her away.

Chapter 16

Drake sank back on the cold stone floor, more miserable than he had ever been in his life. Yesterday had been bad. Today had been worse. He breathed a sigh of relief as the sun went down. His body twitched uncontrollably, his fangs ached. He needed blood. But worse than any of that was the knowledge that Vardin had fed on Elena, and there was nothing he could do about it.

He rested his forehead on his bent knees, thoughts of vengeance and murder chasing through his mind like mice in a maze. Closing his eyes, he imagined driving a stake through his brother's black heart. But it wasn't Vardin who was responsible. True, he had fed on Elena, but it was Rodin who had allowed it to happen. For all Drake knew, Rodin had suggested it. One thing was certain, Elena would not have been quartered with the sheep if Rodin hadn't ordered it.

"Speak of the devil and he appears," Drake muttered as his sire opened the tower door. It took every ounce of what strength he had left to gain his feet.

"I have brought you something to drink," Rodin said.

"I want nothing from you. Nothing but Elena's freedom."

Closing the distance between them, Rodin held up a tankard made of gold. "Drink this."

"No."

"Do not make me force you."

Drake glared at his sire. What would be worse, drinking of his own free will, or resisting? One way or the other, Rodin would have his way, and with that thought in mind, Drake reached for the goblet.

The contents were thick and cold but he drank greedily, his eyes closing as the blood took the edge off the worst of the pain. After draining the goblet, he licked his lips, then met his sire's gaze. "How long are you going to keep me locked up?"

"That is what I have come to discuss with you," Rodin said. Taking the goblet, he tossed it aside.

Drake took a deep breath. From Rodin's tone, it was obvious he wasn't going to like what was coming.

"Tomorrow night, in front of the Council, I will annul your marriage to the mortal female and formally announce your betrothal to Katiya. Since the night of the new moon has passed, you will wed at her pleasure."

"And if I refuse?"

"I will leave you here until your flesh is dry and your veins empty and you beg me for mercy."

"Ever the loving father," Drake said bitterly. "Is that the worst you can do?"

"If you continue to defy me, I will give the woman to Vardin to do with as he pleases."

"He has already fed on her," Drake said, unable to keep the fury from his voice. "Twice!"

"You know what he is capable of. Be grateful he has done her no permanent harm."

It took every ounce of his willpower, honed over five centuries, for Drake to choke back the rage that engulfed him. "I will never forgive you for this."

Rodin nodded. "I have your word that you will do as I have decreed?"

"You will release Elena tomorrow and send her back to Wolfram."

"No. I will release her the day after you and Katiya are wed."

"I have your word?"

Rodin straightened to his full height, his eyes flashing with anger. "Do you doubt it?"

Drake snorted with contempt. "I told Elena you would treat her well, that it was not your way to make war on women."

"I have done what was necessary. I will have your word that you will do as I have commanded."

"You have it, on three conditions. I will marry Katiya, but then the two of us will be free to leave the Fortress."

"So you can abandon her as soon as you are away? Do you take me for a fool?"

"I will not abandon her."

"The woman, Elena, will pay the price if you do."

"I have no doubt of that."

Rodin paced to the far end of the tower, his hands clasped behind his back. Returning to stand in front of Drake, he said, "You may leave the Fortress when Katiya is with child. In the meantime, there is the matter of the Council. . . ."

"That's the second condition. I do not belong on the Council and we both know it. There is no law that says all the members must be of your direct bloodline. Liam would be an admirable addition."

Rodin grunted softly. Liam was a liaison between Rodin and Lucien, the Master Vampire of the Italian Fortress.

"And your third condition?"

"Elena will not be quartered with the sheep, or used as sustenance by anyone. She is to have the run of the

Fortress, and all her needs met. She is . . . was . . . my wife and I will have her treated with the respect she deserves."

"Very well. Now I have a condition of my own. You will not attempt to see her."

"I demand the right to bid her farewell when she leaves."

"Need I remind you that you are in no position to demand anything?"

Drake clenched his jaw, then blew out a breath. "Must I beg for the opportunity to tell her good-bye?"

"No," Rodin said through clenched teeth. "I will allow it."

"I would ask one more favor. She will need someone to take her home."

"I will see that she arrives safely."

"She is to have Wolfram Castle. I will need pen and paper to make it legal."

Rodin nodded.

"I promised her the wherewithal to provide for her needs as long as she lived."

Rodin folded his arms over his chest. "Anything else?" he asked tersely.

"No. If you will do these things for me, then I vow to take Katiya as my bride. I will see that she conceives a child. I will put her happiness before my own. You have my word on it."

"And you have mine." Slipping a heavy glove on his right hand, Rodin touched the thick silver leg iron that bound Drake's ankle to the wall. The manacle fell away with a harsh clatter.

"Come," Rodin said. "Your mother is anxious to see you."

Elena paced the floor of the dormitory, scarcely aware of the other women who were preparing for bed. It had been a very long day, her every thought for Drake. After seeing him last night, she could think of nothing else, could not begin to imagine the pain he was feeling. How did he endure it? How had he even survived? She could not comprehend such torment, or understand how any man, vampire or not, could be so cruel to his own flesh and blood.

They had to get away from here, but how? Drake was helpless as long as he was imprisoned in the tower. There was no way she could break down the dormitory door, or fight her way through a nest of vampires. She shuddered to think what her future would be if something happened to Drake.

She lifted a hand to her neck, remembering the pain, the horror, of being bitten by Vardin. She knew now why the other sheep feared him. He was cruel, oblivious to the pain he caused. Or maybe he simply enjoyed it.

After washing her hands and face, Elena changed into the long white gown she had been given to sleep in and crawled under the covers of her narrow cot. She had been too upset to sit and talk with the other girls while they readied themselves for bed but now, as Northa blew out the last candle, Elena recalled Marta saying it wasn't uncommon for the vampires to come for one of them in the middle of the night.

Elena folded her arms over her chest. How was she supposed to sleep knowing that Vardin or one of the other vampires might come looking for a midnight snack?

She was drifting to sleep when the dormitory door opened. She tasted fear on her tongue as someone stepped into the room. But it was only Liliana.

"Come," the vampire said quietly.

Slipping out of bed, Elena followed Liliana into the clothing room, afraid to ask what was coming. To her surprise, Liliana thrust the clothing Elena had worn to the Fortress into her hands. "Dress quickly. The Council awaits."

The Council. All too clearly, she recalled Drake's words: *The Council judges those who have broken our laws, and executes them, if necessary.* Were they going to execute her for marrying Drake? Or worse, execute them both?

Unable to still her trembling, she removed the nightgown and tossed it aside. She quickly donned her undergarments, then slipped the lavender silk dress over her head and smoothed it over her hips. Sitting on a low stool, she pulled on her heels, thinking how good it felt to wear her own clothes again.

When she started to rise, Liliana put a hand on her shoulder, forcing her back down, and then, to Elena's surprise, the vampire began brushing her hair.

Feeling like a sacrifice being readied for the altar, Elena folded her hands in her lap to still their trembling.

"It is time," the vampire said. "You will keep silent when we reach the Council chambers. Do you understand?"

Elena nodded. Hoping her legs would support her, she followed Liliana up the winding staircase and down the candlelit corridor to the Council chambers. She hesitated when Liliana opened the cathedral-like door. Feeling like a lamb being led to the slaughter, she took a deep breath and stepped inside.

The first thing she saw was Drake. Clad in nothing but a pair of black sweatpants, he knelt in front of the dais, head bowed, hands shackled behind his back. In the light of a hundred candles, the ravages of the sun's heat were clearly visible. His skin was badly burned; in some places, it was almost black.

Rodin sat on his throne, as regal and powerful as any king. A girl sat in the chair beside him. She was young, surely not more than sixteen. Her hair was a rich chestnut brown, her eyes a shade lighter beneath delicately arched brows. She had an aristocratic nose, a generous mouth, a long, slender neck. Her skin was almost luminescent. Liliana's beauty paled beside that of the younger woman.

The members of the Council, dressed in ubiquitous black, sat like statues.

When Elena would have gone to Drake, Liliana put a staying hand on her arm. "No. You must not go near him. You must not speak to him."

And with that admonition, Liliana went to stand beside her husband's chair.

Several moments passed before Rodin spoke. "As Master of the Coven, I call this Council to order. Drake, here present, has violated the laws of our kind in that he has taken a mortal female as his wife. As his sire and Master of this Coven, I hereby declare his marriage void from this night forward."

Elena stared at Drake. He had told her that Rodin wouldn't annul their marriage if it was consummated. Had he lied to her? She willed him to look at her, but his head remained bowed.

"Drake, do you, of your own free will, agree to abide by this annulment?"

"Yes, sire."

"No!" The word was torn from Elena's throat.

Rodin glared at her. "Remain silent, woman! As spoken and agreed, the marriage between Drake and the woman, Elena Knightsbridge, is declared null and void."

As one, the twelve members of the Council said, "As spoken and agreed, let it be done."

"Done and done," Rodin said. "Drake, arise."

The heavy chains binding his wrists rattled as, with an effort, Drake gained his feet.

Rodin stood. He smiled at the young woman sitting quietly in the other chair, then extended his hand. "Come, Katiya."

She rose gracefully, her head high and proud as she took her place at Rodin's side.

"By my will and authority," the Master Vampire declared, "I do hereby approve and affirm the betrothal between Drake Sherrad and Katiya Belova, here present. The marriage will be performed at a time of the bride's choosing. This Council is dismissed."

Chapter 17

Once again, Elena found herself being led out of the Council chambers. But she wasn't taken downstairs to the women's dormitory this time. Instead, Liliana escorted her into a large chamber at the other end of the corridor.

"This will be your room for the remainder of your stay," the vampire said, her voice cool. "Please, make yourself at home. You may have the run of the Fortress during the daylight hours. I would advise you to remain in here, with the door locked, when the sun goes down. You may dine in here, or join the shee . . . the other women at mealtimes. Is there anything you wish?"

Elena clasped her hands, took a deep breath, and said, "I would very much like to see Drake."

"My son is no longer your concern."

Elena bit down hard on her lower lip. It was the only way to stifle the angry words of protest that rose in her throat. She would have gone down on her knees and begged, but she knew doing so would accomplish nothing but her own humiliation. Instead, she straightened her spine and said, "You're right, of course."

Something that might have been compassion flickered

in the depths of Liliana's deep green eyes, and was quickly gone. "There is a nightgown and a change of clothing in the wardrobe. If you have need of anything at all, there will be a drone outside your door. Just tell him what you want."

Elena nodded. A drone? What on earth was that?

"I bid you good night," Liliana said, and with a last look around the room, she took her leave, quietly closing the door behind her.

Elena stood in the middle of the room. It was a far cry from the dormitory where the sheep were housed. Several landscapes adorned the pale yellow walls. Plush beige carpeting muffled her footsteps. A ceramic pitcher and several glasses sat atop an ornately carved three-drawer chest, along with a hair brush and hand mirror. A flowered quilt covered a large brass bed. A wooden shelf held a number of books written in several different languages, as well as numerous DVDs and CDs for the TV and stereo housed in a small entertainment unit. Curious, she opened the door to the left of the bed and stepped inside, surprised to find a small bathroom. There was no tub, just a commode, sink, and shower. A shelf held several towels.

Returning to the main room, she went to the window and pulled back the heavy drapery. A bright yellow moon shone on the snowcapped mountains in the distance. It was too dark to see anything else, but she stood there for several minutes, staring at the wispy gray clouds drifting across the inky sky.

Where was Drake? Was someone caring for him? How long would it take for those dreadful burns to heal? Was he still a prisoner? Would they let her see him again?

So many questions and no one to answer them.

Suddenly overcome with weariness, she sat on the edge of the bed and removed her shoes, then let down her hair.

There would be time enough for answers tomorrow.

* * *

Drake lay on his back on a thick pallet in a cell in the dungeon beneath the Fortress, his arms folded behind his head. It was a dismal place, but preferable to being locked in the tower. A sound of disgust rose in his throat. Trust Rodin to drag out his punishment as long as possible, as if Drake could forget that he was no longer a free man, or that his sire was now making his decisions for him. The thought rankled beyond bearing.

Earlier, Rodin had brought him one of the sheep, but Drake had refused to feed, even though drinking from her would have helped ease his pain and aided in his healing.

It had been a foolish thing to do. He would not heal without feeding, but his anger and his pride had overridden his thirst.

Rodin had glared at him. Though his sire hadn't spoken a word, it was obvious he knew why Drake had refused to feed, and just as obvious that he recognized the gesture for the useless act of rebellion it was.

Drake swore. How had things gone so wrong, so fast? He had badly underestimated Rodin's determination to have his own way. Considering the events of the last two days, it was difficult to believe he was his sire's favorite son, but Drake knew it to be true. The fact that he still lived was proof of it.

He groaned low in his throat as the hunger burned through him. Maybe he should have fed. The pain that wracked him was constant. He could feel his veins shrinking. His fangs ached. His blistered skin throbbed incessantly. But even worse than his physical pain was his need to see Elena, to hold her in his arms, to bury himself in her sweetness.

Closing his eyes, he summoned her image to the

forefront of his mind. How had he lived so long without her? She was like the sun, bringing light into the darkness of his life. He thought of the night they had made love, the way she had given herself to him, the joy he had found in her arms. She had been afraid of what he was, yet she had come to him eagerly, giving him all she had, her love pouring over him as warm and bright as summer sunshine. He remembered the taste of her on his tongue, the way her life's blood had warmed him, turning away the hunger, lighting the darkness of his soul.

What was he to do without her? Where was she now? He tried to find her through the blood link they shared, but he was too weak, the pain too strong, to concentrate.

A cry erupted from his throat, torn from the very depths of his being, a mournful wail that rolled all his pain and loneliness into one long anguished howl that reverberated off the walls and echoed in every room in the Fortress.

And those who loved him heard and wept bitter tears.

Elena woke with an overpowering sense of loss. As much as she might wish otherwise, her brief marriage was over. What was worse, Drake was going to marry someone else. He might insist he didn't want to wed Katiya, but what man—mortal or vampire—would find such a union distasteful? The vampire was beautiful. Her skin was so clear, it almost glowed. Her hair was thick and rich, her figure perfect. Looking at her had made Elena feel as grubby and undesirable as an old worn-out shoe.

If only she could leave this place now! How long would Rodin insist on keeping her here? What if—horrible thought—he made her attend the wedding? She would rather die than watch Katiya become Drake's bride. How was she going to face the future, knowing he was sharing his life with another woman, fathering a child with someone else? No matter how long she lived, she would never forget him.

Swinging her legs over the side of the bed, Elena sat up and stared at the wall. If Rodin sent her away, where would she go? Surely not back to her uncle. Drake had said if the time came when she no longer wanted to be his wife, he would give her Wolfram Castle and the means to support herself for the rest of her life. But he was in no position to do that now, so where did that leave her?

Rising, she went into the bathroom and washed her hands and face while she considered her options.

Whether Drake approved or not, she had little choice but to return to Wolfram Castle when and if she left here. She had nowhere else to go. Maybe she could demand that Rodin provide her with enough money to live on until she could find a job. After all, it was his fault she was now a divorced woman with no visible means of support.

She paused as she dried her hands. Did she really want to go back to the castle when Jenica was buried in the garden? What was she going to do about Jenica? Drake had promised to find her cousin's murderer, but that wasn't going to happen now. And what about her uncle? She would be helpless without Drake to protect her.

Going to the window, she pulled back the curtain and stared outside, a gasp rising in her throat. The view in daylight was spectacular. The Fortress, situated on a mountain peak, overlooked a deep green valley bisected by a narrow ribbon of blue water. Several small cottages dotted the valley floor. How sad for the men and women who were kept here to live in view of such a beautiful place and never be able to see it, never be allowed to go outside to enjoy it.

Turning away from the window, she removed her nightgown, then went to the small wardrobe beside the bed. Opening the double doors, she found a simple green cotton dress with a round neck, long sleeves, and a bell-shaped skirt hanging beside her lavender silk. There was also a pair of jeans and a short-sleeved pink sweater.

Dress or pants? Pants or dress? Deciding the jeans made her feel less vulnerable, she quickly pulled them on and slid the sweater over her head. Liliana had also thoughtfully provided a pair of white sandals. Like the jeans and sweater, they fit perfectly.

Summoning her courage, Elena unlocked the door and stepped into the corridor. A man—a very big man with massive shoulders—stood beside her door. He didn't speak, didn't smile, just stood there like a statue, his gray eyes curiously empty. Was he the drone Liliana had mentioned?

Elena hesitated, then turned and started walking down the hall. Liliana had said she could roam at will. Being curious about the Fortress, she intended to do just that.

She hadn't gone far when she realized the Hulk was following her. To protect her? Or to keep her from stumbling into something she shouldn't?

No matter, she thought, she was going exploring.

The room to the right of hers was a library, larger than any she had ever seen before. Floor-to-ceiling shelves, each filled with books, lined every wall. Several sofas and comfortable-looking chairs occupied the center of the room, along with several low tables. She wandered from shelf to shelf, perusing the titles, noting that there were books in a multitude of languages. She took one from the shelf and thumbed through it. It was in a language she didn't recognize, but thought might be Russian. The pages were edged in gold leaf; the drawings that accompanied the words were breathtaking.

After carefully returning the volume to the shelf, she left the library.

There were two rooms across the hall. The first held numerous works of art. Some were framed and mounted on the walls; other canvases were on easels. Glass shelves held figurines and statues made of blown glass, pewter, onyx, and marble. Picking up a statue of an old woman carved from wood, Elena ran her hand over the smooth oak, marveling at the intricate detail even as she wondered whether the works of art had been created by the vampires.

The next door opened onto a music room. She stood there a moment, her gaze moving from the piano in the far corner to the harp, violins, cellos, flutes, triangles, and drums scattered around the room. Several music stands held pages of sheet music. Did vampires dance? And sing? And play musical instruments?

The room at the far end of the corridor was the Council chamber. There were no pleasant memories in that room and she didn't go inside.

The man continued to follow her as she went in search of the dining room, which she knew was somewhere downstairs. She didn't know if she was too early or too late, but she had the place all to herself. Going into the kitchen, she helped herself to a scone from a covered tray and washed it down with a cup of lukewarm tea. Plucking another scone from the tray, she nibbled on it as she left the dining room.

Behind the next door, she found a laundry room furnished with several washers and dryers, as well as a sink and a long counter. A quick glance, and she moved on.

Remembering that there were no windows in the lower levels, she plucked a fat candle from a wall sconce to light her way before descending the stairs to the dormitories and the day rooms. A lantern hanging from the ceiling provided faint illumination on this floor. She frowned, wondering who the light was for. The drones, perhaps?

The doors were all locked from the outside, of course, but she could hear voices coming from the rec room. She stood there a moment, listening to the muted voices of the women, the occasional laughter. She felt a brief rush of loneliness. The sheep might not be free, but they seemed happy in their captivity, while she had nothing, and no one.

The next floor down was pitch black and eerily silent. She knew immediately that this floor housed the vampires. Was Drake down here? Would she feel his presence if he was nearby? She tiptoed down the long hallway, her footsteps muffled by the thick carpet. She paused at each door but heard nothing. Did Rodin and Liliana live down here with the others, or did they have quarters elsewhere?

At the end of the hallway, she found a narrow wooden door. When she tried to open it, the drone caught her hand. When she looked up at him, he shook his head.

"Dungeon," he said, his voice flat. "You should not go there."

"Liliana said I could go wherever I wished."

The drone looked confused for a moment, as if no one had ever dared defy him before, and then it occurred to her that she was probably the first to do so. Surely the sheep would not disagree with any order given them. When she didn't back away, he shrugged and allowed her to pass.

Elena opened the door, and then hesitated at the top of the stairs. Did she really want to go down there alone? But then, she wasn't alone. The Hulk was right behind her. Still, it seemed the height of foolishness. Who knew what she might find down there? Visions of skeletons and dead rats flashed through her mind. Maybe the drone was right.

With a shake of her head, she was about to close the door when she heard Drake's voice in her mind, as clearly as if he was standing beside her. She peered into the darkness at the foot of the stairs. Was Drake down there?

Chewing on her lower lip, she started down the stairs. The musty scent of rot and decay rose up to meet her. She paused midway down the staircase, one hand on the rail, listening, but all she heard was the sound of the Hulk's breathing coming from behind her.

She had come this far, she thought, might as well see it through. She moved cautiously down the remaining steps, the drone at her heels.

When she reached the bottom of the staircase, she paused. In the eerie glow of the candle, she saw that she was indeed inside a dungeon. Iron-barred cells lined both sides of the room. Did the vampires keep prisoners down here? If so, how did they survive the smell? The air was rank, the low ceiling and stark surroundings oppressive. She shuddered at the thought of humans being locked away down here for days, or perhaps weeks, at a time, where no one could hear their screams for help.

Elena moved forward, her steps sounding overly loud in the silence. She gasped as a rat scurried past her. She was about to turn back when she heard Drake's voice in her mind again.

"Drake!" She hurried forward, her gaze darting right and left. "Drake?"

She found him in the last cell.

He blinked against the light of the candle. "What the hell are you doing down here?"

"I was just exploring, and . . . Oh, Drake." He looked a little better than the last time she had seen him. It was obvious that he had been given the opportunity to bathe and change his clothes, but it still broke her heart to see him locked away in this dreadful place. "How long are they going to keep you here?" she asked, then frowned. He wasn't chained this time. "Why don't you just . . ." She lifted her free hand and let it fall. "You know, just leave?"

"I gave Rodin my word I would do as he wished."

"And that includes letting him torture you? What kind of monster is he?"

"I defied him," Drake said. "For centuries. Whatever fault there is, is mine."

She reached through the bars, needing to touch him.

"Keep away from me."

"Drake, please."

"No, Elena. Whatever we had is over."

"Is it?" She hated the way her voice trembled. "You said you loved me." Why couldn't she be as cool and detached as he appeared to be?

"I do love you. I will love you as long as I live." Unable to resist her tears, he moved toward her, one hand reaching through the bars to wipe the dampness from her cheeks. "Did he hurt you?"

She didn't pretend not to know what he was talking about, just as she knew there was no point in lying. "Yes, but I'm all right." She placed her hand over his, then rubbed her cheek against his palm. "I don't want to live without you."

"You must. I need to know you are alive and well. I have made provisions for ownership of Wolfram Castle to be transferred to you."

"But it's your home!"

"I will be staying here from now on. Rodin will see that you have everything you need."

"I don't want anything from him!"

"Take it. It comes from me, not him." His gaze moved over her face, as if to memorize every line. "I am sorry for the pain I caused you. Had I stayed out of your life, none of this would have happened. Forgive me."

"There's nothing to forgive. You saved me from my uncle. I've loved the time we had together." She blinked back the tears that threatened to fall. "And I love you."

His hand slid down her cheek, his fingers curling around her nape, gently drawing her closer, closer. Murmuring her name, he pressed his lips to hers.

Holding the candle out to the side, she placed her free hand on his shoulder and closed her eyes. His kiss was so tender, so filled with longing, that it brought a fresh wave of tears to her eyes.

Knowing he would not be alone with her again, Drake kissed her harder, deeper, his tongue tasting the sweetness of hers while a voice in the back of his mind urged him to defy his sire, to hold fast to Elena and will the two of them back to Wolfram even though he knew it would be madness. There was no escape. If he defied Rodin again, his sire would hunt him down and destroy him, and Elena, too.

She moaned softly as his tongue tangled with hers. The sound, filled with yearning, fired his desire and he kissed her again and yet again, his rising desire igniting his hunger. His fangs extended. One sharp tip grazed her tongue. The taste of her blood roared through him. It had been days since he'd fed. Need rose up within him, urging him to drag her closer, to drink his fill and, in so doing, ease the dreadful agony that ebbed and flowed with every breath.

Cursing the bars that separated them, he slid his hand over her shoulder and down her arm, his fingers curling over her wrist. He could feel the rapid beat of her pulse beneath his fingertips, hear the quick tattoo of her heartbeat.

Why not take what he so desperately needed? He lifted her arm, ran his tongue over her palm to her wrist. The scent of her warm, living blood called to him, enflaming his hunger, promising an end to his pain. The beating of her heart was like sweet music to his ears. His hand tightened on her arm as his fangs teased the tender skin of her wrist.

"Drake . . . Drake! Stop!"

He was breathing heavily now, the urge to feed riding him with whip and spurs.

Elena struggled in his grasp. She would willingly have

given him what he needed, but he wasn't going to allow her that option. He was going to take what he wanted. For the first time since she had met him, she was in sudden fear for her life.

Muttering, "Forgive me," he bit down, his fangs piercing the tender skin on the inside of her wrist.

Exclaiming, "Forgive me!" Elena jabbed the candle's flame against his neck.

With a howl, he released her and backed away, one hand slapping at the scorched cloth of his shirt collar.

"I'm sorry!" she cried. "So sorry!"

"Go." He forced the word out through clenched teeth. "Go now!"

Sobbing, Elena turned on her heel and bolted up the stairs as if all the hounds of hell were barking at her heels.

She didn't stop running until she was safely in her room, with the door locked.

Chapter 18

"She was here." It was not a question.

Drake nodded. There was no point in lying. Rodin could detect Elena's scent in the air as easily as he.

"You promised not to try to see her."

Drake glanced at his surroundings—the thick iron bars, the stone floor, the corpse of the large brown rat in the next cell—before he stated the obvious. "She came to me."

"You expect me to believe you did not summon her? That she found you without any help?"

Drake shrugged. "Believe what you will."

Rodin lifted his head and sniffed the air. "You drank from her."

Drake's hands curled around the bars, his knuckles going white as he tightened his grip. "I tried."

Rodin grunted softly as he caught the faint odor of burnt cloth. "Are you ready to feed?"

Drake nodded. He was certain Elena would never return to the dungeon, but if she did, he needed to be in control of his hunger.

"I will send one of the sheep to you," Rodin said, approval in his voice. "Is there anyone in particular you would care for?"

"No."

"I have arranged for a meeting between you and Katiya for tomorrow night."

Drake took a deep breath. Then, knowing it was useless, he asked, "Is there nothing I can say or do to change your mind about this?"

"You are my eldest son. You should have taken your rightful place at the head of the Council centuries ago."

"Let Olaf take my place as head of the Council. He has made no secret of the fact he wants it. I do not."

Rodin uttered a short, pithy curse. "I thought we had come to terms on this!"

"Yes, your terms!"

"Did I not agree to your stipulations regarding the woman?"

Drake snorted. "My stipulations? Keeping her safe is nothing more than she deserves. I brought her here as a guest. I expected you to treat her as such."

"Be careful your weakness does not become your undoing."

Drake shook his head. "Be careful your arrogance does not become yours."

"We are much alike," Rodin remarked as he turned to leave. "Perhaps too much." He paused, speaking over his shoulder. "Very well," he said curtly. "I will appoint Olaf as head of the Council until you come to your senses."

Drake stared after his sire. Rodin had changed in the years since Drake had last seen him, but then, change was inevitable, even for vampires.

It was near midnight when the drone known as Number Ten entered the dungeon, with one of the sheep in tow. Drake regarded the girl impassively as the drone unlocked the door.

"Her name is Sophie," the drone said, and thrust her into the cell.

She was tall and slender, with long brown hair and timid gray eyes. He guessed her to be no more than fifteen or sixteen. Had he ever been that young? At the moment, he felt every one of his five hundred years.

He grunted softly as her clean feminine scent filled his nostrils. It was forbidden for vampires who were old enough to reproduce to mate with the sheep. It would be doubly forbidden for him, he mused glumly. He was to save his seed for Katiya in hopes she would conceive and bear a son.

But it wasn't Sophie's body he wanted, tempting as that might be. It was the blood he could hear whispering through her veins.

She took an involuntary step backward when he moved toward her.

Drake stopped, his eyes narrowing. "Is this your first time?"

She nodded, her gaze darting around the room, looking everywhere but at him. He couldn't blame her for that. With his scorched flesh and gaunt cheeks, he must look like he had walked out of a nightmare.

"I am sorry the surroundings are not more pleasant," he muttered with a wry grin.

She said nothing, only stared at him, like a fawn confronted by a wolf.

"I will not hurt you," he said, and hoped it was true. She flinched when he reached for her hand. Swallowing his anger and his humiliation, he drew her down on the pallet. He could smell the terror on her skin, hear it in the rapid beating of her heart. Taking a deep breath, he murmured, "Relax, child," as he wrapped her in his arms.

It took all his willpower to control himself. Her blood called to him. His body urged him to take her quickly, to drink and drink and put an end to the incessant pain that wracked him.

She trembled in his arms, her fear increasing his instinct to hunt, to take it all. She cried out when she looked into his face and he knew his eyes had gone red.

"Do not fight me!" he warned, his voice harsh. "I will not be responsible for what happens if you do."

Eyes tightly shut, she went rigid in his embrace.

Hating himself for what he was about to do, hating Rodin for sending him a woman young and untouched, he lowered his head to her neck and took what he needed so badly, craved so desperately.

Relief was immediate, quickly soothing the pain that burned through him, easing a long and terrible thirst.

He growled when the drone entered the cell, hissed when the girl was wrested from his arms. And then, with a cry, he slammed his fist against the stone floor, despising himself for what he had almost done; indebted, in spite of himself, to Rodin for sending the drone to take the girl away before he drained her dry.

Rodin entered the dungeon two hours later.

Drake regarded his sire through narrowed eyes. Clad in a long wine-colored dressing gown with a high, black velvet collar, the Master Vampire looked like royalty. Which he was, as far as the vampire community was concerned.

Rodin leaned one shoulder against the cell door. "I trust the woman was to your liking?"

Drake shrugged. "They are all the same, as you well know."

"She satisfied your need?"

"Why did you send that particular female to me?"

"She was young and untouched, exactly what you needed for a quick recovery. Judging from your improved appearance, I would say she was just right."

"I almost killed her."

Rodin made a dismissive gesture with his hand. "It happens now and then."

"But you made sure it wouldn't happen tonight."

"One of your brothers fancies her," Rodin said with a shrug. "I promised him he could have her when you were through."

Striving for calm, Drake took a deep breath. The indifferent attitude of his sire and his brothers toward the sheep was one of the reasons he had left the Fortress. He was a vampire, but he had fought against becoming what they were. In some ways, he thought it would be kinder if they killed those they fed upon. He couldn't help thinking that death would be preferable to captivity, knew that he would rather be dead than live the kind of life the sheep led, never knowing freedom, never seeing the outside world, forced to surrender their will to that of their captors. Occasionally, if one of the vampires took a liking to a particular man or woman, they claimed them for their own, a private stash, as it were.

Years ago, one of the human males had led a rebellion against the vampires. It had not ended well for the human population. Many of them had perished here, in the dungeon.

"You are to meet with Katiya tomorrow night," Rodin said. "It will give the two of you a chance to get acquainted. Your mother has requested that we hold a reception in two weeks to honor your betrothal. You will dress appropriately and you will dance every dance with Katiya. When the evening is over, you will escort her to her chambers."

"Am I ever to have any freedom again?"

"That depends on you. You will feed again tomorrow night, and every night until you are wed."

"Send me someone with experience."

Rodin nodded. "As you wish." He turned to leave, then paused. "Do not shame me in front of Katiya's parents," he warned, then vanished from sight.

Drake grasped the bars in his hands. Katiya's father, Cezar, was a Master Vampire in his own land. Rodin and Cezar had been allies for centuries. In the past, they had joined forces to fight off legions of human hunters bearing torches and swords and stakes.

But it wasn't the past that concerned Drake now. It was Elena. For the first time in days, he could sense her whereabouts, knew she was in one of the guest chambers upstairs, sleeping.

And dreaming of him.

Drake smiled faintly. He had promised Rodin he wouldn't try to see Elena, but he hadn't promised not to visit her in her dreams.

Elena stirred restlessly, tormented by dreams of Vardin holding her down, forcibly taking her blood, his eyes a hellish red. And then, abruptly, her dream changed and it was Drake holding her, his voice softly whispering her name, his hands gentle as they lightly stroked her hair, the curve of her cheek. She sighed as he kissed her. Was this also a dream? It felt so real.

"Drake?"

"Yes, love?"

"Am I dreaming?"

"Yes. And no." He kissed her again, kissed her with such aching sweetness it brought tears to her eyes.

His hands caressed her out of her nightgown and then he was lying beside her, molding her body to his, arousing her with strong, masterful hands. She reveled in his touch, her own hands moving over him, reacquainting herself with the width of his shoulders, the swell of his biceps, the taste of his skin on her tongue, the thick silk of his hair.

When he rose over her, his eyes glowing with need, she opened to him gladly. If she lived to be a hundred, there would never be anyone else for her. Only Drake, always and forever, whether they were together or apart.

"I love you," she murmured.

"And I love you," he replied. "Whether you are near or far, you will always be the other half of my soul, the wife of my heart."

He caught her close, their bodies melding, moving together, her heat warming him, his kisses arousing her, until she writhed beneath him, reaching, reaching, for that one perfect moment in time when two became one.

She sobbed with pleasure as he moved deep within her, caught up in the wonder and the magic that sparked between them, bound by the passion between them, bound by the night.

Breathless, she clung to him as pleasure exploded deep within her, cried his name when she felt him withdrawing.

"I love you," he murmured, his voice fading. "I will always love you."

She woke naked and alone in her bed, her cheeks damp with tears.

The woman the drone brought him the next night was in her late twenties. There was no fear in her eyes when Drake took her in his arms, only a kind of weary resignation that twisted like a knife in his gut, flaying him with guilt and regret for what he was, for the need that would not be denied.

He bent her back over his arm, his hand sweeping her hair to the side as he lowered his head to her neck. He took what he wanted with uncharacteristic roughness, and sent her away.

When she was gone, he wrapped his hands around the bars and rested his forehead against the cold steel, grateful that Elena would soon be gone from this place, a place that he hated with every fiber of his being.

Chapter 19

Katiya stood in the middle of her chamber, one foot tapping impatiently as her mother and Liliana fussed over her gown and her hair. She did not want to be there, did not want to marry Rodin's oldest son. She had tried both anger and tears, but, for the first time in her life, her sire had turned a deaf ear to both.

Even her mother had refused to be swayed. "We do not marry for love," Stefanya had replied, her patience quickly coming to an end. "You have a duty to our people to produce as many offspring as you can, while you can."

Katiya heaved a sigh as Liliana and Stefanya stepped back to admire their handiwork. There were no mirrors in the room, but she could see herself reflected in her mother's eyes. The dress, of fine burgundy silk and satin, was exquisite. They had piled her hair atop her head, leaving several ringlets to fall artfully over her bare shoulders.

What would Lord Drake think when he saw her? Not that she cared. She wanted nothing to do with him, or his family, or this impending wedding. She didn't want to live in the Fortress, or—she shivered with revulsion—share Drake's bed.

"You look lovely," Liliana said, smiling.

"Thank you," Katiya muttered. "How long do I have to spend with Drake?"

"Katiya!"

"It is quite all right, Stefanya," Liliana said. "I think we all know that Drake is also opposed to this match."

"Then why must we go through with it?" Katiya exclaimed. "Why must I do this? It is so unfair! I will not even be his first wife!"

"Life is often unfair," Stefanya said calmly. "This will not be the last time you are required to do something you find unpleasant."

"I hate you!" Katiya cried. "I hate all of you!"

The sound of Stefanya's hand striking her daughter's cheek echoed like thunder in the room. "Enough!"

Tears welled in Katiya's eyes and trailed down her cheeks like drops of scarlet rain.

"It is time," Stefanya said. Turning, she opened the door and left the room.

"None of us marry for love," Liliana said quietly. "We do what we must do. You may not love my son, but you will love your children for as long as they let you."

Drake paced the drawing room floor, his strides long and impatient. His future bride was late, adding to his irritation. The sooner she arrived, the sooner they could get on with this farce.

Rodin turned away from the window. "I would remind you that Elena's well-being depends on your behavior this evening."

"You have made that abundantly clear."

Rodin nodded. "See that you do not forget it." He lifted his head, sniffing the air, then strode toward the door. "Your bride is on her way."

Rodin had no sooner left the room than the door opened

again and Katiya glided into the room, a pout on her pretty face. She closed the door behind her, then stood there, her hands clasped in front of her.

"Good evening," Drake murmured.

She inclined her head, acknowledging his greeting.

Mindful that his father could overhear everything that was said if he so desired, Drake forced a smile into his voice. "Would you care for a glass of wine?"

"Yes, thank you," she replied, her voice carefully polite.

"Please, sit down," Drake invited, gesturing at one of the green-and-beige striped silk settees.

He scowled as he moved toward a table that held a variety of crystal decanters and goblets of varying sizes. How long was he supposed to entertain this stranger and what the hell were they going to talk about until he could escort her back to her apartment?

He filled two glasses. Then, schooling his features into a more pleasant expression, he carried them across the room and offered her one.

She took it with a murmured thank you.

Blowing out a sigh, Drake sat beside her. She was beautiful, of that there was no doubt. He supposed he should be grateful for her comeliness, if nothing else.

"So," he said, "how soon are we to wed?"

"Never, if I could have my way," she replied candidly.

Drake stared at her. "You do not want this?"

"No!"

He sat back, his legs comfortably stretched out in front of him as he mulled her response.

"I have no wish to marry a stranger," she said, and he heard the tears in her voice. "I know it is our way, for men and women to mate when the man is of age and the woman is fertile. I know such matches are arranged between families"—she sniffed loudly—"but I have read of other ways to choose one's mate."

"Indeed?" Drake asked, intrigued by her comment.

"Yes! There are places where people are allowed to marry for love."

"I fear that thought is akin to treason," he muttered. Vampire marriages were arranged much like those of royalty in ancient times, mainly to unite families or ensure continued peace between rivals.

Katiya met his gaze for the first time. "You were married before, to that mortal woman. Did you love her?"

"I will always love her," Drake replied quietly, and then he grunted softly. "You are also in love with someone else, are you not?"

"Yes." Her chin lifted defiantly. "Your brother, Andrei."

Andrei! Drake shook his head. He'd had no idea.

"You did not know?" Katiya asked.

"I had no idea. How long has this been going on?"

"Since last November."

Drake grunted softly. Andrei and Drake were half brothers, born to different mothers only a few months apart. "Perhaps this will work to our advantage," he said, thinking out loud. "Perhaps your sire would accept Andrei as your mate. He is far more suitable than I."

Katiya shook her head. "My sire thinks only of power. As the eldest son, you are next in line to rule the Carpathian Coven. My sire thinks to ensure the continuance of our treaty."

Exhaling a sharp breath, Drake took Katiya's hand in his and gave it a squeeze. "Maybe if we try very hard, we can figure out a way for both of us to get what we want," he said, though he didn't really have much hope for either of them.

Drake thought about what he had told Katiya long after he had bid her good night.

Vampires lived a very long time. Once a male had fathered children, his obligation to the Coven was fulfilled. And since vampires married out of a sense of duty and not for love, it wasn't uncommon for couples to go their separate ways once their children were grown.

He raked a hand through his hair. He didn't want to sire a child with a woman he didn't love. Nor could he expect Elena to wait for him until his child was grown. He might not age, but she grew older with every passing day. Dammit! There had to be a way out of this!

He paced the floor in long angry strides. He didn't want Katiya. She didn't want him. What if she simply refused to accept him as her husband? He grinned inwardly. In front of the Council, Rodin had decreed that the marriage would be performed at a time of the bride's choosing. And if she chose not to marry, what then? Would Rodin hold to his word? Could the answer be so ridiculously simple?

Elena sat in the library, a book open in her lap, her gaze on the flames in the hearth. It had been nearly two weeks since she had seen Drake. Their encounter in the dungeon was never far from her mind. What would have happened if she hadn't forced him to stop? If she hadn't had that candle, she would have been helpless to fight him off. Would he have drained her dry?

Driven by the need to see him, to assure herself that he was still alive, she had gone back to the dungeon two nights later, but Drake hadn't been there and she had lacked the nerve to try to find his room for fear of knocking on Rodin's door. Or Vardin's, she thought with a shudder.

Lost in thought, she leaned back and closed her eyes. In two weeks, she hadn't seen anyone save for the drone who stood guard at her door. Eager for company, she would have asked to be quartered with the sheep if there had been anyone to ask.

How much longer would Rodin keep her here?

Elena was almost asleep when the library door opened and Liliana stepped into the room. *Stepped* wasn't really the right word, Elena thought, watching the vampire move toward her. Vampires didn't walk like normal people. They sort of glided effortlessly across the floor.

"I hope I am not disturbing you," Liliana said, her voice as smooth and cool as her ice green gown.

"No, of course not." Elena closed the book in her lap. "I'm glad for the company."

Liliana lifted one brow. "You are lonely?"

"Yes, very."

"Hmm."

"Haven't you ever been lonely?"

"No." The vampire glanced around the room, as if gathering her thoughts. "We are having a reception tonight to celebrate Drake's forthcoming marriage," she said at last. "You are welcome to attend, if you wish."

Elena started to decline, and then she hesitated. The last thing she wanted was to see Drake dancing with his bride-to-be, but if she refused, she might never see him again. Forcing a smile, she murmured, "Thank you, I'd like that."

"You are a most complicated creature," Liliana remarked. "You will find something suitable to wear in the wardrobe. Be ready in an hour. Your drone will escort you to the ballroom."

Elena nodded. She watched Drake's mother glide out of the room, then frowned. She had wandered all over the Fortress but she hadn't seen anything resembling a ballroom. Had she missed something?

Laying the book aside, she went to her room to get ready.

* * *

The formal gown Liliana had left for her was exquisite. Pale blue in color, the full skirt was scalloped around the hem, revealing a dark blue underskirt trimmed in yards of whitc lace. Matching blue ribbons were woven through the neckline of the bodice; a wide sash of the same dark blue as the underskirt circled her waist.

Elena brushed her hair until it shone like ebony, brushed her teeth, sprayed herself with perfume, and told herself she wasn't the least bit nervous.

Nevertheless, her stomach fluttered with anxiety as she followed her drone down the corridor. He paused halfway between the art gallery and the library. Elena looked at him, askance, wondering what they were waiting for, when he placed his hand on the wall. Much to her surprise, a door opened.

She paused before following the drone up a long flight of stairs, wondering, as she did so, if there were other doors hidden in other corridors. Were there bolt-holes here, as well? No time to think about that now.

Chiding herself for foolishly agreeing to attend a gathering where she would be the only sheep among a pack of wolves, she followed the drone down a narrow hallway that opened onto a large, rectangular room. Three of the walls and a good portion of the ceiling were made of glass, affording the guests a splendid view of the valley below and the star-studded sky above.

A trio of long tables covered in gold damask held dozens of crystal decanters and wineglasses. No other refreshments were in evidence.

The room, the view, the vampires—it was the most amazing sight Elena had ever seen. If she hadn't known the truth, she would never have guessed these beautifully coiffed and gowned women and handsome men were vampires. They looked more like movie stars from a bygone era, when an air of mystery still surrounded actors and actresses.

A woman with bright red hair sat at the grand piano located on a small stage at the far end of the room. She closed her eyes as her long, pale fingers flew effortlessly over the keys, never missing a note.

Elena stared at the mirror that took up most of the wall behind the stage. It reflected the woman at the piano and the vampires who stood in clusters around the room, laughing and talking, as well as the couples who were waltzing in the center of the floor.

She frowned. There had been no mirrors in Wolfram. All the myths said vampires couldn't see their reflections, and yet that obviously wasn't true.

A tall, dark-haired man—one of Drake's many brothers by the look of him—approached her, a smile of welcome on his face. "Good evening, Miss Knightsbridge. May I have this dance?"

His request startled her, leaving her speechless.

"I am Andrei. Do you waltz?"

"Not very well."

"Then I shall teach you," he said, and taking her hand in his, he led her onto the dance floor.

"I fear your visit has not been a happy one," he remarked as he guided her around the floor. "For that, I am truly sorry."

"Thank you."

"You are in love with Drake."

It wasn't a question but a statement of fact and she saw no reason to deny it. "Yes, I am."

Andrei nodded. "Our people do not often fall in love. They marry only to beget children."

"I think that's terrible," Elena said candidly, then bit down on her lower lip. "I'm sorry. It's not for me to judge you or your ways."

He laughed softly. "Our ways are changing, much to my sire's vexation."

"Oh? In what way?" She glanced around the room, hoping to catch a glimpse of Drake.

"He is not here yet," Andrei said with a knowing smile. "As I was saying, our ways are changing as more of us choose to leave the Fortress and spend time in the outside world. Some of us, our women especially, are beginning to resent being forced to marry men for whom they have no affection."

"That's very interesting," Elena said politely, "but what does it have to do with anything?"

"Katiya does not wish to marry Drake."

Hope flared in Elena's heart with all the intensity of a Fourth of July sky rocket. Perhaps all was not lost. "Can't she refuse him?"

"She could, but she is young. I fear she lacks the courage to defy both her sire and mine."

"Oh." Having seen Rodin up close, Elena could understand Katiya's reluctance to defy him.

"I understand how you feel more than you know," Andrei said quietly.

"I doubt it."

"Ah, but I do." He laughed, but it rang hollow. "You see, my dear Miss Knightsbridge," he said, swinging her around and around, "I am in love with Katiya."

"I'm sorry," Elena said, though it was hard to speak, he was making her so dizzy.

"And she loves me. So you see, I understand exactly how you feel." He stopped abruptly. "They are here."

The dancers drifted off the floor to line the walls as the piano fell silent.

Rodin entered first, with Liliana at his side. A couple Elena didn't know came next. One look at the man and the woman and she knew they had to be Katiya's parents.

Katiya and Drake came last. She wore an exquisite gown of jade green velvet that showed off her perfect figure. He wore black trousers, supple black leather boots, and a long black coat over a white silk shirt open at the throat. They made a stunning couple. Arm in arm, they walked across the floor, glancing neither to the right nor the left.

Rodin looked every inch the master of his domain as he took the stage. "Good evening to you all," he said jovially. "As you know, we are here tonight to celebrate the forthcoming marriage of my oldest son, Drake, to the fair Katiya. The wedding will take place tomorrow night. . . ."

Elena gasped. Tomorrow night! So soon? She heard Andrei mutter, "Why didn't she tell me?"

Gathering her wits about her, Elena stared at Drake, but he refused to look at her.

". . . and so," Rodin was saying, "let the festivities begin." He smiled expansively. "Please, enjoy yourselves. If the wine is not to your taste, there is other refreshment available upon request."

Elena's stomach churned. "He means the sheep, doesn't he?" she whispered, looking up at Andrei.

He nodded. "There are Master Vampires here from many foreign lands. It is customary to provide nourishment." He took her hand in his cool one. "Come, the music is starting again."

"How can you be so cheerful?" Elena asked. "They're getting married tomorrow night!" She almost choked on the words.

Andrei shrugged one shoulder. "It is all an act. What would you have me do? Throw myself on the floor and wail like a spoiled child? For now, we must make the best of it. Relax, and follow my lead. And try to look as if you are having a good time. It will drive Katiya and Drake crazy with jealousy."

Laughing in spite of herself, Elena glanced around

Andrei's shoulder to see Drake watching her through narrowed eyes as he waltzed by with Katiya.

"Did I not tell you?" Andrei exclaimed. "He is green with envy."

Andrei insisted they dance every dance. Between sets, he kept Elena close to his side, made sure her wineglass was always full. He regaled her with stories of growing up in the Fortress.

"Those were happy times, the days of our youth, before the need for blood overcame every other thought, every other passion. I surrendered to the compulsion several years before Drake. Though he is the eldest, he held out the longest. My brothers and I tormented him terribly."

"Why?"

"We were jealous of his determination to resist the compulsion, envious of his ability to consume mortal food, to roam outside in the sun's light." Andrei's gaze focused on Drake. "Once we poisoned his supper."

"That's terrible!"

"It only made him sick for a short time. He got even with us, though. He fed the sheep absinthe. It didn't hurt the sheep, but it made the rest of us violently ill."

"That's terrible, too," Elena said, but she couldn't help laughing.

It was nearing four in the morning when Elena insisted she needed to sit down. "You might have the staying power of twenty men," she told Andrei, "but I don't."

"Very well." He escorted her to a chair, stood beside her while she rested. She noted the crowd had thinned considerably. Had the vampires retired early? Or were they dining below? She was about to ask Andrei to walk her back to her room when she saw Drake and Katiya gliding toward them.

"Good evening, brother," Andrei said with a slight bow.

"Andrei," Drake replied with a nod. "I wish to dance with Elena."

Andrei darted a glance in Rodin's direction. He stood on the other side of the room, conversing with several men. "Do you think that is wise?"

"No, but it will be my last chance to hold her. I am willing to suffer whatever punishment Rodin sees fit to inflict on me."

"Very well," Andrei agreed. "Katiya, will you dance with me?"

"You know I will." She glanced at Drake. "If Rodin says anything, tell him this was at my request. Come, Andrei."

Drake led Elena onto the floor as the pianist began to play. The music was unlike anything Elena had ever heard—soft and slow, yet there was a dark sensual edge to the notes. She gazed up at Drake as he drew her into his arms. He must have fed well, she thought. The burns and blisters accrued during his stay in the tower had all but disappeared from his face and he looked again like the dashing man she had fallen in love with such a short time ago. How was she going to live without him?

He held her close, his gaze never leaving her face. "Forgive me," he murmured.

"There is nothing to forgive, my lord."

"I could have killed you."

"It doesn't matter now." Nothing mattered now, she thought, and perhaps never again.

"I am not giving up," he said fervently. "No matter how long it takes, I will find a way for us to be together." He caressed her cheek with his knuckles. "Unless you tell me you no longer love me."

Conscious of the curious looks of the other dancers, she blinked back her tears. "I'll love you till my dying breath," she whispered. "And into eternity."

"Elena." He murmured her name and then a curious

thing happened. He swept his gaze over her lips, and even though his mouth was not touching hers, she felt the press of his lips, warm and sweet, on her own.

When the music ended, Rodin stood beside them, his devil dark eyes glinting with barely suppressed fury. Andrei and Katiya appeared as if by magic.

Elena glanced anxiously at the three male vampires. Rodin looked ready to explode. Drake's face was expressionless. Andrei appeared faintly amused.

Katiya smiled at her future father-in-law. "It was my doing," she said, taking Drake's hand in hers and squeezing it tightly. "Please do not blame Drake. I wished to dance with Andrei and Drake graciously permitted it."

Rodin studied her face for several moments, as if trying to determine the veracity of her statement. Katiya met his gaze unwaveringly.

With obvious reservations, or perhaps to avoid a scene, Rodin muttered, "Of course," and then, with a courtly bow, he strode away.

Elena glanced from Andrei to Katiya. It was easy to see they were very much in love. She wondered how Rodin could be so oblivious, but then she recalled Andrei telling her that vampires didn't marry for love. Perhaps one had to experience the emotion to recognize it.

When the strains of another waltz filled the air, Drake reluctantly led Katiya onto the dance floor.

Andrei looked at Elena. "Shall we?"

"No, I think I'd like to go to my room, if you don't mind. I feel a headache coming on."

"Of course." Taking her by the hand, he escorted her from the ballroom. "Maybe all is not lost," he said as they walked down the corridor toward her quarters.

Elena shook her head. "The wedding is tomorrow night."

"There is still hope that Katiya will find the courage to defy Rodin and her sire. I know Cezar has ignored her tantrums at being forced to wed against her will, but if she can find the nerve to say no during the ceremony . . ." Andrei swore softly. "All she has to do is say no. With so many witnesses, her sire may concede."

"Do you really believe that?"

"I have to."

He made it sound so easy, Elena thought when she was alone in her room. Just say no. She didn't know about Katiya's sire, but having seen how Rodin meted out justice, Elena doubted she would have the nerve to disobey the Master Vampire. Nor did she believe that Katiya's father would accept her refusal. But, as Andrei said, it was the only hope they had.

After undressing, she washed her hands and face, pulled on her nightgown, and crawled into bed. She stared up at the ceiling, determined not to cry, but it was no use. Her tears came quickly, burning her eyes, scalding her throat. Tomorrow night, Drake would be forever lost to her. He would marry Katiya and give her children and Elena would never see him again, never lie nestled in his arms, never taste his kisses or experience the wonder of his body melding with hers.

Flopping over onto her stomach, she wailed softly into her pillow, then cried herself to sleep.

Elena woke abruptly, all her senses alert. She didn't know what had awakened her but something—some innate sense of self-preservation perhaps—told her she was no longer alone.

She sat up, reaching for the lamp beside her bed. A scream rose in her throat and was trapped there when a large hand wrapped around her neck.

"Not a word," hissed a voice in her ear. "If you cry out, I will break your neck. Understand?"

Heart pounding like the hooves of a runaway horse, she nodded as best she could.

Cool fingers caressed her cheek. "Ever since that first taste, I have hungered for more of your blood."

Vardin! She shuddered as he ran his tongue along the side of her neck, then bit down hard on her earlobe.

He made ugly sucking noises as he drank, then smacked his lips. "Even better than I remembered." He released his hold on her neck, then pulled her roughly into his arms, his hands sliding suggestively up and down her back and thighs.

"Why me?" she gasped, hoping to divert him. "There are plenty of sheep to satisfy your thirst."

He snorted disdainfully. "I do not want one of the sheep. There is no fire in their blood. I want a tiger."

Knowing he wanted resistance, she went lax in his arms. Perhaps, if she didn't defy him, he would drink from her and let her go.

"Tomorrow night, Drake will wed Katiya, and when it is done, I will see that you are returned to the sheepfold. And then I will claim you as my own."

She stared at him in horror. Could he do that?

"You will be mine until I tire of you." Taking hold of the collar of her nightgown, he ripped it down the front. "But that will not be for a long, long time."

With a hoarse cry, she tried to cover herself, but he trapped both her hands in his and began to kiss her, his tongue plunging into her mouth. Sheer terror welled up within her when he pushed her down on the bed, then covered her body with his.

Certain she would rather die than have him violate her, she screamed as loudly as she could.

The bedroom door flew open almost immediately. In the pitch blackness of her room, she couldn't see much of anything, only a dark blur that hurtled inside, grabbed hold of the man atop her, and flung him against the wall. There was the sound of a scuffle, a sharp gasp of pain, and then silence.

The unmistakable scent of blood filled the air.

A moment later, the light came on and Drake was at her side. Wrapping her in a blanket, he cradled her in his arms. Shaking uncontrollably, she glanced over his shoulder. A body lay on the floor, covered from head to midthigh with the bedspread, now sodden with blood.

A number of other vampires materialized in the corridor and inside the room as if conjured by witchcraft. Rodin and Liliana were among them.

"What is going on here?" Rodin demanded.

"Vardin attacked Elena." Drake's voice was tight with anger as he grabbed Elena's robe from the foot of the bed. Shielding her from view with his body, he helped her into the robe.

Rodin glanced at the body on the floor. A muscle twitched in his jaw. Liliana dropped to her knees beside her son, a harsh cry of denial rising in her throat. A single red tear slipped down her cheek.

Rodin fixed Elena with a hard stare. "Is it true that Vardin attacked you?"

Elena nodded.

"I want her sent home, now," Drake said. "Before anything like this happens again."

Rodin ignored Drake, his gaze still on Elena. "Why did my son attack you?" he asked brusquely. "There is no shortage of nourishment here."

"He said he . . . that he didn't want . . ." She shuddered. "He didn't want one of the sheep."

Liliana glanced up at her husband, a question in her eyes. Rodin nodded tersely. "She speaks the truth."

Stefan stepped forward. "I will take Elena home."

"Thank you," Drake said quietly. "Take Andrei with you." He looked up at Rodin. "Any objections?"

"No." Rodin glanced from Stefan to Andrei. "Take the woman and go. Now."

Elena clung to Drake. The moment she had dreaded had arrived.

Drake looked at his sire. "We will need a moment alone, to say good-bye."

A muscle twitched in Rodin's jaw, but he didn't argue. Two of the vampires lifted Vardin's body and carried it out of the room. Liliana followed behind. Rodin jerked his chin toward the door and everyone else left the room.

"Do not take too long," Rodin said, and closed the door behind him.

Drake's arms tightened around her. "Elena?"

She looked up at him, her eyes swimming with tears.

He wiped the dampness from her cheeks with the pads of his thumbs. "Stefan and Andrei will see you safely home. I have signed a paper deeding the castle to you. I have opened a bank account for you in the city. A large amount will be deposited to your account every month."

She nodded, but the only thing that registered was that he was sending her away.

He caressed her cheek with his knuckles. "Be happy, Elena. I will never forget you."

"Don't make me go!" She hated the pleading note in her voice, but she couldn't help it. The thought of being parted from him was unbearable.

"It is impossible for you to stay here," he said. "You must realize that."

"I know." She sifted her fingers through his hair, slid her fingertips over his lips. "Kiss me good-bye."

Cupping her face in his hands, he kissed her ever so gently. "I will love you as long as I draw breath."

She nodded, unable to speak past the lump in her throat.

Drake pulled her close and she clung to him, memorizing the feel of his hard-muscled body against hers, the scent that was his alone. He kissed her again, hard and quick, and then Rodin was striding into the room, ordering Drake away.

What happened next passed in a blur. Andrei and Stefan materialized in the room. With a reassuring smile, Stefan took Elena in his arms. There was a familiar buzzing in her ears, a sense of hurtling through time and space, a queasiness in the pit of her stomach.

When she came to herself, it was early morning and she was lying in her bed in the castle, alone.

Elena rolled onto her side, her cheek pillowed on one hand, and stared at the wall. She wondered without really caring if Stefan and Andrei were still in the castle or if they had returned to the Fortress.

She had known Drake such a short time. How was it possible that he had made such a drastic impact on her life?

She had fallen in love with him.

She was one of the few mortals alive who knew that vampires existed.

Wolfram Castle belonged to her now.

She had a marriage license proving she had married Drake Sherrad. No one would ever know that Rodin had annulled her marriage. . . . She frowned. Where did Drake's sire get the authority to end her marriage, anyway? No matter. Drake was lost to her. She could tell people he had died on their honeymoon and no one could disprove it. The castle was hers now. She could live here for as long as she wished. If she desired, she could hire a cook and a housekeeper to help care for the castle. Doing so would not only provide her with household help, but company, as well. She could travel the world, go anywhere she pleased.

But none of that mattered because she was, and always would be, in love with Drake.

And tonight he was marrying someone else.

Chapter 20

"It is time."

Drake glanced over his shoulder to find his mother standing in the doorway. She looked as beautiful as always. Sometimes it was hard to think of her as his mother, since they appeared to be about the same age. Tonight, she wore a gown of cloth-of-gold that made her pale skin glow and added shimmering highlights to her long blond hair.

"Are you ready?" Liliana asked.

Drake snorted. "I will never be ready."

She blew out an impatient breath. He could see her gearing up for another argument, could almost see the wheels turning as she sought for some way to make what must be done more amenable.

He decided to save her the trouble. Putting on his coat, he said, "Let us get it over with."

"It is for the best." Liliana brushed her hand over his coat, removing a miniscule bit of lint. "Katiya will make you a good wife. She is lovely, well mannered, and will provide the Coven with children."

"How can you defend this way of life?" He hadn't meant to argue with her, but the words poured out of him, coming hard and fast as his anger and frustration rose to the surface. "I know there is no love between you and my sire. There never has been. Yet you stay with him, and condemn me to the same misery you have endured for centuries. Why?"

"We are vampires, Drake. The only way you will ever find peace is to embrace what you are. No way of life is perfect. Do you think all mortals find happiness in their marriages?" She shook her head. "Happiness lies in family, in tradition, in shared beliefs. I stay because my sons and daughters are here, because this is my home."

"This was never my home," Drake said bitterly. "It never will be."

"I would spare you this, if I could." A sigh of regret whispered past Liliana's lips. "Your bride awaits."

With a nod, Drake followed his mother down the corridor to the Council chambers.

Weddings among his kind were not romantic affairs. There was no music, no flowers, no guests other than the bride and groom, their parents and siblings. As Master of the Coven, Rodin would perform the ceremony.

Drake glanced briefly at his brothers as he entered the chamber. Notable by their absence were Vardin, Andrei, and Stefan. Earlier that evening, Vardin's body had been disposed of, the ashes buried in the small cemetery located in the forest behind the Fortress. Drake assumed Andrei and Stefan were still at Wolfram with Elena. He would have given everything he owned to be there with her.

Liliana took her place beside Katiya's parents.

Drake took a deep breath. With Vardin's death, he had hoped for a reprieve, but he should have known better. His people had no mourning period. They burned their dead and never spoke their names again.

His last hope was that Katiya would find the courage to defy her father's wishes. If she refused to go through with the ceremony, Rodin would have to accept her decision.

Taking his place beside Katiya, Drake reached for her hand. Her skin was cooler than usual. He could feel her trembling. She didn't look at him; instead, she stared at the floor.

Rodin's gaze moved over those assembled in the room. "You have been called here to witness the union of Drake Sherrad and Katiya Belova, here present. Drake, will you have this woman to be your life mate, to care for her and protect her so long as you shall live?"

Drake thought fleetingly of the nights and days he had spent with Elena, of the love they had shared, the light she had brought to his life, her willing acceptance of what he was.

It was his undying love for her, the very real fear that Rodin would make good on his threat to do Elena harm, that made Drake say, "I will."

"Katiya Belova," Rodin said solemnly, "will you have this man to be your life mate, to care for him and bear his children?"

Drake held his breath as he waited for her answer.

Katiya stared at Rodin and then at her sire, her eyes wide and scared, like a doe caught in a trap. She swallowed hard, then lowered her gaze and murmured, "I will."

Drake blew out a sigh of resignation. There would be no reprieve.

Rodin pulled a small golden goblet from inside his jacket and placed it on the table in front of him. Taking Drake's hand in his, he used his thumbnail to make a shallow cut in Drake's palm, then held Drake's bleeding hand over the goblet. He made a similar cut in Katiya's hand, adding her blood to the cup.

Lifting the goblet, Rodin offered it first to Drake, who took a swallow, and then handed the cup to Katiya. She closed her eyes, drank quickly, and returned the goblet to Rodin.

"By the exchange of blood," Rodin intoned, "and by my authority as Master of the Carpathian Coven, I hereby decree that from this night forward, Drake Sherrad and Katiya Belova are life-mated." Rodin embraced the bride and then the groom. "May you be blessed with many healthy sons and daughters."

Drake endured his sire's embrace in taut silence; then, holding Katiya's hand, he walked out of the chamber, his back rigid.

One of the drones had moved Katiya's belongings into Drake's quarters earlier that evening. His rooms, once spare and uncluttered, were now littered with female paraphernalia. Colorful pillows were scattered across the sofa. Half the wardrobe held her dresses and shoes. Bottles of perfume, sweet-smelling shampoo, brushes and combs occupied half the countertop in the bathroom. Flowered towels hung on the rack beside his own navy blue ones. He had seen a sheer black nightgown, most likely bought by the bride's mother, spread across the foot of his bed. He grimaced at the memory.

Closing the door, Drake shrugged out of his jacket and tossed it over a chair, then turned to face his bride, his hands clenched at his sides. "Why did you not just say no?" He bit off each word.

"I was going to— I wanted to, but I lost my nerve when I saw my father watching me."

Drake blew out an angry breath. Why was life never easy? If she had just refused to accept him, he could be on his way back to Wolfram Castle and the woman he loved.

Dropping down into the chair in the corner, he stretched his legs out in front of him and regarded his new wife over his steepled fingers.

She stood in the middle of the living room, looking lost, obviously as unhappy about their union as was he.

So. He had kept his word. He had wed Katiya. Elena was

safely away from the Fortress. As far as he was concerned, she was still his wife and always would be. Rodin might have the power to perform weddings and proclaim annulments here, in the Fortress, but that authority carried no legal weight in the outside world. According to the laws of Transylvania, Elena was still his wife. And would remain so, if he had anything to say about it.

"What are we going to do now?" Katiya asked.

A slow smile spread over Drake's face. "I have a plan. We are going to spend as much time as needed pretending to fall in love. Once we have convinced Rodin that we are happily married and have accepted things as they are, we are going to leave the Fortress for a belated honeymoon."

"Leave?" She shook her head. "I was told you were going to take a seat on the Council."

"One of the terms of my agreeing to this marriage was that Rodin find another to take my seat in the chamber."

She considered that a moment before asking, "How long must we pretend to be happily wed?"

"That, my dear unwanted bride, remains to be seen."

Elena had expected to be unhappy without Drake, but she hadn't expected to feel so empty inside, as if someone had ripped out her heart and left a bleeding, gaping wound behind. She couldn't stop thinking about him, but she had expected that, had known she would miss him, that she would grieve for him almost as if he had died. She had expected that, too. It was the depths of her misery that surprised her. She told herself she hadn't known him very long, that it wasn't as if they had been in love for years and years. And yet it felt as if she had lost a vital part of her being.

Stefan and Andrei did their best to cheer her up. And they were good company, but it was hard to be around Drake's brothers night after night. How was she supposed to forget Drake when Andrei and Stefan looked so much like him, when she was living in Drake's house, sleeping in his bed? Maybe she should move, but where would she go? And even as she considered it, she knew she would never leave Wolfram Castle. She had no way to get in touch with Drake. Her only hope of ever seeing him again was to stay here in case he should one day decide to return.

For once, Elena would have welcomed the presence of the cat, but he was nowhere to be found.

One afternoon, needing a change of scene, Elena decided to take the car and drive to the city. She found the keys to the Porsche, grabbed her handbag and a sweater, and left the castle.

What had seemed like a good idea faded somewhat once she was behind the wheel. She knew how to drive a stick shift. She had learned in school. But she had never driven more than a few miles from home. So, she thought, switching on the engine, this would be an adventure.

It was inevitable that thoughts of Drake would fill her mind as she drove, ever so carefully, toward the city. It was there she had learned the truth of what he was. Funny, how unimportant that had seemed once she realized she was in love with him. She wondered now what they would have done when she grew old and he did not. Would he have stayed with her, taken care of her until she passed away? Or would he have left her for someone else when she became a burden?

Well, she would never know now.

Arriving in town, she parked the car and strolled along the sidewalk. Now that she was here, she had no idea why she had come. When they first arrived at Wolfram, Andrei had given her an envelope that contained more money than she had ever seen.

"From Drake," Andrei had told her.

Drake. Just the mention of his name made her heart ache with loneliness. He had once told her to make any changes she wanted in the castle, but she liked it just the way it was, although electricity would be a nice addition.

With a sigh, Elena continued down the street. When she came to a store that sold housewares, she stepped inside. An hour later, she had purchased a set of flowered china, sets of silverware and glasses, and several new pots and pans. She also bought a pretty blue cloth for the table in the kitchen, and a pale green one for the trestle table in the main hall. It seemed strange to be able to buy whatever she wanted without having to ask permission or worry about the cost. After a clerk helped her carry everything out to the car, she strolled on down the street.

Passing by a bookstore, she stepped inside and bought every vampire book she could find.

Elena was making her way back to the Porsche when she saw her uncle step out of the hotel across the street. With a gasp of alarm, she quickly turned to look in the window behind her. Had he seen her? Heart pounding, she stared at his reflection, breathed a sigh of relief when he moved on down the street.

Hurrying to the car, Elena stowed everything on the floor and the passenger seat, slid behind the wheel, and drove for home as fast as she dared.

It wasn't until the city was far behind that she breathed a sigh of relief. She had been so lost in her own misery, she had forgotten all about Dinescu. What was even worse, she had forgotten about Jenica.

* * *

Drake knew it wouldn't be easy to convince his father that he had decided to make the best of things where Katiya was concerned, so he took it slow, knowing that, if he went too fast, Rodin would be suspicious. For the first few weeks, he remained cool and aloof with his bride. He was polite when they were in the presence of others. He treated her with respect, but not affection. Only gradually, did he become more relaxed. He began to smile at her. He held her hand. Once, he let Rodin catch him kissing Katiya in one of the corridors.

Katiya played her part as well. In the beginning, she made sure to let her mother know that she was not pleased to have Drake as her husband, and that Drake was equally unhappy at being forced to marry her and then, as time went on, she, too, began to smile more often.

Six weeks after Drake married Katiya, Andrei returned to the Fortress.

Drake sought him out the next night. "Elena," he said, "is she well?"

"She misses you, of course. She cries a lot." Andrei grinned. "She's been reading vampire books."

"Vampire books!" Drake exclaimed.

Andrei nodded. "None of them are close to being accurate. She asks a lot of questions. And then she cries some more."

Cursing softly, Drake shook his head. Why on earth was she reading vampire books? If she'd had questions, she could have asked him, he thought irritably. But then, once she had found out what he was, they hadn't had a lot of time alone.

"So, how are things going here?" Andrei asked. "Is the plan we agreed upon working?"

"I believe so. Yes."

"How is Katiya?"

"She worries a lot."

"I cannot say as I blame her."

Drake grunted softly. "Rodin is hosting a feast tonight for Marcos."

"Why?"

"Marcos has taken over the Fortress in England. He is coming here to propose a new treaty with Rodin."

"So, Marcos now rules the Fortresses in England and Spain."

Drake nodded. It was an old story. Vampires lived a very long time. Often, when they grew bored, the very old ones challenged each other for territory. Such fights were always to the death. In the course of Rodin's long existence, he had defended the Carpathian Fortress over a dozen times.

But Drake had other things on his mind tonight. "Katiya is fully ripe. I am certain she will conceive tonight. Once that is accomplished, there will be no reason for my sire to insist we remain here."

"And if Rodin still refuses to let you leave?"

Drake clenched his hands at his sides. "Pray that he doesn't," he said, his voice little more than a hoarse whisper. "I cannot stand being here much longer."

The reception began at midnight. Marcos and his entourage, apparently desiring to make a grand entrance, arrived an hour later. Rodin took the stage to introduce his guests, and everyone present came forward to pay their respects, starting with Rodin's sons.

When that was done, Drake took his father aside.

"I hope you will not be offended," he said, "but Katiya and I desire to retire early."

"Is something wrong?" Rodin asked, his voice curt. "You have not yet danced with your bride."

"The night is young, and we have another dance in

mind," Drake said with a smile. "The woman is ripe and willing, and I am eager."

"Then go with my blessing!" Rodin said exuberantly. "She will bear lusty sons and beautiful daughters."

"Of that I have no doubt," Drake replied.

Moments later, he took Katiya by the hand. Smiling at each other, they hurried out of the ballroom, arm in arm.

Chapter 21

Time passed, one day blending into another. Elena kept busy as best she could. There was always something to do in the castle—a bit of dusting or sweeping, windows to clean, tapestries that needed airing and beating, clothes and sheets to wash and dry.

Once, leaning over the wooden washtub in the kitchen, she grinned, remembering how she had once contemplated doing her laundry on a rock in the river.

The nights were better. She had only Stefan for company now. Stefan claimed he didn't know why Andrei had returned to the Fortress, but she didn't believe him for a minute. Something was going on.

But she was too unhappy to wonder or care what it was. Drake belonged to someone else now. What else mattered?

One night, a month after Andrei's departure, she coaxed Stefan into accompanying her to the lake. It was as beautiful as she remembered, but it lacked the magic she had felt when Drake had taken her there, and she realized then that it hadn't been the lake or the moonlight that had cast the magical spell on the place, but Drake's presence beside her. Had she loved him even then without knowing it?

"You are very quiet tonight," Stefan mused when they were seated side by side on a fallen log.

"Will I ever stop missing him?" she asked. "Will the pain ever go away?"

"I know little of the ways of mortals," he replied, gazing out over the water. "Sometimes I think it would be a blessing to be human."

"How so?"

"You may miss Drake for decades, but I have centuries to grieve."

"Have you lost someone you cared for?"

"Yes, but it was long ago."

"But you're still mourning for her, aren't you?"

He nodded.

"Would you like to talk about it?"

"No. It only freshens the pain."

They sat in silence for several minutes. Elena gazed into the distance, thinking how sad it was that the only place where men and women lived happily ever after was in fairy tales.

"Are you truly immortal?" Elena asked after a while. She couldn't imagine living forever. Of course, if you never got sick and never got old, it might not be so bad. But to live forever—when you had been everywhere and seen everything, what else was left?

"Not exactly immortal," he said. "Everything that lives can be killed. But some of us take a lot of killing."

"Drake is five hundred. How old is Rodin?"

"He turned one thousand and one this year."

The number was staggering, she thought. "How many children does he have?"

"I am not sure how many his other wives have borne him, but Liliana has given him five sons and three daughters."

"I thought Drake said female vampires were only fertile for a short time."

"They are fertile four months of the year, but many have difficulty conceiving or carrying a child full-term." Stefan laughed softly. "Liliana is obviously not one of them."

"Would it be rude of me to ask how old you are?"

"Only mortal women are vain about their age," he said, grinning. "I am four hundred and fifty-three."

She pondered that a moment, then sighed. "Do you think he misses me?"

"I know he does."

"Why can't vampires and humans have children together?"

"I do not know," he said with a shrug. "I am not sure it has been tried very often. The penalty for mating with a mortal is death. If not for the fact that Drake is Rodin's favorite, and the favorite of our mother, he would be dead now."

"How many wives does Rodin have?"

"Twenty. He has taken two wives every fifty years for the last five centuries. Our women outnumber the men, so it is not uncommon for a Master Vampire to have more than one wife. Liliana is Rodin's first, and his favorite."

"Do they all live at the Fortress together?"

"No," Stefan said, laughing. "When Liliana comes to the Fortress, the other wives go elsewhere."

"I can't say as I blame them. Oh! I'm sorry. I shouldn't have said that."

"It is all right. Liliana never loved Rodin, but she is extremely jealous of the other wives and refuses to have them under the same roof. As the first wife, it is her right. She has always been good to me, spoiled me because I was her youngest son, but she can be cruel and uncaring to those not of her family."

Stefan glanced at Elena, his expression solemn. "Trust me, you are well out of it. Take my advice. Forget this place. Forget Drake. Start a new life somewhere else. Somewhere far from here."

Elena was thinking about what Stefan had said the following morning when the clang of the bell at the front door announced a visitor.

She opened the door cautiously, then stood there, staring at a man in overalls and the enormous moving van that loomed behind him.

"Miss Knightsbridge?"

"Yes?"

"Got a delivery for ya. Sign here."

She glanced at the clipboard, noting her name and directions to the castle were neatly typed in the space that said, *Deliver to.* "But I didn't order anything."

"Well, somebody did. I got a truckload of goods here, all paid for."

The words had barely escaped his lips when four big burly men began carrying furniture into the castle: bedroom sets in gleaming walnut and antique oak, an oak dining room table with eight chairs, an enormous flat-screen TV, an entertainment center, three antique oak curio cabinets, flowered sofas and matching love seats, overstuffed chairs, oak end tables and coffee tables, and lamps. Except for the TV and the entertainment center, all the pieces appeared to be antiques, which was only fitting, she thought, considering the age of the castle.

An hour later, she stood in the middle of the main room surrounded by more furniture than she had ever seen in her life. Who had sent it? What was she going to do with it all? And how was she supposed to get it up the stairs?

A short time later, the bell rang again and a man stood on the steps. His eyes grew wide when he looked past her. "Holy hel . . . heck," he muttered. "This place really is a castle. I'm gonna need a lot more help," he said, pulling a cell phone from his back pocket.

"Excuse me?"

"Got a job order from the power company to wire this place." He shook his head. "You must know somebody mighty important, that's all I can say. We'll get started as soon as I get more help. Won't be done for a couple of weeks, big as this place is, and that's pushin' it. We'll try to stay out of your way as much as possible. Like I said, it'll take time, but we'll get ya hooked up, never fear."

Elena nodded. Then, feeling as though she was living in the twilight zone, she closed the door.

A short time later, men were swarming around the outside of the castle, like ants at a picnic.

The biggest surprise of the day came with the setting of the sun. There was no knock at the door this time. Elena was sitting on one of the new sofas, reading a book, when there was an odd ripple in the air and suddenly Drake, Katiya, and Andrei were standing in front of her.

"Drake." She murmured his name, her gaze devouring him. She was certain she was dreaming until he swept her off the sofa and wrapped her in his arms.

"Elena! How I have missed you!" He held her close, crushing her body to his until she could scarcely breathe. But she didn't care—he was here. He was real, and nothing else mattered.

"I missed you, too." Tears fell unchecked down her cheeks as she hugged him close. He was here. "Oh, how I missed you!"

She didn't know how long they stood like that, just looking at each other—a moment? A lifetime?—before she noticed that Andrei and Katiya were also embracing.

"Elena, beloved, let me look at you." So saying, Drake put her on her feet and held her at arm's length. "You are more beautiful than ever."

"How long can you stay?" she asked, dreading the answer.

"As long as you wish."

She glanced at Katiya. "I don't understand."

"I want to be your husband," he said. "Always, if you will still have me."

"But . . . how is that possible? And what about Katiya? She's your wife now."

"Rodin's decree has no authority in the outside world. According to the laws of the land, you and I are still man and wife."

"So, what is Katiya doing here?"

"We left the Fortress together. Rodin believes we are on a belated honeymoon."

"And Andrei is here because . . . ?"

"He is here because Katiya is here," Drake replied, as if that explained everything.

Elena continued to stare at him while her mind tried to process what he had told her. But none of it seemed to register save for one fact—he was still her husband, if she wanted him.

"Say something," he demanded. "I do not like your silence."

"Drake." She caressed his cheek, ran her fingertips over his lips. "Read my mind."

His gaze met hers, a moment only, and then he swept her into his arms again and carried her swiftly up the stairs.

A thought closed and locked the door and they were alone in the bedroom.

Drake set her on her feet ever so slowly and then he stood there, just looking at her. "Never again," he vowed. "Never again will I be parted from you."

Fresh tears welled in Elena's eyes.

"You are my heart, my soul." He drew her into his arms again. "There is no life for me without you."

Pressing her face against his chest, Elena closed her eyes, her hands moving restlessly up and down his back. "Drake . . . ?"

"Yes, wife?"

"I can't wait any longer."

He murmured her name and the next thing she knew, they were in bed, lying naked in each other's arms.

She smiled into his eyes. "And to think, I once refused to take you to my bed."

He laughed softly. "Tonight, it will be even better than the first time."

"I don't think that's possible."

"You doubt me?" He rose over her, his eyes blazing red with his desire.

"Oh, no, my lord," she exclaimed.

"See that you do not," he warned with mock fierceness. "I am no puny mortal who grows weary after one encounter. Or two. Or three."

"I remember," she said, grinning. "Shall we try for four?"

"As you wish, my sweet wife. As you wish."

Elena awoke with a smile, and a fervent hope that the night past hadn't been a dream. But no, for Drake was there, asleep beside her. He loved her. He had vowed never to be parted from her again.

Last night had been so wonderful, she wished they could make love again, now. But he was resting and she really needed a shower.

She was about to get out of bed when his fingers curled around her wrist.

"Where are you going, wife?"

"Well, it's morning, and I'm hungry—"

"As am I."

"I don't think we're hungry for the same things," Elena remarked dryly.

"No. Were you not just lusting after my body?"

"I wouldn't say *lusting*, exactly," she replied, choking back a laugh.

"Wishing for?"

"Perhaps. A little."

"If you want me, woman, you had better take me now, before the sun climbs any higher in the sky."

"Take you?" she asked with a grin.

"Every way you can," he said, his grin matching hers as he pulled her under the covers. "As long as I can reciprocate."

It was midafternoon when Elena slipped out of bed. Humming softly, she grabbed her robe and went downstairs.

To her amazement, most of the furniture that had cluttered the main room was gone. The old sofas and couches and tables had been replaced with the new ones. Only the scarred trestle table remained. Did it have some special significance for Drake, that he had kept it? And where was all the old furniture?

Going down to the kitchen, she could only stare in wonder. The old oven was gone and a shiny new one stood in its place. There was also a small refrigerator. The old sink with the pump had been replaced by a stainless steel basin and a new counter. An apartment-sized washer and dryer just barely fit at the end of the counter.

Elena shook her head. It was amazing. How had Drake accomplished it in such a short time?

The ringing of the bell at the front door drew her back upstairs.

"Morning, miss," the electrician said cheerfully. "We'll be needing to work inside today."

"Of course." Elena stepped back to allow the man and his crew into the castle.

"You might want to consider getting rid of that bell pull and installing a real doorbell," he said.

She nodded. "That's a wonderful suggestion. Thank you."

While the men were at work, she went upstairs and discovered where the rest of the furniture had gone. Apparently, while she slept, Drake, Andrei, and Stefan had carried the bedroom furniture upstairs. All the bedrooms had beds now, as well as chairs, nightstands, and throw rugs. And dressers, Elena noted. Dressers with mirrors. She would have to ask Drake about the whole reflection-in-the-mirror thing.

She spent an hour making all the beds, then went downstairs to see how the electrician was doing.

"Just about finished in this room," he said. "You'll need a cable hookup for the TV, but the stereo and DVD player will work just fine."

"Thank you."

"Tomorrow, we'll begin wiring the kitchen."

Elena nodded. Then, realizing it was late afternoon and she had skipped breakfast and lunch, she went downstairs to the kitchen for something to eat, thinking how wonderful it would be when the electricity was hooked up in all the rooms. She could hardly wait to fill the new refrigerator with meat and cheese and eggs and milk. And ice cream.

She was sitting at the table, finishing a peanut butter and jelly sandwich, when the big gray cat hopped on the chair beside hers.

"Smoke!" she exclaimed. "Where have you been?"

The cat yawned, then curled up on the chair.

"You are a most peculiar creature," Elena murmured. "Drake said you're not his, yet when he's not here, neither are you. . . ." She frowned, remembering the night she had asked Drake about the cat, and he had replied that he didn't own one. Yet Drake had returned only last night. And this afternoon the cat was back. Was it possible? No, the very thought was absurd.

Still puzzling over the odd comings and goings of the remarkable cat, Elena went up the stairs to the main hall. After slipping a DVD into the player, she stretched out on one of the new sofas. Moments later, Smoke joined her there. He rubbed up against her arm, licked her cheek, then curled up beside her and closed his eyes. What a life he led, Elena thought. All the creature did was sleep.

It was near sundown when the cat jumped off the sofa and padded out of the room.

Sitting up, Elena rubbed her eyes, and then she smiled. Drake would soon be here. A thrill of excitement bubbled up inside her, and then he was there, striding toward her, tall and dark and handsome. Wordlessly, he pulled her up into his arms, one hand cupping her buttocks to draw her tight against him while he kissed her. And kissed her again, until she clung to him, breathless.

"So, wife of my heart," he said, "did you miss me while we were apart?"

"You know I did."

"What do you think of the new furniture?" he asked, glancing around. "Do you like it? If not, I will send it all back."

"I love it. But why did you decide to furnish all the rooms upstairs when there's just the two of us?"

"Andrei and Katiya will be staying with us for a while." He stroked her hair, his gaze moving over her face. "Do you mind?"

"Of course not. What about Stefan? Will he be staying here, too?"

"No." He settled on the sofa, drawing her down beside him. "He has gone back to the Fortress. But I thought he should have a room, should he return."

"How did you persuade Rodin to let you leave?"

"Katiya and I convinced him that we had decided to make the best of things."

"And he believed you?"

"Yes, but only after Katiya conceived."

Elena stared at him, shock rolling through her like an icy wave. "She's pregnant?"

He nodded. "It was the only way."

She shook her head, unwilling to believe that Drake had slept with the vampire.

"Elena. Wife. The child is not mine."

"No?"

"No. Andrei is the father."

"Andrei? How did that happen?" she asked. But the answer was obvious. "You had this all planned out, didn't you?"

Drake smiled smugly. "Katiya is quite a good actress. We spent the first month of our marriage pretending to dislike each other," he said with a laugh. "Although it didn't take much pretending, at least in the beginning. Gradually, we let people think we were growing fond of each other. Katiya told her mother that she was falling in love with me. Her mother naturally told mine. We were quite convincing."

"And when you had convinced everyone, Andrei returned to the Fortress."

"He had returned every night since the wedding. He slept in my bed. I slept in his. No one knew. I think she must have conceived the first night. A clever plan, do you not agree?"

"I guess so, but what will happen if Rodin finds out?"

"That, I cannot predict."

"Nothing good, I bet," Elena muttered.

"Of that you can be sure," Drake agreed. "But let us not worry about that now. We are together. Let us make the most of it."

"Your cat came back."

"Have you forgotten what I told you?" he asked with a laugh. "I do not have a cat."

"It's you, isn't it?" she asked, stabbing him in the chest with a forefinger. "You're the cat."

He grinned at her. "Finally figured that out, did you? It took you long enough."

"How is that possible?"

"Those of us born to Liliana are able to shape-shift. It is a rare ability, but useful, when you have a stranger in the house."

"You could have told me!"

"It was more fun this way. And it allowed me to watch over you during the day."

She blew out a sigh, wondering if she would ever learn all there was to know about this extraordinary man. But there was no time to ask now, because he was kissing her again, leading her up the stairs, pressing her down on the bed, his body covering hers. And there was no more need for thought.

Later, lying in his arms, Elena ran her fingers down the crooked scar along his neck. "How did you get that?"

"Does it matter? It is an old wound."

"I thought vampire wounds healed without a scar."

"Most do, but not ones inflicted with silver."

"Oh. I'd still like to know how you got it."

He looked past her, as if traveling backward in time. "Many years ago a band of gypsies camped down by the lake. I heard their music one night, and because I was lonely, I went down to watch them dance. Luiza was one of the dancers. She was young, no more than fifteen or sixteen, and very beautiful, with clear olive skin and long red hair. I went back to their camp every night for several weeks, drawn by the music and the dancing. They were a happy people, filled with the kind of joy that was lacking in my own life, in my own kind.

"One night, Luiza followed me home. She declared she was in love with me. I told her there was no future for us, that her band would be leaving in a few days and that I could not go with them. She begged me to make love to her." He shook his head. "She was too young. For all her flirtatious ways, she was innocent in the ways of men and women."

"What happened?" Elena asked.

"I sent her away. Late that night, she came to the castle. I was on the ramparts, watching the gypsies pack, when she burst into the room. She told me she did not want to live without me. She pulled a dagger out of her sleeve and dragged the blade over her wrist. I do not think she meant to cut so deeply, but she was young and foolish and the dagger was very sharp. I am afraid the scent of her blood brought out the vampire in me.

"Luiza stared at me, her eyes wide. I imagine my own eyes had gone red by then. She backed away from me. I tried to tell her not to be afraid, that I would not hurt her. I knew I had to get to her soon, to stop the bleeding. When I reached for her, she flailed wildly with the knife. When

I reached for her again, she stumbled and fell on the blade. It pierced her heart."

"That's so sad," Elena murmured. "But it wasn't your fault."

He grunted softly. He had carried the guilt for Luiza's death for centuries. It was one of the reasons he had stayed away from people, never letting himself get too close, never letting himself care, until Elena wandered into Wolfram Castle and turned his life and his world upside down.

Chapter 22

Tavian Dinescu stared up at Wolfram Castle. He had seen the delivery trucks wending their way up the long path to the old place, seen the utility vans of other vendors coming and going. Had Lord Drake sold the place? That seemed the only logical explanation for the sudden flurry of renovations and repairs that had been going on the last few days.

He rubbed a hand over his jaw. Were there also people working in the old garden behind the kitchen?

Perhaps it was time he paid an official visit to the castle's residents. After all, as chief of police, it was his duty to know what was going on in his jurisdiction.

Elena poured herself a cup of coffee, her gaze moving around the kitchen. Funny how a few modern appliances and some new furniture had changed a drafty old castle into a comfortable home. She could hardly wait until the electricians had completed wiring the castle.

Andrei and Katiya had disappeared into one of the bedrooms soon after they arrived, and as far as Elena knew, they hadn't come out since.

As soon as she finished her coffee, she was going to drive into the city for a few things. It would have been much faster and closer to shop in town, but she didn't want to risk running into her uncle.

The thought had no sooner crossed her mind when the new doorbell rang. She was smiling when she opened the door, thinking it was one of the workmen, only to come face-to-face with the devil himself.

A bolt of fear raced through Elena when she saw her uncle standing there. She told herself there was nothing to fear. Drake had warned her uncle to leave her alone, yet here he was, at her door.

"Elena!" Dinescu said jovially. "How well you look, my dear. May I come in?"

"No!" She tried to slam the door, but he blocked it with his foot.

"Now, now," he said, barely suppressed anger in his voice. "Is that any way to treat the man who took you in and raised you as his own daughter? Who fed you and clothed you and cared for you all those years after your parents died? Surely I deserve a little hospitality in return."

Elbowing past her, Dinescu strode into the room. He glanced around, noting the costly wall-mounted TV, the fancy entertainment center, the expensive new furniture.

"You've done very well for yourself, haven't you?" he remarked, his eyes narrowing. "How did you manage to snag such a catch, I wonder? Were you sleeping around behind my back like that slutty cousin of yours?"

"I . . . no . . . how dare you!" she sputtered. "Get out of here!"

"You were to be mine." Grabbing Elena by the hair, he forced her head back. "Mine!"

"I would rather die," she said, gasping for air. "Let me go!"

He laughed, a harsh, ugly sound, and she knew in that moment that he intended to kill her or worse.

Spurred by fear, Elena stomped down on her uncle's instep as hard as she could, then kicked him in the shin. He grunted with pain, loosening his hold on her hair. She twisted her head to the side, jerking her hair free of his grasp, although it felt as though she left a handful behind.

Freed of his hold, she ran for the door, but he was right behind her.

"Oh, no, you don't!" he roared.

Her hand was on the latch when he caught her. Face distorted with lust and rage, he grabbed her T-shirt and ripped it down the front, exposing her bra and the bare expanse of her belly. "I will have you," he repeated with a leer. "Right here. Right now. And then I'll take you to visit Jenica."

Elena opened her mouth to scream. She knew the vampires were resting and likely wouldn't hear her, but she prayed one of the workmen would come to her aid. Before she could make a sound, Dinescu slapped one ham-sized hand over her mouth, trapping the cry in her throat.

He had her bent backward over his arm when the cat came barreling down the stairs. Snarling, Smoke launched himself at Dinescu, his claws raking both sides of the man's face, slicing his cheeks open to the bone.

With a shriek of pain, Dinescu released Elena and bolted out the front door.

Elena sank to the floor, her arms wrapped around her waist. She stared at the cat, wishing for sunset. She needed Drake to hold her, needed to tell him what her uncle had said.

Smoke padded quietly toward her, bright yellow eyes staring up at her. "That was a brave thing you did," she said, stroking the cat's head. "Thank you."

At her touch, there was a ripple in the air and Drake knelt beside her, stark naked.

Elena blinked at him, then burst out laughing, but her laughter quickly turned to tears. "Did you hear what he said?"

With a nod, Drake gathered her into his arms. A glance closed and locked the door, and then he carried Elena up the stairs, tucked her into bed, and slid under the covers beside her. "Are you all right?"

"He killed her, didn't he?"

"There is little doubt of that now."

"But can we prove it?" she asked anxiously. "If he killed Jenica, he has to pay for what he's done."

"He will," Drake said, his voice filled with quiet menace. "Never doubt it for a minute."

The town lay dark and quiet under a bright yellow moon when Drake knocked on Tavian Dinescu's front door.

Standing on the porch, Drake watched the lights go on inside the house, heard the man's heavy footsteps as Dinescu shuffled toward the foyer.

Drake caught the faint scent of metal and gun oil, heard the rapid beat of Dinescu's heart just before the door swung open.

Dinescu's bulk filled the doorway. He would have made a comical figure, clad in a white T-shirt and a pair of loose-fitting pajama bottoms, save for the large pistol held in one meaty fist.

"You!" Dinescu hissed. "What the devil do you want?"

"Do not ever threaten my wife again," Drake said.

"Your wife," Dinescu said, sneering. "Your widow, you mean."

"Are you threatening me now?"

"No threat," Dinescu said, bringing up the gun. "I'll just shoot you where you stand, then drag your body inside and claim self-defense."

"What makes you think you will get away with it?"

"There's just you and me. And you'll be dead. Besides, who's going to doubt the word of the chief of police?" Dinescu asked smugly, and pulled the trigger.

Drake absorbed the impact without flinching, then plucked the smoking pistol from the astonished man's hand.

Dinescu stared up at him, a fine sheen of sweat dotting his brow. "What are you?"

"Listen to me," Drake said, exerting his preternatural power over the man's mind. "You are going to turn yourself in for murdering your daughter. And you will confess to any other crimes you may have committed. You will write your confession out, in detail, and deliver it in the morning."

Dinescu nodded. "In detail."

"If anyone asks why you have decided to come forward, you will tell them you cannot live with your guilt any longer. And if, for some reason, they do not find you guilty, you will come to me, and I will mete out the justice you deserve. Do you understand?"

"Understand. Yes."

"See that you do as I have instructed. My justice will not be as swift or as merciful as that of the court."

Chapter 23

The confession of the chief of police was the lead story in the local paper and on the nightly news. According to reporters, he had confessed to killing his daughter, Jenica Dinescu, as well as Emil Bramwell, the banker's son.

The police arrived at Wolfram Castle early that morning with a warrant to search the grounds for the body. Drake had warned Elena to feign ignorance of the location of the corpse, saying it would only complicate matters if she told the police where to look, and might cause problems in the future when the police wondered why she hadn't come forward to report finding the body.

When questioned, she told the officers what she had once thought of as the truth—her cousin had run away from home with one of the boys from town.

"It's what my uncle told me the morning Jenica went missing," Elena said. "I had no reason to believe otherwise."

There was no pretense in her tears when they exhumed her cousin's body, placed it in an ugly black bag, and carried it away. They found Emil Bramwell, too, buried in a far corner of the garden, as well as another, unidentified body.

It fell to Elena to arrange for Jenica's funeral, which was held two days later. Nearly everyone in town attended.

They offered Elena their sympathy, murmuring words of kindness, of disbelief, that a man like Tavian Dinescu could have done such a terrible thing.

The following day, Emil Bramwell was laid to rest. Again, the townspeople turned out to pay their respects and offer their condolences to the family.

Elena felt duty-bound to attend Emil's funeral. She stood at the grave site, feeling lost and alone, and wishing that Drake could be at her side. He had been a great comfort in the past few days. She missed him now, missed his arm around her, giving her strength, his calm assurance that everything would be all right.

Standing there, she had an inkling of how he must feel when he was among mortals. He looked human, but he didn't really belong. And it occurred to her that as long as she lived with him, there would always be a gulf between her and her own kind.

She stayed at the funeral only as long as necessary, and then hurried up to the castle on the hill where a big gray cat waited to greet her.

"I am sorry I could not be there for you," Drake said later that night. They were sitting on one of the new sofas in front of the fire, his arm draped around her shoulders, her head resting against his arm.

"I know. They're both at peace now," Elena said, and hoped it was true. "They still haven't identified the third body. It's been there much longer than . . . than the others. I overheard one of the townspeople say he thought the body belonged to a young woman who had stayed at the inn eight or nine years ago. She went missing, though she had left all her belongings behind."

She took a deep breath, wishing this was all behind her,

but there was still her uncle's trial to get through. "Do you ever think about death? About dying?"

"Not often."

"Stefan said your father is over a thousand years old."

Drake nodded.

"I can't imagine living that long. Does he ever get bored, do you think?"

"With twenty wives and dozens of children? I doubt it."

"So, you have other siblings besides those on the Council?"

"Yes." He lifted a strand of her hair and let it slide through his fingers.

"Why did he choose those twelve?"

"They are his favorites. Many of the others live elsewhere, as do his other wives whenever Liliana stays at the Fortress."

She grinned. "That's what Stefan said."

"She is very jealous. I always found that odd, since she claims to have no love for her husband."

"Do you believe that?"

"Not entirely. I believe she cares for him as much as she is able. As much as he will allow."

"We'll never have children, will we?"

"It is doubtful. As far as I know, no mortal woman has ever given birth to a child sired by one of us." His hand stroked her nape. "Does that bother you?"

"A little. Doesn't it bother you?"

"No. You are all I need." His hand cupped her cheek and then he was pressing his lips to hers, his tongue slowly teasing hers, until her stomach quivered with excitement. His hands caressed her, gently, tenderly, and then with greater and greater urgency, until she lay beneath him, her legs wrapped around his waist. She had no idea where her clothes had gone, didn't care about anything but the urgent need that grew inside her.

He whispered love words to her in a language she didn't

understand, but there was no mistaking their meaning, or the desire behind them.

She moaned when his tongue slid along the side of her neck, closed her eyes when she felt his fangs lightly scrape her skin.

"Elena?"

She heard the question in his voice, the need, and had no thought to refuse him. Murmuring, "Yes," she clung to him, caught up in a sensual whirlwind that carried her away to a place where she had never been, a mystical place where there were no doubts, no fears for the future, only the incredible pleasure of his bite and the magic of two souls blending, bonding, to become one.

Chapter 24

Katiya lay wrapped in Andrei's arms, her head resting on his shoulder. Since their arrival at the castle, they had not left this room except to hunt. She would have been happy to stay there the rest of her life, to spend her days sleeping at Andrei's side, and her nights in his arms.

Yet always, in the back of her mind, was the fear that her happiness would be short-lived. With the passing of each day, she worried that Rodin and her father would arrive at the castle and drag them all back to the Fortress. If that happened, Andrei's life would be forfeited. Perhaps hers and Drake's, as well.

She trailed her fingertips over Andrei's chest, felt his lips move in her hair.

"Do you think they will come after us?" she whispered.

"Is that what you are worrying about?"

"I cannot help it. I know we agreed not to let it ruin our time together, but . . ." She blinked back her tears. "I am so afraid of what will happen if they find out we have deceived them." She could lie to her father. She could lie to Rodin. But Rodin had only to read Elena's mind to ferret out the truth.

Andrei stroked her hair. He was a realist. Whether he liked it or not he knew that, before long, Drake and Katiya would have to return to the Fortress to continue their charade as a happily married couple. Of course, there was always the possibility that Rodin would send someone to check up on them before that or, worse yet, decide to come for a visit himself. The most they could hope for was another few months together. Katiya would have to return to the Fortress to give birth. As Drake's wife, it would be expected.

Andrei placed his hand over Katiya's womb. His child rested there. Whatever happened in the future, nothing could change that. If the truth came to light, retribution would surely follow. Rodin could choose to punish Andrei or destroy him. He might torture Drake for his deception, but Katiya would be exempt from any punishment, at least until their child was grown.

Beside him, Katiya wept. There had to be a way for them to stay together, Andrei thought desperately, a place where no one would find them, where they could raise their child in peace. Where they could live together in love. He shook his head. It was only a pipe dream, he thought ruefully.

"Katiya, beloved," he murmured, wiping away her tears. "Please do not cry. Even if the worst happens, I will never regret the time we have spent together."

Chapter 25

Tavian Dinescu's trial was the talk of the town. He had been charged with murder, attempted murder, and attempted rape.

People who knew him were shocked to discover he had killed his own daughter, as well as the banker's oldest son. Of course, there were those who said they had known all along that there was something wrong with Tavian, that they had never believed his story about Jenica running off with Emil.

Stories came out about his past. A woman remembered catching eight-year-old Tavian cutting the head off a dead rat. A man recalled a time when Tavian had been a few years older and set a kitten's tail on fire. An old school chum recalled Tavian's fascination with torturing small animals and how he had once held a puppy underwater to see how long it would take the animal to drown.

During the course of the trial, Elena was called upon to testify. Sitting in the witness stand, her hands folded tightly in her lap, she refused to look at her uncle as she related her testimony. Yes, her uncle had often made improper advances toward her. Yes, it had frightened her and she had run away from home. Yes, he had come to the castle two weeks ago.

"And what did he say at that time?" the prosecuting attorney asked.

"He said 'I will have you.' I told him I'd rather die, and . . ." She swallowed hard, her cheeks growing hot. "He ripped my T-shirt down the front."

"This T-shirt?" The prosecuting attorney held it up and offered it as exhibit A.

"Yes." She bit down on her lower lip. "He told me he was going to . . . to have me then and there, and then he said, 'I'll take you to see Jenica.'"

"And what happened next?"

"My cat attacked him, and he ran out of the castle." She glanced at her uncle for the first time. He looked prosperous in a new, dark blue suit. Both cheeks were bandaged where Smoke had scratched him.

In light of Dinescu's confession, combined with the DNA evidence found on all three bodies, the defense had little to build its case on.

The jury deliberated only a short time. When they returned, they declared that they found Tavian Dinescu to be criminally insane and recommended that he be sent to Borsa Castle. Borsa had once been the summer home of the Banffy family. At the end of World War II, the Communists had thrown the family out. It was now an asylum for the insane and, some said, for people no one else wanted.

In spite of all he had done, Elena was overcome with pity for her uncle. She had heard stories of Borsa, which was rumored to be the most monstrous mental institution in all Romania. He would have no one to visit him, no one to offer the attendants food and gifts in exchange for better care.

She blew out a sigh. There was nothing more she could do for him. Whatever happened to her uncle now was his own fault. He had brought it all on himself.

A week after the trial ended, her uncle's lawyer knocked on the castle door. "Good afternoon, Miss Knightsbridge."

"Mr. Balescu. What brings you here?"

"May I come in?"

"Of course." She took a step backward, and almost tripped over the cat. "Smoke, get out of the way," she murmured, and grinned when he licked her ankle. "This way, Mr. Balescu," she said. "Please, sit down."

She sat on one of the sofas in front of the hearth, the cat at her side. The lawyer took a seat on the sofa across from her. He was a middle-aged man, impeccably dressed in a dark blue suit, with light brown hair, hazel eyes, and a wispy mustache.

"Is something wrong?" she asked.

"I am here to settle your uncle's estate." Setting his briefcase on the coffee table between them, he opened it and withdrew several sheets of paper. "According to the terms of your uncle's will, the house and all its belongings were bequeathed to your Aunt Catalena. If she died first, his property was to go to Jenica. And then to you."

"No." Elena shook her head. "No. I don't want it."

"You can dispose of his holdings in any way you wish," Mr. Balescu said. "But first you need to sign these papers." He pushed them across the table toward her, and offered her a pen. "There's also a small savings account."

Elena read the papers over carefully, asking questions when there was a clause she didn't fully understand, then signed where the lawyer indicated.

Mr. Balescu tucked the papers into his briefcase and closed it with a flourish. "If you have any questions, please, do not hesitate to call. It will take a few weeks to transfer the title on the house into your name."

"Thank you."

Rising, he sketched a bow.

When she started to get up, he waved her off. "I can see myself out. Good day to you, Miss Knightsbridge."

Elena stared after the lawyer, then looked down at the cat. "I never expected that."

The cat rubbed his head against her thigh.

"I'll sell the house," she said, thinking out loud. "And whatever else he has. If I donate it to the asylum, maybe they'll make his life easier."

With a hiss that could only be disapproval, the cat jumped off the sofa and ran up the stairs.

Elena blew out a sigh of exasperation, then followed the cat.

She found Drake waiting for her in bed, the sheet pooled in his lap.

"You think I'm wrong?" she asked. Sitting on the edge of the bed, she kicked off her shoes.

He shook his head. "I am only amazed at your kindness."

"What kindness?"

"Mortals are strange creatures. Dinescu would have killed you without a qualm. You wanted him to be punished. You testified against him and now, when he has been sent to the worst hellhole in the country, you want to do what you can to make his life more comfortable." He shook his head. "My people are not so kind. Any one of us who did what your uncle did would have been destroyed, and that would have been the end of it."

"I guess I wouldn't make a very good vampire."

"No," Drake agreed, pulling her toward him, so that her back rested against his chest. "But you make a perfect wife."

"What will happen when you don't go back to the Fortress? You aren't going back, are you?"

"I am afraid we must. It is the only way to continue this charade. The only way for Andrei and Katiya to be together."

"What if Rodin finds out what you've done?" She had asked him that before, and he had said, *That, I cannot predict.*

Today, he said, "I will appeal to Liliana for mercy for you and for Katiya."

Elena looked over her shoulder, her gaze searching his face. "What will he do to you?" Remembering how Rodin had punished Drake before, she hated to ask, but she had to know.

He thought about it a moment before replying. "I do not know. I promised I would marry Katiya. I promised that she would conceive a child, and that I would put her happiness before my own. I have kept those promises," he said with a wry grin. "I married her. She is with child, and she is happy."

"Maybe that will mollify Rodin," Elena said hopefully.

"Maybe," Drake replied. But it was doubtful. Forgiveness was not one of Rodin's virtues.

"What will happen to your brother?"

"I do not know. Andrei's mother is currently out of favor with Rodin."

"You don't have the same mother?"

"No." He ran his fingertips along her arm, then lifted her sweater over her head and tossed it aside. Her bra and jeans followed. "Let us not worry about the future now," he said, his voice a low purr. "I can think of better ways to spend the afternoon."

"Shouldn't you be resting?" she asked primly.

"Later. Right now, I need you here, in my bed, in my arms."

"And what will we do in your bed?"

His laughter filled the room. "Exactly what you are thinking, wife," he said as he pulled her under the covers and showered her with kisses.

Chapter 26

The day after Elena received the title to her uncle's house, she drove down the hill for one last look. Walking from room to room, she tried to remember the happy times she had spent in this house, but they were few and far between, and had ended abruptly when her Aunt Catalena had passed away.

Elena spent a few minutes in her old bedroom. She didn't have much in the way of belongings—her clothes, a dozen or so CDs, a handful of old school books, a few knickknacks, a couple of movie posters. Seven years of her life, she thought, glancing around, and the only thing she wanted to keep was the music box her aunt had given her one Christmas. It was a lovely thing, white with pale pink flowers painted around the edge. When she lifted the lid, a tiny blond ballerina wearing a fluffy pink tutu twirled round and round.

Carrying the music box into the kitchen, she placed it on the table with the other items she wanted to keep—her Aunt Catalena's Bible, the silver candlesticks her mother and father had given Catalena as a wedding gift, her aunt's favorite teapot, a gold crucifix on a chain that had belonged to Jenica.

Sad, Elena thought as she placed the items in a box and stowed them in the back of the Porsche, that there were so few happy memories from her childhood.

The next day, she put the house and all its contents—including Dinescu's clothes and her own, the furniture and appliances—up for sale. After meeting with the Realtor, she drove away from the house and didn't look back.

Later that afternoon, she called Mr. Balescu and informed him that the money from the savings account, as well as the net proceeds from the sale of the house, were to be sent to Borsa Castle to be used for her uncle's care.

Done and done, she thought as she ended the call. She had no ties left to her uncle. She had done her best by him, which was more than he deserved, and now, at last, it was over.

The next few weeks passed peacefully and life at Wolfram Castle settled into a pleasant routine. They had electricity now. It was such a pleasure, Elena sometimes went from room to room flicking the lights on and off, just because she could. She spent her days caring for the house. There was plenty to keep her busy—clothes to wash, furniture to dust, floors to vacuum and sweep. Having music playing in the background made the chores seem less like work. She rarely went into the garden, although she did plant a chestnut tree in the place where she had discovered her cousin's body.

And when she got lonely during the day, the cat was there. Somehow, he always knew when she needed company.

"When do you sleep?" she asked Drake one night. "During the day, you're here in your cat form, and at night, you're Drake."

"You forget how much the cat sleeps," he replied with

an easy grin. "I love those catnaps. And I sleep at night, when you do."

As time went on, Elena grew increasingly fond of Andrei and Katiya. They were very much in love, anyone could see that, and excited at the prospect of becoming parents. If it weren't for the fact that the other people in the house slept by day and didn't eat, she might have forgotten they were vampires.

Some nights, the four of them played cards. Some nights they played chess, a game that Drake invariably won. Other nights they walked in the moonlight or went swimming in the lake, or spent a quiet evening at home, reading. They often watched movies until the wee hours of the morning.

Elena's favorite way to pass the night was dancing with Drake. She loved being close to him, reveled in the sense of wonder she felt whenever he was near, the way he looked at her, his dark eyes filled with love and longing. And a distant sadness she often saw reflected in her own eyes when she looked in the mirror.

She tried not to think of the future, of the time when Drake and Katiya would have to return to the Fortress, but it was always there, in the back of her mind, a nagging worry that Rodin would somehow discover the truth, that he would torture Drake again, or worse, execute him.

It seemed the harder she tried not to think about the future, the more often it popped into her mind, and when she was successful at keeping her worries at bay during the daylight hours, they turned her dreams into nightmares. Nightmares that became increasingly more real, more vivid.

In her dreams, Drake was again locked in the tower. Only this time there was no reprieve and Rodin left him there, to be slowly burned alive, until nothing remained of the man she loved but a pile of gray ashes. Night after night, she woke screaming or in tears.

And then, all too soon, the night she had been dreading arrived.

Elena and Drake were sitting in front of the fire, taking turns reading *Wuthering Heights* aloud, when Stefan appeared. One look at his face, and Elena knew he had brought bad news.

"You are needed at the Fortress, immediately," Stefan said. "Gerret has challenged Rodin for leadership of the Coven."

"Gerret!" Drake exclaimed, rising. Gerret was the Master of the Irish Fortress. "I do not believe it."

"It is true, nevertheless. Liliana sent me to bring you back."

Drake swore. If his mother wanted him home, she must be apprehensive about the outcome of the battle. He could understand that. If Rodin lost, she would have to leave the Fortress, as would all the vampires who lived there. As for the sheep, they would become prey for Gerret and his Coven. He doubted Liliana cared one way or the other what happened to the sheep, but she considered the Fortress home.

"What brought this on?" Drake asked. "Gerret has never shown any interest in acquiring more land or more power."

Stefan shrugged. "Who can say? The meet is set for the day after tomorrow at midnight. Gerret's second-in-command is already at the Fortress. Rodin has named you as his second."

Drake uttered a short, pithy oath.

"What shall I tell him?"

Andrei materialized in the room and took his place beside Drake. "I do not like this. I smell treachery."

Drake nodded.

Elena's gaze darted from one man to the other. "What kind of treachery?"

Andrei shook his head. "Something is off. Gerret has never expressed any interest in expanding his holdings." He looked at Stefan. "Who did he send as his second?"

"Florin."

Andrei and Stefan exchanged glances.

"What?" Drake asked sharply.

"If you spent more time at the Fortress, you would know what is going on," Stefan said, a faint note of accusation in his tone. "This is not about territory. It is about revenge."

"What kind of revenge?" Elena asked.

"Florin is the son of Rodin's fourth wife, Nadiya Korzha," Andrei explained. "He got into a fight with Olaf over one of the sheep and Rodin banished Florin from the Fortress. Nadiya has never forgiven him for that. Gerret took Florin under his wing. Florin does not care who wins the upcoming battle. All he wants is a way into the Fortress. If Gerret destroys Rodin, so much the better. As far as I can tell, Florin's only interest is in avenging himself on Olaf."

"Which will cause more tension between Liliana and Nadiya," Stefan remarked.

Drake raked his fingers through his hair. "All this because of one of the sheep?" he muttered irritably.

"There is more to it than that," Stefan said. "Rodin gave the sheep to Olaf. Rather than stay with him, she killed herself. It is said that Florin was in love with the girl."

"In love?" Drake exclaimed. "With one of the sheep?"

"Like I said, if you spent more time at the Fortress, you would know what is going on. Many of the younger ones are not happy with our current laws. Our young men and women do not like being told who to marry."

"I can understand that," Drake muttered.

"Our men and women often want more from the sheep than nourishment."

Drake swore under his breath. "Why tell me all this? It is Rodin who should hear your complaints, not me."

"He will not listen."

"Back to the matter at hand," Drake said, glancing at his brothers. "Who else knows about Florin's plan for revenge?"

Stefan shook his head. "No one."

Drake glared at Stefan. "And you left Olaf there, with no one to protect his back?"

"I told Ciprian that I did not trust Florin and ordered him to shadow the intruder's every move until I return."

Drake nodded. Ciprian was another of his half brothers.

"Something troubles you," Stefan said.

"Florin is not the type to risk his life over a woman."

Stefan frowned thoughtfully. "You think he intends to challenge Rodin for banishing him from the Fortress?"

"Florin has no chance in battle against Gerret and even less against Rodin, but if Gerret should win, Florin would again have access to the Fortress. Gerret might even put him in charge of the Fortress and its people." Drake shook his head. The odds of Florin besting either Gerret or Rodin in battle were slim to none.

"Stefan, stay here with Elena. Andrei, you and Katiya will come with me."

"Wait a minute!" Elena said. "I'm going with you."

"No."

"Yes!"

"Elena, be reasonable," Drake said. "I cannot take you to the Fortress with me."

She bit back her protest. He was right, of course. If Rodin saw her with Drake, it would give rise to questions they dared not answer. But how could she stay here? "Are you going to fight?"

"I am going to watch Rodin's back while Andrei watches Olaf."

"What if Rodin loses?" Elena asked. "What then?"

With a reassuring smile, Drake pulled her into his arms and kissed her. "Pray that does not happen."

Rodin demanded an audience the moment Drake and Katiya returned to the Fortress. After spending time with Elena, Drake found it difficult to go back to pretending that he and Katiya were happily wed and joyfully antici-pating the birth of their first child, but both Rodin and Liliana seemed convinced.

After the initial greetings were over, Katiya and Liliana left the men to converse alone.

"So," Rodin said, sitting back in his chair. "Married life agrees with you."

"We get on well together." Drake sat in his mother's chair, his legs stretched out in front of him.

"Stefan told you about Gerret?"

"You are not worried about the outcome of the chal-lenge, are you?"

Rodin snorted. "The Irishman is no threat. It is obvious that Florin set this up to accomplish his own agenda."

"I will take care of Florin."

"If I lose the fight, you must challenge Gerret. I do not want your mother to have to leave the Fortress."

"Of course," Drake said, frowning. "But that will not happen."

"I cannot control this Coven and the Irish territory, as well. When I have defeated Gerret, your mother and I will move to the Irish Fortress temporarily. She has always wanted to visit Ireland. You will take over the Coven here until we return. It will make a good home for you and Katiya and your child."

"No." Drake shook his head emphatically. "No. I do not want to live here. Nor do I wish the responsibilities of being a Master Vampire."

"You are the oldest and the strongest of my sons. You have pledged your life and your allegiance to me, and you will do as you are told."

Drake sat back, his mind spinning. "And if I refuse?"

"You will not."

With Drake gone, Elena couldn't sit still. She moved from one thing to another, unable to concentrate on anything. She tried to watch a movie, she tried reading a book, playing solitaire, baking a cake. She couldn't concentrate on the movie or the book, she tossed the cards on the floor, she burned the cake.

She talked Stefan into helping her rearrange the furniture in the main hall, but quickly lost interest.

"I can't stay here," she said, arms akimbo. "It's killing me, not knowing what's going on!"

"What do you want me to do?" Stefan asked.

"Take me to the Fortress."

"No way. Drake would have my head, if Rodin did not take it first."

She dropped down on the sofa, which was now in the center of the room. "How do vampires fight, anyway?"

"With swords."

"Swords! How positively medieval."

"You have no idea." He took a seat on the nearest chair and stretched his legs out in front of him.

"Drake said they fight to the death."

Stefan nodded. He had seen a few challenges in his

time. Some were quickly over. Others turned into blood baths. Either way, they were not pretty.

"Will Rodin win?"

"Undoubtedly. There is no one better with a sword except perhaps Drake."

"Swords," she murmured.

"What did you expect?"

"I don't know. Something otherworldly." She paused a moment. There had been no swords involved when Drake killed his brother. "How did Drake kill Vardin?"

Stefan leaned forward, his expression solemn. "Are you sure you want to know?"

"I think so," she said, then frowned. "Why wouldn't I?"

"It was not as quick as a sword thrust, or as merciful."

"So, what did he do?" she asked, her curiosity piqued.

"Drake ripped his heart out."

She swallowed hard. "With . . . with his hands?"

Stefan nodded. "You look a little pale. Can I get you anything?"

"No. No, I'm fine." She recalled the body lying under a blanket on the floor of her room in the Fortress, the awful bloody stain on the blanket, and on the rug beneath.

Wrapping her arms around her middle, she whispered, "I think I'm going to be sick."

In a blur too quick for human eyes to follow, Stefan left the room, only to return a moment later, chamber pot in hand.

She grabbed it just in time.

He left again, returning with a damp washcloth, a dry towel, and a glass of warm water. She quickly wiped her face, then rinsed her mouth. "Thank you."

"No problem," he said, grinning as he took the chamber pot and soiled linen and left the room.

Elena sighed. She didn't know which was worse, throwing up, or doing so in front of Stefan.

"I'm sorry," she murmured when he returned. "I guess vampires don't throw up."

"No. Not a pretty sight."

"I suppose not. Are you sure Drake isn't going to fight?"

Stefan's gaze slid away from hers.

"Stefan?"

"He will not fight. Unless Rodin is defeated."

Chapter 27

The atmosphere in the Fortress was subdued that night. Everyone knew about the upcoming challenge, though no one spoke of it openly. Even the sheep knew. But then, it seemed as if they always knew what was going on. Drake had often wondered about that. Did they have some sort of telepathy of their own? Or were they just in tune with what went on around them? He thought it more likely that they eavesdropped on what their captors said. They certainly didn't learn anything from the drones, those poor, unfortunate humans who were little more than zombies.

Too keyed up to sit still, he prowled the corridors for hours before going to his apartment.

Katiya looked up when he entered their quarters. "Have you seen Andrei?"

Drake nodded. "He is shadowing Olaf. He told me to kiss you good night."

She laughed softly, her cheeks flushing as Drake dutifully brushed a kiss across her lips.

"Did you see Florin?" she asked.

"No. He has wisely chosen to stay in his room. One of the drones is keeping watch outside his door, ostensibly to do his bidding. Ciprian is also watching over him, from a distance, of course."

"And Rodin?"

"He is sequestered with Liliana."

Drake paced the floor, then dropped into one of the chairs, his hands braced on his thighs. "I have a bad feeling about this whole thing."

"You are not afraid Rodin will lose? He has defeated every challenger who has ever come against him."

Drake nodded. Maybe he was worrying for nothing. Maybe it was being away from Elena that had his insides tied in knots.

"Listen," he said, rising quickly to his feet. "I need to see Elena."

"You are leaving?" Katiya asked, her eyebrows rising in disbelief.

"I will be back before dawn. If anyone comes looking for me, you do not know where I am."

Elena had gone to bed early, only to toss and turn. A glance at the clock showed it was almost 2 A.M. Would this night never end? With a sigh, she closed her eyes, wishing Drake was there beside her.

"Elena?"

"Drake?"

"I could not go to sleep without kissing you good night."

She threw her arms around him. "Oh, Drake. I hate it when we're apart."

He gathered her close, a sense of peace stealing over him as he inhaled the scent of her hair and skin, heard the familiar beat of her heart, tasted her lips with his own. Without his knowing how it had happened, she had become the most important thing in his life, his only reason for living. After five hundred years, he felt as if he had found the other half of his soul. Love, he thought, it was more binding than blood.

When she would have spoken, he silenced her with a kiss. It lit the fire between them as quickly as a match ignites tinder. She wrapped her arms and legs around him, holding tightly, while his hands caressed her back, her shoulders, the sweet curve of her thigh, the swell of her breast.

He growled something under his breath, and the next thing she knew, her nightgown and his clothes were gone and he was rising over her. There was no need for foreplay. She sensed the urgency within him, but it was as nothing compared to her own need. They came together in a rush, his mouth crushing hers, her fingers digging into his back, urging him on.

Just when she was certain it couldn't get any better, she felt his fangs at her throat. She moaned softly as pleasure exploded deep within her, spreading outward like ripples in an ocean, until she was certain she would expire from the sheer wonder of it all.

His tongue laved her neck, and then he was kissing her again, carrying her over the edge of pleasure into ecstasy.

Elena sighed as she turned onto her side, her head pillowed on Drake's shoulder, one arm across his chest, one leg sprawled over his. For this moment, he was hers, and only hers.

But it was a moment fated to end too soon. She sensed the change in him, knew he was getting ready to leave.

"Do you have to go so soon?"

His hand lightly massaged her neck and shoulders. "I promised to be back before dawn. The challenge is tonight at midnight."

"Please take me with you. Can't you hide me somewhere in the Fortress?"

"No. Have you forgotten what happened the last time I took you there? I will not willingly put your life in danger again."

"I'm not afraid." It was a bold-faced lie, but she was desperate to be with him.

"I will return to you as soon as I can." He caressed her cheek with the back of his hand, then kissed her slowly, deeply. "Stay close to Stefan."

Determined not to cry, she sat up, watching him as he dressed, thinking it was a shame to cover that perfect masculine body, wishing he had time to make love to her again.

"Thank you, wife," he said with a wicked grin. "I will fulfill that wish when I return."

"I'll hold you to it."

"Please do."

Fully clothed, he bent down and kissed her again. "Do not worry. Rodin has never lost a battle."

She nodded, but she couldn't ignore the shiver of unease that speared through her when Drake vanished from her sight. Was it only her fear making itself known? Or a premonition of something worse?

The bad feeling was still there when she awoke in the morning—afternoon, she amended when she looked at her watch. It was a little after one thirty. Ten and a half hours left until Gerret challenged Rodin for control of the Fortress.

Rising, she went down to the kitchen. Too upset to eat, she drank three cups of coffee, then wandered out into the garden.

A good cry, she thought. That's what she needed. But the tears wouldn't come.

Feeling thoroughly depressed, she sat on the wrought-iron bench and stared at the fountain. What was Drake doing? Was he resting? What of Liliana? And Katiya and Andrei? How could any of them rest when Rodin was going to fight another vampire to the death?

She should be there. She had to be there. She didn't know why, but she couldn't shake the feeling that Drake needed her.

She lost track of time as the certainty grew within her that she needed to go to the Fortress. Unfortunately, she had no idea where it was.

But Stefan knew.

She drummed her fingertips on the arm of the bench.

Stefan knew.

Eventually, hunger drove her back into the kitchen. She fixed a sandwich, ate it with a glass of milk while she warmed several pots of water on the stove.

When she finished eating, she bathed in the wooden tub. When this was over, she was going to ask Drake about having a bathroom installed in their bedroom.

Wrapped in her bathrobe, she went upstairs to get dressed, only to come to a halt in the doorway when she saw a large brown cat curled up on her pillow.

"Stefan?"

"Meow."

She frowned. She had never seen Stefan in his cat form before. Why now? Moving to the bed, she sat on the edge of the mattress.

The cat rolled onto its back, inviting her to scratch his belly.

"I'm not sure Drake would approve," she muttered as she rubbed the cat's belly.

The cat purred loudly.

Elena stretched out on the bed, her hand still stroking the cat, who continued to purr, even after she had fallen asleep.

Elena woke with a start. What was she doing in bed? She had come up here to get dressed. A glance at her watch told her that had been over five hours ago. She frowned, remembering how she had found the cat in her bed. There was something supernatural about purring cats, she thought. They inevitably put her to sleep.

Rising, she pulled on a pair of jeans and a sweater and went downstairs.

Stefan was waiting for her in the main hall.

"Why did you do that?" she asked.

"You were driving yourself crazy. I thought I would save you a few hours of worry."

"Oh. Thank you. I think."

"It will be over soon."

"Where will they fight?"

"There is a clearing below the Fortress. They will meet there at midnight, with their seconds."

"Just the four of them?"

"No. There will be four other vampires, summoned from other Fortresses, who will serve as witnesses."

"So, it's outside?"

"Yes."

"Take me there."

"No."

Grasping his shirt in both hands, she shook him as hard as she could. It was like trying to move a mountain. "You have to take me! Drake needs me. I know it! Please, Stefan."

"Dammit, Elena, do you know what he will do to me if anything happens to you?"

"Do you know what will happen to me without him?"

Stefan swore long and loud. Not all of it was in English, but some words sounded the same in any language, and she knew she had him.

He paced back and forth in front of the fireplace for a moment, then turned to face her. "All right," he said. "I will take you. But you will have to stay out of sight. And after he kills me, I expect you to put flowers on my grave."

"I promise."

Moving quicker than her eye could follow, he wrapped her in his arms. "Hang on tight, Mrs. Sherrad," he whispered in her ear, and then he swore again. "I know I am going to regret this."

Elena closed her eyes as a familiar feeling of dizziness and nausea swept over her. There was the sense of flying through time, of freewheeling through space, and then nothing. When she opened her eyes, she was standing under a tree, wrapped in Stefan's arms.

He smiled down at her. "You know," he said, hugging her closer, "I could get used to this."

"What?" She looked up at him, her thoughts obviously elsewhere.

"Nothing." He pointed up the mountain. "Look."

At first, Elena didn't see anything. But, gradually, she saw flickering lights moving down the side of the mountain, slowly growing larger, brighter, until she could make out four vampires carrying torches. Behind them, coming single-file, she saw Rodin and Drake, and following them, two other vampires she didn't recognize. All eight wore long black cloaks. And then, trailing far behind, she saw another dark shape that cut away from the group and quickly disappeared into the trees.

"Do not move." Stefan whispered the words. "Try not to breathe."

"Did you see the other vampire?"

Stefan nodded. "It was Liliana. She is not supposed to be here, either."

Elena wrapped her arms around her waist. What if Liliana had seen them? Well, said a little voice in the back of her mind, what if she had? She couldn't say anything without incriminating herself. That knowledge should have been comforting, but it wasn't.

The vampires in the clearing were moving, spreading out. The four torchbearers formed a circle around Rodin and his opponent. In the bright silver glow of a full moon, she easily identified Drake. Taller than the others, he stood outside the circle, behind Rodin. The eighth vampire took a similar stance behind the challenger.

Rodin tossed his cloak aside and Elena saw that he wore a pair of black leather pants and boots and nothing else. His opponent was similarly attired. Each carried a sword. The long silver blades glinted in the moonlight.

Silver, Elena thought. It would make each cut doubly painful for the vampires.

One of the torchbearing vampires moved to stand between Rodin and his opponent. "Rodin Sherrad, Master of the Carpathian Fortress," he intoned, his voice carrying clearly in the quiet. "Be it known that Gerret Lynch, Master of the Irish Fortress, has come here this night to lay down a challenge for your lands and holdings. Do you accept? Or concede?"

"I accept."

"Florin Korzha. Drake Sherrad. You have been chosen as seconds. Come forward."

Drake and Florin took a step forward. Drake inclined his head, and Florin did likewise.

"All those required to be in attendance are here present," the torchbearer said solemnly. "Let whatever blood is shed this night be done with honor." And so saying, he returned to his place in the circle.

For a moment, it was as if the vampires in the clearing were frozen in time.

Elena shivered as a low, keening wind sprang up, rattling the leaves of the trees, causing the torches to flicker erratically. She looked up at Stefan. His eyes burned red as he stared at the scene in the clearing.

Without taking her eyes from the combatants, she asked, "Why is Florin's last name Korzha if he's Rodin's son?"

"Only Liliana and her children carry his surname." Like Elena, Stefan kept his attention on Rodin and his opponent. "His other children take their mother's maiden names."

There was no signal given that Elena could see, but suddenly Rodin and his opponent were moving. The ring of metal against metal was very loud in the stillness of the night. As the blades met, the wind howled through the trees.

Elena shivered again. She risked a look at Drake. His hands were clenched at his sides, his face like something carved from stone.

She turned her attention back to the battle. The vampires moved so swiftly, there were times when they were little more than a blur so that she couldn't tell one from the other.

Power shimmered through the air as sword met sword. When the scent of blood filled the air, the two vampires parted, and Elena saw that the challenger was bleeding from a long gash in his left arm.

The two combatants came together again and again.

It was like being caught up in a nightmare. The wind howling. The blood in the air. The ringing of metal striking metal. The blazing red eyes of the vampires, the light of the torches casting eerie shadows on the ground.

It seemed as if the fight would go on forever when Rodin suddenly feinted left, pivoted in a circle, and drove his sword through his opponent's heart. The other vampire fell backward, his sword dropping from his hand. Before

Gerret hit the ground, Rodin's blade swung again, cleanly severing the challenger's head.

Retching, Elena turned away, her arms folded over her stomach. Stefan had been right. She should have stayed home.

From behind her, someone shouted, "Stop him!"

In the distance, Elena heard a scream filled with such pain, such agony, it raised the short hairs along her nape.

Beside her, Stefan hissed, "No!"

Afraid of what she might see, Elena glanced over her shoulder. Rodin lay on the ground, a long wooden stake protruding from his chest, exactly where his heart would be. A dark stain pooled beneath him.

In the blink of an eye, Drake had Florin by the throat.

And Liliana was kneeling at Rodin's side, a look of horrified disbelief on her face.

One of the torchbearers drew a sword from beneath his cloak and took a step forward, clearly intending to take Rodin's head.

With a wild cry, Stefan propelled himself across the field. Grabbing the sword from the other vampire's hand, Stefan drove the blade into his heart, then whirled around, ready to fight the remaining vampires, if necessary. The three remaining torchbearers dropped their cloaks to the ground. None of them carried weapons.

Elena stared at the grisly scene and then, slowly, lifted her gaze to find Drake staring at her over Florin's shoulder.

Chapter 28

Elena knew a moment of fear when Drake's gaze met hers. Eyes burning red, fangs bared, he stared at her over the head of the vampire struggling in his grasp. She wondered what had possessed the other vampire to stab Rodin from behind, but it was immaterial at the moment.

She had forgotten how frightening Drake's vampire mien could be. With her, he had always been so gentle and tender, it had been easy to forget that beneath his courtly exterior there lurked a deadly predator who lived on human blood.

One of the torchbearers stepped forward. After pulling on a pair of gloves, he reached into the pocket of his trousers and withdrew a pair of silver handcuffs.

Florin ceased his struggles once the shackles were locked in place.

Elena remained where she was, her heart pounding with trepidation. She knew Drake wouldn't betray her presence, but other vampires were arriving now, followed by a handful of drones. One of them picked up Gerret's body and carried it away.

In the flickering light, Elena recognized some of the vampires as members of the Council. They formed a large, silent circle that encompassed Drake, Florin, Stefan, Liliana, and the fallen Master Vampire.

And then Liliana rose to her feet. Eyes blazing, cheeks streaked with scarlet tears, she picked up her husband's sword. "Rodin, Master of the Carpathian Fortress, has been destroyed by treachery." Her voice rang out in the darkness. "I seek a champion to avenge his death and return the Fortress to its rightful heirs."

Every member of the Council took a step forward, as did Stefan and Drake.

Hidden in the shadows, Elena murmured, "No. Oh, no," as Liliana offered the sword to Drake.

Liliana nodded. "As Rodin's eldest son, I honor you with the task of avenging your sire's death."

With a nod, Drake took the sword from her hand.

"According to our laws," Liliana said, "you may challenge Florin Korzha, or you may execute him for his treachery. The choice is yours."

Drake removed his cloak and shirt and tossed them aside. "Release him," he said, his voice as lethal as the weapon in his hand. "An execution is too swift. Too merciful."

One of the drones stepped forward and removed the shackles from Florin's wrists. Even in the dim light, Elena could see that Florin's skin had already blistered and blackened where the silver had touched him.

Drake glanced at his brother. "Stefan, give him your blade."

Stefan glared at Drake, then threw Gerret's weapon on the ground.

Florin's gaze darted from left to right as he picked up the bloodstained sword. Then, lips peeled back to reveal his fangs, he sprang toward Drake.

Elena took a step forward, hardly daring to breathe. Rodin had fought swiftly, skillfully, meting out more punishment than he had received. Florin was not as adept. His moves were slower, less confident.

Drake fought coldly, precisely, his sword slicing into his opponent again and again. Aside from the exquisite pain of silver biting into preternatural flesh, the blade inflicted no lasting damage, the vampire's wounds healing almost immediately, though there would be scars.

Elena choked back a cry as Florin's sword opened a long gash across Drake's chest. He seemed immune to the pain as he parried Florin's next thrust. As the fight went on, Elena realized that Drake could have ended it at any time. He was deliberately prolonging the battle in order to inflict as much pain as he could before delivering the final coup de grâce.

When the end came, it came swiftly. The sword in Drake's hand moved faster than her eye could follow, opening dozens of deep gashes on Florin's arms, legs, back, and chest before a well-placed thrust drove Drake's sword into his opponent's heart.

There was a collective sigh from the watching vampires as Florin staggered backward, then spiraled slowly to the ground.

Knowing what was coming, Elena turned her back. It did little good. Perhaps it was because she had been focused so strongly on Drake, perhaps it was simply because of the bond they shared, but she heard the whisper of the sword slice through the air, saw the blade cut easily through preternatural flesh as Drake severed Florin's head.

She swallowed hard, but she wasn't sick this time. Instead, she was only grateful that the man she loved still lived.

Drake came for Elena later, after Rodin's body had been carried away by the members of the Council.

His gaze burned into hers. "What the hell was Stefan thinking, to bring you here?"

"I begged him to do it. Don't be mad at him."

"I told you to stay home."

"I . . . I thought . . . I had this horrible feeling that something was wrong, that you needed me." She squared her shoulders and stiffened her spine. "I guess I was wrong."

The hurt in her eyes melted his anger. Murmuring her name, he pulled her into his embrace. "I will always need you, but you should not have come here." He shuddered to think what would have happened to her if she had been discovered by a vampire who didn't know who she was. Out here, alone, she would have been mistaken for a runaway sheep. Those who tried to escape were beyond the protection of the Fortress and were considered easy prey for any who should find them. She would have been drained before she had time to mention his name or explain who she was. The thought made him hold her closer, tighter.

"Drake, I can't breathe."

"Sorry." He loosened his hold immediately. "Come with me. I will take you to my quarters. Katiya is there. Promise me you will not leave."

"I promise."

Keeping his arms around her, he willed the two of them to his apartment.

Katiya looked up, her expression troubled. "I heard what happened to your sire. I am sorry."

Drake nodded. Rodin had been destroyed. It was unthinkable. Unbelievable.

"What will happen now?" Katiya asked.

"The Council is meeting in an hour." He glanced from Katiya to Elena. "I want both of you to stay here. Keep the door locked. Do not open it for anyone."

"Except Andrei," Katiya said.

"Andrei will not knock," Drake said. After bolting the door, he kissed Elena on the cheek, and vanished from the room.

Elena blinked, amazed, as always, at how quickly vampires could come and go.

"What are you doing here?" Katiya asked.

"I felt that I needed to be here, for Drake. I guess I was wrong."

"Do sit down and make yourself comfortable," Katiya said. "Can I get you anything?"

"No." Elena worried her lower lip with her teeth. "What do you think they're doing?"

"The Council will decide who is to take Rodin's place. Tomorrow night, all of Rodin's wives and children will gather here. His body will be cremated and they will never speak of him again."

"Never?" Elena asked.

"It is our way."

"Are you happy, being a vampire?"

"I was, until I came here. Rodin ruled his Fortress differently than my sire rules his."

"Differently?"

"Rodin ruled as if he were a king and his wives and children and those who took refuge here were his subjects. His word was law. My sire's rules are less stringent, our people given more freedom, except when it comes to marriage," she said, her voice suddenly tinged with bitterness. "That is where all vampires are the same."

"So, vampires never marry humans? Never have children with them?"

"Not to my knowledge." Katiya canted her head to the side, her expression thoughtful. "There was one case, where one of Rodin's sons impregnated a mortal female."

"Which son?"

"I do not know. I am not supposed to know it even

happened. All I know is that it did not end well. The mother and baby both died in childbirth. The strange thing was, the vampire was fifty years shy of being five hundred. He should not have been able to father a child at all."

Elena sighed, wondering if she would ever learn all there was to know about this strange society. And then she frowned. "A drone carried Gerret's body away, but Florin's body was left in the clearing. What will happen to it?"

"In the morning, the sun will burn it up."

"Oh." The more she learned, the less she wanted to know. Sitting back in the chair, she folded her arms over her chest and prayed that Drake would return soon.

Clad in unrelieved black from head to foot, Liliana sat in her chair on the dais in the Council chamber. Drake stood beside her, his arms crossed over his chest, his face like stone as he watched the Council members file into the room and take their places.

Earlier, he had met with Andrei and Ciprian, who'd informed him that Olaf was missing, no doubt destroyed by Florin's hand.

But at the moment, Drake had a more pressing concern on his mind. He held his breath as Liliana rose to her feet.

"You all know why we are gathered here." Though she spoke quietly, her voice echoed off the walls. "My husband has been killed. We will lay him to rest tomorrow night. But appointing someone to assume his position cannot wait. There is only one among us who is old enough, wise enough, strong enough, to take Rodin's place."

Drake went still as every head in the room turned in his direction.

"It is no secret that Rodin's firstborn son is the only one qualified to take his sire's place. I ask—nay, I demand—

that the Council name Drake Sherrad as Master of the Carpathian Fortress. How say you? Yea or nay?"

As one, the members of the Council stood. Heads bowed, each one said, "Yea."

Liliana faced her son for the first time. "So be it, Lord Drake. The Fortress is now yours."

As one, the members of the Council bowed their heads again. "As spoken and agreed, let it be done."

With a faint smile, Liliana embraced her son.

One by one, the members came forward to declare their allegiance to Drake before leaving the Council chambers.

"You knew I did not want this," Drake said when he and his mother were alone in the room.

"It was your sire's wish. And mine also."

"You will regret it," he said, and with a courtly bow in her direction, he stalked out of the room.

Chapter 29

Katiya's face lit up with a smile of welcome when Andrei materialized in Drake's apartment. Cupping her face in his hands, Andrei kissed her once, twice, three times before acknowledging Elena's presence.

"Where's Drake?" Elena asked anxiously. "Is everything all right?"

Andrei wrapped his arm around Katiya's shoulders. "My brother is not particularly happy just now. Liliana demanded the Council name him as Master of the Coven. It is a position he never wanted."

"So, where is he?" Elena asked again.

"I cannot say for sure, but I think he has left the Fortress to meditate."

"Left?"

"Only to go outside," Andrei said. "I believe he needs some time alone to come to terms with all that has happened." He shook his head. "Although why he needs to think about it is beyond me. He must have known there was a chance, however slim, that Rodin would one day be defeated in battle. As the eldest son, he should have known he would be first in line to take our sire's place."

Elena nodded. She didn't know what to think, what to

say. Couldn't begin to imagine how this would affect her relationship with Drake. Would he be expected to stay here now? Permanently? What of Katiya? And Andrei? What of their child? She hadn't seen any vampire children in the Fortress, nor had Drake ever mentioned them. Were they that rare?

"I need to go home," Elena said.

Katiya and Andrei stared at her.

"I can't stay here," Elena said. Rising from the chair beside the sofa, she began to pace the floor. She didn't belong in this place, and she never would. "And if Liliana finds out I'm here. . . ." She shook her head. "I don't even want to think about that."

Suddenly nauseous, she sat down again.

"Elena, are you ill?" Katiya asked.

"I'm fine. It's just all this stress," she said with a shrug, "plus I haven't had anything to eat."

"Of course," Katiya said. "How thoughtless of us, not to offer anything. Andrei, please find her some nourishment."

With a nod, he left the room, only to return moments later with a tray bearing a roast beef sandwich, a bowl of sliced fruit, and a cup of tea.

Murmuring, "Thank you," Elena picked up the sandwich.

Katiya and Andrei sat side by side on the sofa, trying not to stare at her as she ate.

Elena did her best to ignore them, but she couldn't help wondering if they ever missed solid food. She loved malts and chocolate milk and orange juice, but she wouldn't be happy living on a liquid diet, especially one as stringent as theirs. Malts were good, but so was chicken and French fries and steak, not to mention pie and ice cream.

Katiya cleared her throat. "Andrei, what do you think Drake will do now?"

"I have no idea, but I would not be surprised if he turned the Fortress upside down."

Elena was trying to figure out what he meant by that when Drake entered the room.

"Not now, Andrei," he said, seeing the curiosity in his brother's eyes. "I am in no mood to answer questions. All I want is to spend what's left of the night with Elena." Taking her by the hand, he drew her to her feet. "If that is all right with you?"

"It is more than all right, my lord," she murmured.

"Andrei, we will need to use your apartment."

"As you wish. My lord," he added with a grin.

Drake glared at his brother; then, wrapping his arm around Elena, he transported the two of them to Andrei's quarters.

"What now?" Elena asked. She glanced around the living room. It was sparsely furnished with a brown leather sofa and matching chair, a pair of glass-topped ebony end tables, and a large, wall-mounted TV. Through an open doorway, she saw a king-sized bed covered with a brown velvet spread.

"What now?" Drake repeated. "I wish I knew." He paced away from her, then stood staring at the pair of paintings over the sofa. Both pictures depicted an ocean— one by day with the sun shining brightly on an expanse of clear blue-green water; the other by night, with the moon's silver light reflected on troubled black waves.

Elena stood in the center of the room, not knowing if she should follow her heart and put her arms around him, or leave him alone.

"I will take control of the Fortress tomorrow night," he said at last.

"Oh?"

He turned to face her. "You need to decide what you want to do."

"Do?" She frowned at him. "About what?"

"About us."

"I thought I had already made that decision."

"Things are different now. I am not sure how what I have planned will be received."

"Whatever happens, I want to be with you."

He didn't say anything, just wrapped her in his embrace. He sighed, and she felt the tension drain out of him.

"Did you think I would leave you?"

"I cannot think of a single reason why you would want to stay. Your life has been anything but peaceful since the night we met."

"And I've loved every minute we've spent together," she said. "Well, almost every minute. So, are you through being the master for the night?"

He arched one brow. "That depends. Is there something you desire?"

"You," she whispered. "Only you."

"Granted. Do with me what you will."

"So, it's okay for me to do this?" Rising on her tiptoes, she pressed herself against him. "And this?" Cupping her hand around his nape, she kissed him, long and slow, then drew back so she could see his face. "Any complaints?"

"None so far. What else have you got?"

She ran her tongue across his lips, then kissed him again.

"And if I was to sweep you into my arms and carry you to bed, do you think you could find something for us to do there?" he asked with a wicked grin.

"I can guarantee it."

"Show me," he said, his voice low and husky with de - sire as he swung her into his arms and carried her swiftly to bed.

* * *

Elena awoke slowly; then, remembering where she was, she turned to study the man sleeping soundly beside her. Whatever else might happen, after last night she had no doubt that Drake loved her completely and that he would do everything in his power to ensure that they could be together.

Rising, she showered, then dressed. Last night, Drake had warned her not to leave Andrei's apartment, then told her that one of the drones would bring her something to eat at 10 A.M. A glance at her watch told her the drone would be there any minute. A moment later, there was a knock at the door.

Though it was unnecessary, Elena thanked the drone, then locked the door after him, though she doubted it would keep the vampires out. It was sure to arouse suspicion if any of the vampires learned food had been delivered to Andrei's quarters, especially during the day, when he was supposed to be sleeping. But she was too hungry to worry about that now.

After a meal of French toast, scrambled eggs, and bacon, she wandered around the apartment, which consisted of four large rooms—bedroom, bathroom, living room, and library. The library was stocked with books, CDs, DVDs, magazines and newspapers in several languages, and an assortment of crossword puzzle books. A desk held a computer with a large monitor. There was also a state-of-the-art stereo system.

Elena turned the stereo on low, found the latest Frankenstein novel by Dean Koontz, and lost herself in another world.

When she tired of reading, she went in search of a movie, surprised to find that Andrei had what looked like every movie John Wayne had ever made. She was watching *Hondo* when the drone delivered her lunch.

She was browsing through Andrei's CD collection when

a whisper of power flowed through the room, making the short hairs on her arms stand at attention.

"Drake." She knew he was there even before she turned around.

She sighed when he drew her into his arms, closed her eyes as his mouth covered hers, whispered "more" when he would have let her go.

He kissed her again, longer, deeper, then brushed his knuckles across her cheek. "I need to go," he said. "I have business to attend to. One of the drones will come for you in an hour or so."

"What are you going to do?"

"You will be there when it happens." He cupped her cheek in his palm. "Say a prayer for me."

"What should I pray for?"

"Success." He kissed her again, quickly, and then he was gone.

A short time later, Katiya and Andrei appeared in the apartment.

"I brought you something to wear," Katiya said. "I think it will fit."

"It's lovely," Elena said. "Thank you." The dress, of dark mauve, had a velvet bodice and a long satin skirt.

Katiya reached into her pocket. "I brought a brush for your hair, as well."

"Thank you."

"I will see you soon," Katiya said, and vanished from sight.

Elena looked at Andrei, who had taken a seat on the sofa. "Do you know what's going on?" she asked as she ran the brush through her hair.

"Knowing how Drake feels about this place, I have a fair idea."

"He seemed worried earlier."

"I would be surprised to hear otherwise."

Elena found little comfort in his words.

The gown Katiya had lent her fit Elena as if it had been made for her. She had barely finished changing clothes when a drone knocked at the door. Elena ducked out of sight when Andrei went to answer it.

"Lord Drake requests your presence in the Council chamber immediately," the drone said.

Andrei blew out a breath. "Here we go."

A million nervous butterflies took wing in Elena's stomach as she followed Andrei down the hall toward the Council meeting room. When they reached the door, Elena grabbed his hand. "Are you sure he wants me here?"

"Very sure," Andrei said, and opened the door.

Elena's gaze swept the chamber in a single glance. Drake, dressed all in black, sat in Rodin's chair on the dais. Liliana, also dressed in black, sat on his right. Katiya, looking young and lovely in pale blue, sat on his left. The Council members were seated.

Drake rose when he saw her. "Please, come in."

Taking a deep breath, Elena entered the chamber at Andrei's side.

Liliana rose. "What is this outrage?" she demanded, her voice as cold and brittle as arctic ice.

"Liliana, sit down," Drake said, his voice equally cold. "She is here at my request."

Liliana glared daggers at her son, but she did as he said.

Impressive, Elena thought.

"As you all know," Drake said, "Rodin has been destroyed. As the new Master of the Carpathian Coven, I have decided there are changes that need to be made."

He cast a warning glance at Liliana, who had started to rise. Fury radiated from her eyes but she remained silent and seated.

"Katiya," Drake said. "Come forward."

Rising, she stood beside him. She looked cool and unruffled, her face serene, making Elena think that Katiya was well aware of whatever change Drake was about to make. Aware and in agreement.

"As Master of the Coven, I hereby renounce my marriage vows to Katiya Belova. How say you, Katiya? Yea or nay?"

"Yea, my lord."

"So let it be recorded," Drake said. "So let it be done."

"So let it be recorded," the Council members said. "Done and done."

Leaving the dais, Katiya took a seat in the back of the room.

"Elena Knightsbridge, come forward."

Heart pounding, she moved toward the foot of the dais.

Drake smiled at her. "Come, stand beside me."

"No!" Liliana's voice echoed through the room like rolling thunder.

"Be still!" Drake shot a quelling glance at his mother. "If you interfere again, I will have you removed." He held out his hand to Elena. "Come."

Praying that her legs wouldn't fail her, Elena took Drake's hand and stepped up on the dais.

Drake faced the Council. "Rodin Sherrad annulled my marriage to Elena Knightsbridge. As Master of the Coven, I hereby revoke that annulment. From this time forward, Elena Knightsbridge will be my wife. All who wish to shelter here will accord her the respect to which she is entitled as my consort. So let it be recorded. So let it be done."

"So let it be recorded," intoned the Council members. "Done and done."

Taking Elena in his arms, Drake kissed her lightly. "I love you," he said quietly. "Please take your place."

Fully aware of Liliana's fulminating gaze, Elena took the chair vacated by Katiya.

"Andrei Lazarescu," Drake said, "come forward. As Master of the Coven, I now unite Andrei Lazarescu and Katiya Belova as husband and wife by my hand. Andrei, how say you? Yea or nay?"

"Yea, my lord."

"Katiya, how say you? Yea or nay?"

"Yea, my lord."

"So let it be recorded," Drake said, smiling. "So let it be done."

"So let it be recorded," the Council members said. "Done and done."

Hand in hand, Andrei and Katiya left the room, smiling.

"Liam Tarasova, come forward."

The vampire who strode toward the dais was of medium height with short, dark brown hair and heavy-lidded brown eyes.

"Liam Tarasova, as Master of the Carpathian Coven, I appoint you as the thirteenth member of the Council. Do you accept the responsibility this task entails, and do you now swear to uphold our laws? Yea or nay?"

"Yea, my lord."

"So let it be recorded," Drake said solemnly. "So let it be done."

"So let it be recorded," the Council members said. "Done and done."

"One last matter of business," Drake said. "I have never approved of keeping humans as sheep. It is my intention to offer them their freedom."

This announcement elicited a gasp from everyone in the room, including Elena.

Liliana stood, her whole body quivering with outrage. "You have no right—"

"I have every right," Drake retorted sharply, "given to me by your own hand. Sit down."

Liliana glared at him, her eyes burning bright red, and then she vanished from the chamber.

"I intend to give the sheep their freedom if they so wish it," Drake said again. "If they choose to stay, they will no longer be prisoners. They will be allowed the run of the first three floors of the Fortress. They may stay or go at their pleasure, but those who decide to leave will have all memory of this place and what happened to them here erased from their minds. Further, I revoke the decree making it unlawful for humans and vampires to marry."

This announcement was met with gasps of surprise as well as exclamations of disbelief from those present.

"So let it be recorded," Drake said solemnly. "So let it be done."

There were whispered murmurs from the members of the Council before they gave their unanimous approval.

"I declare this convocation closed until further notice."

As one, the Council members filed out of the chamber, followed by Liam, until only Drake and Elena remained.

He stood there a moment, his head bowed, before he reached for her. "So, wife, what say you?"

"I don't know what to say. Your mother . . ."

"Reacted exactly as I expected," he said.

"I don't know which upset her more, your decision to free the sheep, your decision to give Katiya to Andrei, or your declaration that our annulment was stricken."

"She will accept my decisions or not. If she refuses to abide by my laws, she will be banished."

"You'd make your own mother leave here when you know how much she loves it?"

"My first loyalty is to the Coven. If I cannot enforce my laws, if I cannot command obedience and respect from my own mother, then I do not deserve to be Master of the

Coven." He ran his fingertips over her lips. "No more talk of vampire business tonight."

Before Elena could respond, they were in the living room of Drake's apartment. There were dozens of red roses in a sparkling crystal vase on the coffee table. Soft music played in the background, candlelight illuminated the room with a pale golden glow.

"Are you hungry, wife?" he asked.

"Famished," she murmured.

"What are you in the mood for?"

"I'm not sure."

He quirked an eyebrow at her. "How about something tall, dark, and dangerous?"

"Perhaps," she said, frowning. "Of course, almost every man in the Fortress seems to be tall, dark, and dangerous."

Drake growled at her in mock anger. "Careful, wife."

"Yes, my lord." She slipped her hands under his shirt, then splayed her fingers across his chest. "Is this careful enough?"

He nipped the lobe of her ear. "I warn you, you are playing with fire."

"Will you show me the flames?"

"Just look into my eyes."

Sweeping her into his arms, he carried her into the bedroom. There were more roses in here, as well as a pair of candles on the bedside table, along with a bottle of red wine and two cut-crystal goblets. Red rose petals were scattered over the bed.

Elena looked up at him, a question in her eyes.

"I hoped we would end up here sometime tonight," he said, grinning.

"Well," she purred, "here we are."

"And here we will stay," he said, lowering her onto the mattress, "at least for a few more days."

"Then what?"

"Let us not talk of that now."

He wished away his clothes and her own. Pulling her into his warm embrace, he kissed her. At the first touch of his mouth on hers, she forgot everything but her need for this man above all else.

She ran her hands over the broad expanse of his chest, along his arms, dragged her fingertips across his belly, loving the way he responded to her touch, the way his muscles bunched and flexed beneath her questing fingertips as she trailed her hand lower, lower. He groaned deep in his throat as he stretched out on his side, then aligned her body with his, so that they were pressed intimately together from shoulder to thigh, their legs entwined.

Her breath caught in her throat as he began a slow, sweet exploration of her body, his hands trailing fire, his tongue a flame as it dueled with hers.

She clutched his shoulders when he rose over her, lifted her hips, eager to receive him, to feel the welcome weight of his body covering hers as two became one, joined flesh to flesh, and heart to heart.

Chapter 30

Elena spent the next day much as she had spent the previous one—reading, watching movies, listening to music, thumbing through the daily papers, thinking how strange it was that people lived their lives never knowing that vampires dwelled in their midst. Time and again, she glanced at her watch, willing the hours and minutes to pass more quickly.

Drake appeared in the living room shortly after she finished dinner. Taking her in his arms, he kissed her. "How was your day?"

"Lonely, without you."

"You must know I would spend my days with you if I could."

"I know."

"For now, I have business to attend to. Do you wish to accompany me?"

"Of course!"

"Come along, then," he said, and taking her by the hand, he led her into the dining hall.

Elena was surprised to see the sheep assembled there. Tables had been added to accommodate several couples with babies and young children. She had never seen children in the Fortress.

The tension in the hall practically crackled when Drake walked through the door. Glancing at the faces of the sheep, Elena noticed that they all wore the same wary expression, like patients awaiting bad news.

Drake's gaze swept the room, and the tension in the hall grew thicker.

"As you know," he said without preamble, "there has been a change in leadership. I am now the Master of the Coven and as such, I have instituted several changes, most of which do not concern you. There is, however, one change that will affect you all."

Elena watched the sheep. Some stirred restlessly, as if sensing danger. Several of the couples held tighter to their children, their expressions fearful. Northa and Marta looked at Elena. She smiled, hoping to reassure them.

"I realize you have been born here," Drake went on, "and that you have known no other life but this one. I am now offering you a choice. You may stay here, if you wish, or you may leave."

The sheep stared at Drake and then at each other.

"I am sure you have questions," he said. "Feel free to ask them."

And still the sheep stared at him as if he were speaking a foreign language.

"I am offering you your freedom," Drake said.

Finally, one of the men spoke up. He was young, perhaps nineteen. A little girl with pigtails sat on his lap. "Where would we go? Who would take care of us?"

"Who would feed us?" asked another man.

"We don't know anything of the outside world," Marta said. "Who is going to teach us what we need to know?"

"If you wish to leave, we will teach you how to survive in the outside world," Drake said. "If you wish to stay, you will no longer be prisoners. You will be permitted access to the first three floors of the Fortress and to go outside when you wish. But you will not be permitted to pass beyond a certain point."

"Then aren't we still prisoners?" one of the men asked.

"It is for our protection," Drake said. "And yours. If you wish to leave, you may do so at any time, but we must know first."

"Will you still feed off us?" Northa asked.

"Yes, in exchange for feeding and housing you, but you will no longer be compelled to go with anyone you dislike. Nor will you be punished for refusing. Think about what I have said. You do not need to make any decisions tonight. Until decisions have been made, you will continue to stay in your rooms. That is all."

"Do you think any of them will stay?" Elena asked when they returned to Drake's apartment.

"Who can say? What would you do?"

Sitting on the sofa, she kicked off her shoes. "I don't know. If I'd never lived anywhere else, never had the freedom to do as I pleased"—she shook her head—"I think I'd be afraid to leave, even though I think I'd want to."

"You were brave enough to run away from your uncle."

"That was different. I wasn't a prisoner in his house. And I wasn't going outside for the first time."

Drake nodded as he took the seat beside her.

"What do you think they'll do?" Elena asked. "And if they all leave . . . ?" She wasn't quite sure how to phrase the next question, but Drake knew what she meant.

"I think the single men and some of the women will go. I know several of the females have strong feelings for some of my brothers. I think they will stay. Perhaps the couples, as well. As for what we would do if they all left . . ." He shrugged. "Every Coven has a Fortress like this one, but not all of them provide nourishment for those who live within its walls."

"Oh." She shuddered to think of the unsuspecting people who were helpless prey to the hunger of the vampires. "Have you spoken to your mother lately?"

"No. She has left the Fortress."

"Where did she go?"

"I have no idea. I only heard of her departure late last night."

Feeling suddenly queasy, Elena bit down on her lower lip. Drake was supposed to be his mother's favorite son. But what if that were no longer true? Drake had destroyed Vardin. He had annulled his marriage to Katiya, resumed his marriage to a woman his mother did not approve of. And now he was bringing change to the Fortress.

Elena shivered. She recalled all too clearly the outrage in Liliana's eyes the night before when Drake had assumed command of the Fortress—the fury in her voice, the way she had vanished from the Council chamber in a fit of anger.

People made jokes about their in-laws all the time, Elena thought, but there was nothing funny about an angry mother-in-law, not when she was also a powerful vampire.

As it turned out, Drake was right. The four breeding pairs, who had five children between them ranging in age from three months to fourteen years, decided to stay, as did most of the single women. All but one of the men opted to leave.

Those who had chosen to leave were schooled in how to survive in the outside world. Drake was elusive when Elena asked who was teaching them, but when she pressed harder, he told her that the vampires waited until the sheep were sleeping, then spoke to their minds, giving them the information they needed to live in the outside world.

"It is quicker and more effective than trying to teach them while they are awake," he explained. "But most of the sheep are bright and learn quickly, since my sire selected only the best and the brightest for breeding. They made better companions."

Breeding, Elena thought. With Drake as her husband, there was no chance of having children of her own. The thought made her stomach churn. Hurrying into the bathroom, she leaned over the commode.

Drake followed her into the bathroom. "Are you ill?"

"I must be catching the flu." She rinsed her mouth, washed and dried her face. "I'll be all right."

Surprisingly, it only took a little over three weeks to prepare the sheep who had decided to leave the Fortress. Stefan and Liam were in charge of transporting them to various small towns in the area. Once they arrived at their destinations, the vampires erased all memories of their life at the Fortress and all memory of the vampires from their minds.

Elena was pleased with the changes Drake had made in the Fortress. It was far less lonely for her now that the sheep—she had to stop calling them that!—could move freely about the first three floors of the castle.

For the first time since she had been there, people walked the corridors during the day. The dining hall was no longer silent. The laughter of children echoed off the walls. Elena spent the daylight hours with Northa, Elnora, Marta, and some of the other women. Elnora was very much in love with Dallin, and since Drake had abolished the law forbidding vampires and humans to marry, she had high hopes that Dallin would propose. Marta held the same hopes for Cullin. Northa had elected to stay because she enjoyed the sensual pleasure of the vampire's bite, and because she was afraid to leave the only home she had ever known.

"There's no reason to leave now," Northa said one afternoon. "Since we're free to come and go as we please, and to go outside. . . ." She spread her arms wide. "Living here now is like being a princess in a castle."

"I just wish my prince would ask me to marry him," Elnora said with a sigh.

"Maybe you should ask him," Northa said with a wink and a smile.

"Maybe I will!"

"Elena, you're married to a vampire," Marta said. "Is it wonderful?"

"Drake is wonderful," she replied, smiling, and then she thought of Vardin. "But I don't know if all vampires make wonderful husbands."

Returning to their apartment, Elena curled up on the sofa and picked up a magazine. She thumbed through a few pages, but she kept thinking about what Marta had said. Would she have felt the same about Drake in the beginning if she had known what he was? Would she have had the courage to take the time to get to know him? Or would her fear of what he was have kept her from trusting him?

She wanted to think she would have loved him the same no matter what, and yet there were times, when she let herself think about the future, that she wished he was human, that they could share a meal, bask in the sun, return to Wolfram. Have a child.

"You are looking very pensive this evening," Drake said.

"What?" She looked up, surprised to find him in the room. Usually, she sensed his presence almost before he appeared. "I was just thinking about . . . things."

"Unpleasant things, from the expression on your face."

She started to deny it, then realized it was useless. He would know if she was lying. "Not unpleasant," she said. "Just . . . It doesn't matter."

Sitting beside her, he reached for her hand. "Of course it matters. I want no secrets between us."

"Isn't that impossible when you can read my mind?"

"Yes, I suppose it is, but I have been making an effort not to intrude on your thoughts. So, tell me, what troubles you?"

"Nothing, really. I was just wishing for things that can't be."

"What kinds of things?"

She made a vague gesture with her hand, as if to push them away. "Nothing major, except . . ." She blew out a breath. If he didn't want any secrets between them, then she would tell him the truth. "I was wishing we could have a baby."

"Ah."

"It doesn't matter, not really," she said quickly.

But they both knew she was lying.

Elena met Northa in the drawing room the following afternoon. She was relating the conversation she'd had with Drake the previous night when she bolted for the bathroom.

What was the matter with her? This was the third time she had thrown up in the last few weeks. It wasn't the flu. She couldn't be pregnant, and she didn't really feel sick, but if there was nothing wrong with her, why was she throwing up?

"Are you all right?" Northa asked when Elena returned to the drawing room.

"I don't think so. Is there a doctor here?"

"One of the drones is a doctor."

"Really?" Elena exclaimed. "How is that even possible? They all look like . . . like, I don't know."

"Like zombies," Northa said.

"Exactly."

"All the drones have special occupations—doctors and dentists and pediatricians. Once the vampires release them from their spell, the drones become regular people again and don't remember being enthralled. Are you really sick?"

"I hope not." Elena didn't care how skilled the drones might be; she didn't want any of them examining her.

She said as much to Drake when she saw him that night.

"Why do you need a doctor?" he asked, his brow furrowed with concern.

"I've just been feeling kind of . . . I don't know . . . sick to my stomach lately. But it isn't the flu. I don't have a fever or anything."

"I will take you to Brasov tomorrow evening."

"Never mind. I feel fine now."

"Tomorrow evening," he repeated.

Drake stood at the foot of the bed, watching Elena sleep. Lying there, with her hair spread like black silk across the white satin pillowcase, her dark lashes like fans against her cheeks, she looked like a fairy-tale princess waiting for the prince to awake her with love's first kiss.

He watched the rise and fall of her chest, listened to the faint whisper of her breathing, the slow, steady beating of her heart. He had rarely known fear, but the thought that she might be ill—perhaps fatally so—filled him with dread. He had never expected to fall in love. Before Elena came into his life, he had resigned himself to marrying a woman of his sire's choosing, having children, watching them grow to maturity. He had never thought beyond that. And then Elena had wandered into Wolfram Castle and it was as if sunlight had taken residence in the old place. He had basked in her glow, delighted in her innocence, reveled in her love. Even now, it was hard to believe that she wanted him, that she loved him. How would he live without her?

True to his word, Drake took Elena to a doctor in Brasov the next evening. There were several people in the waiting room, but after Drake spoke to the receptionist, Elena was immediately taken into an examination room and handed a white plastic cup.

"For a urine sample," the nurse explained, and directed her to the nearest restroom.

When Elena returned to the room, the nurse instructed her to undress and put on a paper gown.

A short time later a middle-aged woman with curly brown hair and kind blue eyes entered the room. She introduced herself as Doctor Mary Arcos. She listened to Elena's heartbeat, took her temperature and her blood pressure, checked her eyes, ears, nose, and throat, drew some blood, and, lastly, did a pelvic exam that Elena found embarrassing and uncomfortable.

"You can sit up now." The doctor removed her glove and tossed it into the wastepaper can.

"So, is everything all right?"

"You're very healthy," the doctor said, smiling. "And very pregnant."

Elena blinked at the physician. "Excuse me?"

"Pregnant. About twelve weeks."

"But . . ." Elena shook her head. "That's impossible."

"Are you telling me this is a virgin birth?" the doctor asked with a wry grin.

"No, of course not, but . . . that's . . . Are you sure?"

"Very sure. I hope it's good news."

"Oh, yes," Elena murmured. "The very best news. Thank you so much."

"You may want to thank your young man," the doctor said, chuckling. "You may get dressed now. Be sure to start taking prenatal vitamins right away. Get plenty of rest. Try not to do any heavy lifting. And come and see me again in four weeks."

"Yes, I will. Thank you."

Smiling, the doctor left the room, closing the door behind her.

Pregnant, Elena thought, removing the paper gown. She placed her hands over her stomach. How could she be pregnant? She recalled Katiya telling her that one of the vampires had impregnated a human and that both the mother and child had died. She shook the thought aside. Just because it had happened to someone else didn't mean it would happen to her.

She dressed quickly and stepped into her shoes. What would Drake think when she told him? *Please,* she prayed, *please let him be as happy as I am.*

Drake was pacing the floor of the waiting room when she entered. He went to her immediately, his dark eyes searching her face. "Are you all right?"

She couldn't stop smiling. "I'm fine. Let's go."

"What did the doctor say?"

"I'll tell you outside." Her cheeks were starting to hurt from smiling so much.

Taking her by the hand, he hurried her out the door and around the corner of the building. "All right, what did she say?"

"She said I'm going to have a baby."

"This is no time for jokes, Elena."

"I'm not joking. I'm pregnant."

He stared at her.

Elena's smile faded. "Say something."

But he didn't speak. Instead, he placed his hand over her womb, his expression intense. "It is a girl."

"What?"

"The baby," he said, his voice filled with awe. "It is a girl." He shook his head. "If I hadn't been so involved with events at the Fortress, I wouldn't have missed the echo of your heartbeat."

"You can hear the baby's heartbeat?"

He nodded.

"How do you know it's a girl?"

"I know."

"You don't look very happy."

He drew her into his arms. "Of course I am."

"But?"

"I did not think it was possible. I know it has happened occasionally in the past, but so rarely that I put the thought out of my mind." His arms tightened around her. "I love you, wife."

Lowering his head, he kissed her, hoping to avoid any more conversation, at least for the moment. And all the while, in the back of his mind, he was remembering Stefan and how devastated his brother had been when the mortal woman he loved had died in childbirth.

When they returned to the Fortress, Drake sent Elena to their apartment, then called a meeting of the Council. He also bid Andrei and Katiya to attend, as well as his brother Stefan.

"I am leaving the Fortress," Drake announced when those who had been summoned were seated. "Andrei will be in charge while I am away. His word is to be obeyed as my own. Stefan, you will be second-in-command."

"Where are you going?" Andrei asked.

"Back to Wolfram with Elena. She is with child. I do not want her here."

"She is pregnant?" Katiya exclaimed. "Oh, but that is wonderful."

Drake nodded, aware that Stefan was watching him closely. "Let us hope so."

Chapter 31

"Leaving?" Elena stared at Drake. "Where are we going?"

"Back to Wolfram."

"But . . . why?"

"Would you rather stay here?"

She bit down on the corner of her lip. Did she want to stay at the Fortress? She had few friends back home. She loved Wolfram, but she knew she would miss Andrei and Katiya, Northa, Marta, and Elnora. And Stefan. But Wolfram was home, and it would be nice to be alone with Drake.

"No," she said. "I guess not. Is it all right for you to leave?"

"I am the Master of the Coven," he said. "I can do whatever I choose. And I choose to leave. Are you ready to go?"

She grinned. Sometimes she forgot that her husband didn't need mortal transportation, that he could simply will himself wherever he wished to be. "I'm ready," she said, then frowned. "It won't hurt the baby?"

"No. Is there anything you want to take with you?"

Elena shook her head. There was really nothing here that belonged to her. Except Drake.

He folded her in his embrace, kissed the top of her head, and once again, she felt herself being carried away through time and space.

When the world righted itself, they were in the living room at Wolfram.

"You look tired," Drake said, brushing a lock of hair from her cheek. "You should go to bed."

"Only if you come with me."

He smiled, a real smile for the first time since he had been appointed Master of the Coven.

"Always my pleasure," he murmured.

"I think I'd like a bath before we go to bed. Which reminds me. Do you think we could install a bathroom upstairs? A real bathroom, with a tub and a shower and a sink and a toilet."

"Is tomorrow soon enough?"

She made a face at him. "I guess so, if you can't do it tonight."

He swatted her on the rump. "Go, take your bath. I will be back soon."

Elena nodded. He was going out to feed. She would have to get used to that, now that there were no sheep to satisfy his hunger.

Elena had bathed and changed into her nightgown by the time Drake returned. She tried not to think of where he had been, or wonder who he had fed on, or what it tasted like, but the questions flooded her mind. She would always be curious about that part of his life, always wonder what it was like.

"You could come with me next time," he remarked, sitting beside her on the sofa.

"I don't think so. Hey! I thought you weren't going to read my mind anymore."

"Sometimes I cannot help it."

"Hmm." She canted her head to the side. "Is feeding on a stranger different than drinking from me?"

"Very much so."

"Why? Blood is blood."

"With you, it is more than easing my hunger. Though I do not expect you to understand, it is a way of making love."

"Do vampires drink from each other?"

He nodded. "It is a pleasurable experience."

"Better than drinking from humans?"

"It depends on who is drinking from whom." He trailed his fingertips along the side of her neck. "Nothing equals what I feel when I taste you."

"Are you hinting for a taste now?"

"Would you mind?"

"No. I like it when you do it."

Smiling, he took her by the hand. "I think we should continue this conversation in bed."

Excitement fluttered in the pit of Elena's stomach as they walked up the stairs. There had been times in their relationship when she had been afraid that Drake was lost to her, that she would have to spend the rest of her life without him. But those days were behind them now. They were back in Wolfram where they belonged, with a baby on the way.

She put all thoughts of the past behind her when Drake drew her gently into his arms. Whispering that he loved her, he kissed her as he backed her toward the bed, then slowly lowered her onto the mattress.

They undressed each other with impatient hands.

She closed her eyes and gave herself into his keeping, sighing as he rained kisses on her cheeks, her brow, the length of her neck. She moaned when his fangs pricked her skin, sighed as their bodies came together, fell asleep with the sound of his voice whispering that he loved her more than life itself.

The next day, Elena couldn't think of anything but the baby. A girl, Drake had said. After breakfast, she went down the hall to the bedroom next to their own. This would be the nursery. Standing in the middle of the floor, she imagined how she would decorate it. Yellow for the walls, she thought. White furniture. The crib near the window where her daughter would be able to see the sun and the sky. A rocking chair in that corner. New carpeting for the floor, new curtains for the windows. Perhaps a mural on one wall. Maybe a country scene, with baby animals frolicking in a green pasture, or perhaps scenes depicting the Disney princesses. After all, her daughter lived in a castle and would be viewed as a princess in her own right by those in the Fortress.

They would definitely need a bathroom now, Elena thought as she returned to her own bedroom. There was no way she was going to bathe a new baby in that wooden tub!

Anxious to begin remodeling the nursery, she dressed quickly in a sweater and a pair of jeans, grabbed the keys to the Porsche, and drove into the city.

She wandered through the furniture store, looking at cribs and high chairs and bassinets. There were so many styles to choose from, how was she ever to decide?

She had better luck in the paint store. She found exactly

the shade of yellow she wanted, bought two gallons of Summer Sunlight paint, a quart of white for the door, brushes, masking tape, paint thinner and a roller, and headed for home.

Drake was waiting for her in the main hall when she arrived.

She smiled when she saw him. "Hi, I've been—"

"I know where you have been."

She frowned, puzzled by his harsh tone. "I'm sorry I didn't tell you I was leaving. I didn't want to disturb you."

He crossed the room, his movement so quick it was little more than a blur. "Elena, you must be careful."

The warning in his tone made her heart skip a beat. "Why? Is something wrong?"

"No." His hand smoothed her hair. "Forgive me. I am overreacting."

"I'm sorry," she said, confused by his attitude. "I didn't mean to worry you, but why are you so upset?"

He smiled at her. "Worrying too much," he said lightly. "I have never been this close to being a father before. I cannot help feeling anxious when you are away. So, what did you buy in the city?"

"Paint, for the nursery. I left it in the car."

"I will get it later." He ran his hands up and down her arms, as if to assure himself that she was all right. "I spoke to a contractor on the phone today. He and his men will be here tomorrow to install the bathroom."

"That's great!"

"I have requested they install the bathroom between our room and the one next to it so it will be accessible from both rooms. They are also adding a closet in the nursery."

"Sounds wonderful."

"Is there anything else you want?"

"A kiss?"

A slow smile spread across his face as he drew her into his arms. "I do not need a contractor for that," he replied, and lowered his head to hers.

Elena had never truly appreciated the benefits of being wealthy until she saw how quickly money could get things done. She had seen some evidence of it when the castle was wired for electricity. Due to the age and size of the castle, it had taken a considerable amount of time. But that was then and this was now. She had expected it to take many weeks, perhaps several months, to build a bathroom and a closet where none had existed before. But money could buy miracles and manpower, and the renovations were accomplished in less than a month.

Elena stood in the middle of the floor, turning slowly as she admired her new bathroom. The floor was gold-veined white marble. There was a white oval tub with a Jacuzzi, a square shower big enough for two, a toilet that flushed automatically, recessed lighting, and two sinks set in a granite countertop. She had not yet decided on a color for the walls.

Since the rooms were so large, the contractor had suggested adding a walk-in closet for the master bedroom. It was, Elena thought, big enough to be a room of its own. Drake moved their old wardrobe into one of the other bedrooms.

The new bathroom, walk-in closet, and smaller closet in the baby's room made the nursery a little smaller, but Elena had assured Drake that wouldn't be a problem. When their daughter grew older, she could simply move into one of the other, larger bedrooms.

Elena thought of little else besides the baby. How strange, to think that she carried a living being inside her.

She could hardly wait to hold her daughter in her arms. What would their child look like? Would she have her father's blue eyes or her mother's brown ones?

Drake drove her into the city the evening after the renovations were complete. He agreed with her choice of the white crib and the rest of the furniture and arranged to have it delivered at the end of the week.

"You're going to spoil me, you know," Elena remarked on the drive home.

"That has always been my intention," he replied, squeezing her hand. "Whatever you want, whatever you need, you have only to ask."

Elena spent the next day painting the nursery and thinking she had never been happier than she was now. The man she loved slept in the next room. They were having a baby. A girl, she thought, smiling. Life was good. No, it was better than good. It was perfect.

She had just finished painting the window seat when Drake appeared in the doorway.

"You have been busy," he remarked, glancing around the room.

"Do you like it?"

He nodded. "Yes, but should you be painting in your condition?"

"I'm pregnant, silly, not sick. Besides, it's nice to have something to do to pass the time while you rest. I was thinking of painting the bathroom the same shade of yellow as the nursery," she mused aloud. "Or maybe a light blue. What do you think?"

"Whatever you decide is fine with me."

"I think, in deference to your masculinity, I'll paint it blue."

"Thank you," he said, chuckling. "What would you say to a walk down by the lake?"

"The same thing I always say," she replied with a saucy grin. "Yes!"

The lake was beautiful, as always. Stars winked on the black blanket of the sky like the twinkling lights on a Christmas tree.

Kneeling on the shore, Elena dipped her hand into the water, and quickly jerked it out. "I was hoping to go for a swim, but it's too cold."

"Is it?"

"Feel for yourself."

He shook his head. "I believe you, but if you want to swim, then swim we shall."

Elena heaved a sigh as he quickly undressed. Being a vampire, she supposed he was immune to the cold.

"Are you coming, wife?"

"No. It's like melted ice in there."

"Will you not trust me, my sweet?"

With a sigh, Elena pulled her sweater over her head, stepped out of her shoes, socks, and jeans, removed her underwear, walked into the lake. And shrieked when the chilly water swirled around her ankles. When she would have retreated, Drake captured her hand in his and gently tugged her toward him.

Surprisingly, as she waded out closer toward him, the water grew warmer. "Why is it warmer out here?" she asked suspiciously. "You didn't pee in the pool, did you?"

Drake threw back his head and laughed. "No, my love. I merely infused a little preternatural power into the water to warm it for you."

Elena sighed with amazement. Truly, there was nothing this man couldn't do.

Holding her against his side, he carried her out to deeper

water. Once, she had been frightened to be out so deep, but no more. Nothing could happen to her while Drake was there. Leaning against him, she gazed up at the stars.

"What shall we name our daughter?" she asked after a while.

"I have not given it any thought, but I think you have."

"I was thinking about naming her after my mother, if it's all right with you. Unless you'd rather name her after your mother."

"No. What was your mother's name?"

"Kaitlyn."

"A fine old-fashioned name," Drake said. "I like it."

"I looked it up. It means 'pure.'" She smiled up at Drake. "Are you as happy as I am?"

"Never doubt it for a moment." He brushed a kiss across her brow. "You have given me more happiness than I deserve."

"Drake! What a thing to say. You deserve to be happy, just like everyone else."

"I am pleased that you think so, but there are incidents in my past, things you do not know." He thought of the people he had killed when he was a new vampire. His lack of compassion. Of Luiza. "Events I regret that I can never make right."

"Shh." Elena twined her arms around his neck and kissed his cheek. "I don't care what you've done in the past, or why you think you're unworthy of happiness. It's over and done and none of it matters now. Got it?"

"Yes, wife," he replied solemnly.

"Good. You're my hero. My knight in shining armor. And I won't have you thinking otherwise."

"Tarnished armor," he said with a wry grin.

"Stop that!"

"I will do my best not to let you down." How could he do

otherwise when she was looking at him like that, as if he were Superman and Albert Schweitzer all rolled into one.

She kissed him then, her lips achingly sweet and filled with love, and in that kiss he found hope. And an encompassing warmth that felt like forgiveness.

Chapter 32

The next day, Elena called the furniture store and asked if it was possible to have their order delivered that night. The salesman said he didn't think so, but after asking her name, he quickly changed his mind and assured her that it would be there by nightfall. She was grinning when she hung up the phone. Amazing, she thought, the miracles that could be obtained just by mentioning the Sherrad name.

They were arranging the furniture in the nursery later that night when the doorbell rang.

Elena looked at Drake. "Are you expecting someone?"

He shook his head and turned away, but not before she saw the worry in his eyes.

She followed him down the stairs, hanging back a little when he opened the door.

It was Andrei.

"Is something wrong?" Drake asked after inviting his brother inside.

"Liliana has returned to the Fortress," Andrei replied. "I thought you would want to know."

Drake lifted one brow. "You came here to tell me that?"

"No." Andrei nodded at Elena before returning his attention to his brother. "Stefan has left the Coven."

"Where has he gone?"

Andrei shook his head. "No one seems to know."

"When did this happen?"

"I am not sure. I have been busy looking after Katiya and making sure your new rules are upheld. Cullin has claimed Marta for his own. She is now living in his apartment. I was not aware that Stefan was missing until Liam informed me last night. The last time anyone remembers seeing Stefan was four nights ago."

"Perhaps he has gone hunting," Drake suggested.

Andrei sat on a corner of the coffee table. "He would not leave the Fortress without telling someone. I thought perhaps he had come here."

"No. I have not seen him."

"Katiya thinks . . ."

"Thinks what?" Drake asked.

"That with you and me being happily married, and our wives pregnant . . ."

"You told Katiya about Stefan?" Drake asked sharply.

Andrei shrugged. "Not intentionally."

"What about Stefan?" Elena asked, perching on the arm of the sofa. "Oh!"

Drake looked at her, his eyes narrowed. "Oh, what?"

"He's the son, isn't he? The one who got a girl pregnant and the girl and the baby died."

"Katiya told you that?" Drake asked.

"She didn't mention his name when she told me. She didn't know which brother it was."

"Well, she seems to know now," Drake muttered. "Dammit!" He paced the floor from one end to the other.

"Do you have any idea where he might go?" Andrei asked.

"He once talked about going to America," Drake replied.

"America!" Andrei exclaimed. "Do you really think he would go that far?"

"Would that be so bad?" Elena asked, glancing from Drake to Andrei and back again.

"He would have no one to protect him there," Drake said. "No place to go should he be injured or in need of refuge."

Elena was contemplating what Drake had said when there was a ripple in the air, like lightning before a storm, and Liliana appeared in front of the hearth. She looked like an ice princess in a long white gown, her blond hair streaming down her back, her pale face like something carved from ivory.

She glared at Drake. "This is all your fault!" she cried. "Had you accepted your responsibility to Katiya and the Coven, Stefan would not have run away."

"He ran away because he is still grieving for a woman my father refused to allow him to wed," Drake retorted. "Had my father been less of a tyrant, Stefan would be here now." Even as he spoke the words, he wondered if Katiya had the truth of it, and that Stefan had left the Fortress because he couldn't abide being around Katiya and Andrei because they were constant reminders of what he had lost.

"Your father knew what was best for our people, best for the Coven. You have changed our laws, laws that made our people strong. You are nothing like your father," Liliana said, her voice dripping with malice.

"Well, thank goodness for that," Elena exclaimed, then clapped her hand over her mouth.

Andrei grinned, then quickly covered it with a cough.

Drake laughed out loud.

Liliana glared at Drake. "If anything happens to Stefan, it will be on your head." Her voice was every bit as cold and unforgiving as her expression.

"So be it," Drake said, his voice equally cool. "Go home."

Tension flowed between Drake and his mother, so strong that Elena was surprised the room didn't burst into flame.

Liliana scorched them all with a final glance and then, with a wave of her hand, she was gone as if she had never been there.

"Well, she is going to be loads of fun to live with now," Andrei muttered.

"If you hear anything of Stefan, you will let me know immediately," Drake said.

"Sure." Andrei smiled at Elena. "Good to see you again, sister. Married life seems to agree with you."

"It does indeed." Rising, she slipped her arm around Drake's waist. "Tell Katiya hello for me."

"Will do," Andrei said, and then he, too, was gone.

"Must be fun, being able to zap yourself wherever you want to go, just like that," Elena said with a snap of her fingers.

"It has its advantages." Drake kissed her cheek. "I hope Stefan will be all right."

Elena nodded. "Are you really worried about his safety?"

"I am confident he can take care of himself."

"But you're still worried." She sat on the sofa, one leg curled beneath her.

"Yes." He dragged his hand over his jaw, his expression thoughtful. "Stefan has spent most of his life at the Fortress. He has never had to defend himself, never had to make any effort to hide what he is, with one exception."

"When he fell in love with a mortal girl?"

"Yes."

"Was she one of the sheep?"

"No. He had gone to Bucharest with my brother, Ciprian. Stefan met Cosmina in a nightclub. When Ciprian returned to the Fortress, Stefan stayed behind. I do not know the full story of all that happened, only that Cosmina became pregnant and passed away. It never should have happened. Stefan was not old enough to father a child."

"Maybe he was just mature for his age," Elena mused.

"Perhaps. He has not been with a woman since then."

"Hmm."

"What does that mean?" he asked, taking a seat beside her.

"Have you been with a lot of women?"

Drake stared at her, taken aback by the question and wondering why she hadn't asked it before. And how he was going to answer it now.

"Well?" Elena asked.

"Define a lot."

"More than . . . ?" She paused. He was five hundred years old, handsome, virile, charming. A chick magnet. If he'd been with just one woman a year . . . the number was staggering.

He laughed softly as he drew her into his arms. "I do not remember any of them."

"Why don't I believe you?"

"Believe me," he said, his finger tracing the curve of her cheek. "I have not looked at any other woman, or wanted any other woman, since you came into my life."

She gazed into his eyes, those deep, dark, penetrating eyes, and knew he was telling her the truth.

The next few weeks passed without incident. With the nursery ready, Elena went shopping for baby clothes. With Drake's money behind her, nothing was out of reach. She bought fluffy pink blankets, diapers, nightgowns in a variety of colors, booties and socks, hooded towels and washcloths. Baby shampoo and soap and powder. And dresses. Dozens of pink dresses in varying sizes. And one delicate lace dress in white for the baby's blessing.

In addition to baby clothes, she bought maternity clothes for herself. It seemed she grew hungrier and heavier with every passing day, and even though she told herself she was eating for two, she began to worry that she would outgrow her smocks.

Drake had laughed when she'd told him that.

"Well, it could happen," she lamented. "I'm as big as a horse."

"Nonsense."

"Well, I *feel* as big as a horse."

"You are beautiful, more beautiful than ever. And I shall love you whether you weigh a hundred pounds or a thousand."

She stuck her tongue out at him. "I'll hold you to that."

She was happy, happier than she had ever been. She loved the castle, loved being pregnant, loved her husband.

Life was perfect, she thought as she drove into town to buy groceries. Better than perfect. It was paradise.

She nodded at people she knew on the street, took a few minutes to chat with the owner of the grocery store.

She was walking back to her car when she saw the headline in the local paper.

FORMER CHIEF OF POLICE ESCAPES BORSA CASTLE

Elena pressed her hands over her swollen belly as she read the headline again. And then again.

Paradise was gone, she thought numbly.

The snake had returned.

Chapter 33

"You don't think he'll come here, do you?" Elena asked.

"He will regret it if he does," Drake assured her. "Stop worrying."

"The newspaper said he killed a patient and a doctor before he escaped." She worried the hem of her skirt. "He's been gone for three days."

"It would not make sense for him to come back here," Drake said, taking her hands in his. "This is the first place they will look."

"Of course. You're right. I know you're right." She folded her arms protectively over her womb. She couldn't forget the barely veiled threat in her uncle's cold gray gaze when he'd looked at her in the courtroom, the hatred in his eyes when the judge handed down his sentence.

"I think you should stay close to home until Dinescu is apprehended," Drake said. "I will drive you into town when you need to go."

"I thought you said he wouldn't come here."

Drake shrugged. "He will not, if he is smart, but I would rather be safe than sorry."

* * *

In the days that followed, nothing else was heard of Tavian Dinescu. The newspaper speculated that he had left the area, and then other stories, more current, took over the front page.

Elena told herself there was nothing to worry about, that Drake would protect her, that her uncle wouldn't dare come to the castle after what had happened the last time.

Still, she spent her days inside the castle or in the garden. She took up knitting, intending to make a blanket for the baby, but it kept getting bigger and bigger, until she had an afghan.

No matter how hard she tried, she couldn't shake a sense of impending doom, and she began having nightmares. Sometimes her uncle showed up in the castle, intending to do her harm in ever-changing ways that grew increasingly grotesque as time went on. Sometimes he destroyed Drake before coming after her. Sometimes he waited until her baby had been born, and then he murdered her little girl first.

She tried to hide her worry from Drake, but that was impossible. He could read the anxiety in her eyes. And in her mind. Nor was there any way to hide her nightmares from him, not when she woke up screaming or crying every night.

One night, after a particularly horrible dream, Drake suggested they return to the Fortress until Dinescu was caught. The idea held a certain appeal, except that Elena didn't want to have her baby there, didn't want to be anywhere near Liliana's corrosive influence.

As the days slipped into weeks and then became a month, Elena's fears gradually subsided. Worry over her uncle receded into the background as the reality of the baby she carried grew more real with her growing waistline. She could feel the baby moving now and thought how awesome it was that she carried a new life beneath her heart, a child born out of her love for Drake. Although the idea of being a mother was a little frightening, she could hardly wait to hold the baby in her arms. She'd had little to do with babies. Never taken care of an infant, only held them on rare occasions when she was growing up.

Sitting in front of the fire one night, with Drake's arm around her shoulders, she gave voice to her fears. "I don't know how to be a mother," she said, gazing into the flames. "I've never even changed a diaper. How will I know what to do? Babies are so fragile and need so much care. I scarcely remember my own mother."

"Elena, you will be a wonderful mother. You have a tender heart, a generous nature. You will love our child and that will be enough." He brushed his knuckles across her cheek. "You should be more worried about the kind of father your child will have."

"What do you mean?"

"I come from a family where expressions of love and affection were rare. My father ruled the Fortress with an iron hand. He had little time for us, or for my mother. His neglect made her bitter and she took it out on us. Once we reached maturity, we saw little of our parents. I know nothing of children. You have given me the only real love I have ever known."

"We make a fine pair, don't we?" she asked with a rueful grin.

"We will learn as we go along," he assured her. "People have been having babies for thousands of years. Most of them survive, one way or another. Ours will be rich in love, if nothing else."

Rich in love, Elena thought. Perhaps that would see them through. But, to be on the safe side, she had Drake drive her to the bookstore in the city the following night.

Drake shook his head as she handed him one book after another. "Are you sure we need all of these?" he asked, perusing the titles—*Your Baby from Birth to Teen*, *Doctor Spock's Baby and Child Care*, *Your Baby's First Year*, *How to Be a Successful Parent*, *Do's and Don'ts of Rearing Your Child*, *The ABC's of Baby Care*.

"I just wish they had a few more."

"More? Good Lord, woman, we are only having one child."

"I want to know everything there is to know."

Wisely, he didn't argue, just paid the bill, and prayed that the baby would be born strong and healthy and that Elena would survive the birth of their child.

For the next two weeks, Elena immersed herself in reading. She'd known she had a lot to learn, but she had no idea how much she didn't know.

She said as much to Drake when they were in bed one night.

He laughed softly as he stroked the curve of her cheek. "You do not have to learn all of it before the baby comes," he said. "You only need to learn what you need right now. No point in worrying about raising a teenager until the time comes."

"You're right," she said with a sigh. "I know you're right. It's just such an awesome responsibility, raising a baby." Taking his hand in hers, she placed it over her womb. "Feel that?"

"Quite a lusty kick for a little girl," he remarked. Surely that was a good sign. "I hope she looks like you."

"Drake?"

"Yes, wife?"

"What will she be?"

He knew what she was asking, knew she was wondering if their daughter would follow in her father's footsteps when she turned twenty. "I do not know if she will become vampire, Elena. To my knowledge, there are no half-vampires in existence."

"Does that mean they are born either human or vampire?"

He drew her closer, afraid to tell her the truth, yet certain that keeping it from her would do more harm than good. She needed to be prepared for the worst, should it happen.

"Drake?"

"As far as I know, no child conceived by a vampire and a human has ever survived."

Elena stared at him, her hand pressed tightly, protectively, over her stomach. "No! No! That can't be true!" Tears flooded her eyes. "I don't believe you!" she said, sobbing. "I won't!"

He drew her into his arms and held her close. He should have taken precautions, he thought, should have remembered what had happened to Stefan, but matings between vampires and humans were rare, and conceptions rarer still. . . . He cursed softly. If anything happened to Elena or their baby, he would never forgive himself.

Tavian Dinescu huddled under a tree in the forest behind Wolfram Castle. Clad in rags, his body gaunt from lack of food, his beard thick, he stared at the lights burning in the window on the second floor.

He had hidden here for days, leaving the cover of the trees only late at night to scavenge in the forest, or creep down the hill to the town to steal whatever food he could find.

Sitting there, shivering in the cold, he tried to make sense of his muddled thoughts, but it was hard to think, hard to concentrate. He recalled the trial, but could not remember why he had confessed. Even when they showed him the confession, written in his own hand, he could not remember writing it. Deep in the far recesses of his mind, a faint memory niggled, something to do with the lord of Wolfram Castle, but when he tried to remember, it made his head hurt.

He hated all of them, hated the whole town for their treachery. He had protected them, kept them safe, and they had all turned their backs on him.

But the worst offender was Elena. He had opened his home to her, fed and clothed her, offered her his name and what had she done in return? She had testified against him, the ungrateful brat! Sent him to that awful place for crazy people. He clapped his hands over his ears, shutting out the echo of tormented cries in the night, the moaning and groaning of the sick, the dying, the sobs of the hopeless, the helpless.

They would pay, he thought, rubbing his hands together with anticipation. Oh, yes, they would all pay. And Elena most of all. When the moment was right, he would strike. She would not escape him again.

Chapter 34

November turned to December, bringing a flurry of snow that quickly covered the ground and clothed the trees in gowns of white. In spite of the fireplaces and heaters in every room, the castle was chilly. Elena spent most of her time in the main hall, curled up on the sofa in front of the hearth, sometimes reading, sometimes napping.

Strangely, Drake, in his cat persona, had returned. He spent his days sitting beside her, or stretched out along the back of the sofa, sleeping. She was glad for the company.

She had asked Drake about the return of the cat the first time it appeared. He had said only that he missed her during the day and wanted to be near her. She suspected it was more than that. Her uncle was still out there, somewhere, and even though Drake claimed not to be worried, she knew he was.

Drake appeared late one afternoon, when the sky had turned dark and overcast. "This will be our first Christmas together," he said, helping her into a heavy winter coat. "I thought we should have a tree."

Excited at the idea, Elena pulled on a pair of fur-lined boots and gloves, put on a fur-lined hat, and followed him outside, where he picked up an ax and laid it on his shoulder. "Ready?"

"Ready," she said.

She followed him down a path he had cleared earlier to the edge of the forest.

"Which one do you like?" he asked.

She glanced from tree to tree. "That one," she said, pointing. "But how will you ever carry it into the house?" she asked, and then grinned sheepishly. To a vampire, carrying a ten-foot tree was akin to a mortal carrying one-half that size.

It took only a few strokes of the blade to bring the tree crashing down.

Returning home, he shook the snow from the branches, then carried the tree into the main hall. "Where do you want it?"

"There," she said, pointing to the far corner of the room.

He quickly built a stand and nailed it to the base of the tree.

"We don't have any ornaments," Elena said. "Or lights."

"We'll take care of that tomorrow night," he said. "For now, you need to get warmed up."

"I'm fine."

"Of course you are." Even as he was speaking, he was helping her out of her coat, boots, and hat, settling her on the sofa, covering her with the afghan she had made, bringing her a cup of hot tea.

Elena smiled up at him, thinking he was the most wonderful, sweet, caring man in the whole world.

She was about to tell him so when she sensed a familiar ripple in the air. Moments later, Andrei materialized in the room.

Elena's smile of welcome faded when she saw the expression on his face. Something was wrong. Terribly wrong.

"The baby was born tonight," Andrei said, his voice flat.

He didn't have to say anything else. She saw the sorrow in his face, the pain in his eyes.

"He came too early, and lived only a few minutes. Just long enough"—Andrei swallowed hard—"long enough for me to hold him."

"How is Katiya?" Drake asked.

"For a time, I thought I would lose her, too. But she will be all right."

"Andrei, I'm so sorry," Elena murmured. "Is there anything we can do?"

"No." He sank down on the edge of the sofa beside Elena, his head cradled in his hands. "Her mother sent me away, told me Katiya needed to rest. I wandered around outside the Fortress and then"—he shrugged—"I found myself here. We were happy here."

Feeling helpless, Elena looked up at Drake, who was standing near the hearth. *What can we do?*

He shook his head. *He needs time.*

"I should go back," Andrei said. "I just thought you should know."

Biting down on her lower lip, Elena slid her arm around Andrei's shoulders. To her surprise, he turned into her embrace, his arms going around her waist. He held on tight, his body shaking uncontrollably as sobs racked his body.

"She'll be all right," Elena said, patting his back. "She's young and strong. And she loves you."

Andrei took a deep breath, then drew back. "Forgive me."

"There's nothing to forgive."

Andrei rose heavily to his feet. "I must go back."

"You may stay, if you wish," Drake said.

Andrei shook his head. "Katiya will be missing me."

"How are things at the Fortress otherwise?" Drake asked.

"All is well. Your plan to free the sheep was a good one. The transition has gone smoothly. I must go." He bowed in Elena's direction, and then he was gone.

"Poor Andrei," Elena murmured.

Drake nodded. He had never fully understood Stefan's pain, he thought, perhaps because he, himself, had never been in love, never lost anyone he cared for, but he understood it clearly now. He had seen Stefan's pain reflected in Andrei's eyes.

Needing to hold Elena, he sat beside her and drew her into his arms as he faced the very real possibility that he could lose Elena, and the baby, too.

Later, lying in the dark in Drake's arms, fears about her baby, about the birth itself, rose in Elena's mind. Katiya had been young and healthy, in her prime for bearing a child. If Katiya could not conceive and carry a vampire child, what chance did a mortal woman have? Elena placed her hand over her womb. Would her baby be born too early, as well? Take a few breaths, then slip away, its life over before it had even begun? And what of her own life? Andrei said they had almost lost Katiya. If a vampire, who had the strength of twenty and was nearly invincible, was at risk, how much more so was she?

"Elena, you must not worry."

He was reading her mind again, but she didn't care. She hadn't wanted to worry him with her fears, but now that they were out in the open, she needed to talk about it, needed his reassurance.

"Do not be afraid for our little girl," he murmured, stroking Elena's hair. "She will survive. I can hear her heart beating, strong and steady."

Elena nodded.

"She already knows your voice," he said. "Whenever

you speak, her heartbeat speeds up a little. I know she is eager to see your face, to be in your arms."

His words brought tears to Elena's eyes. True or not, it was what she needed to hear. Content to be in his arms, she closed her eyes. How blessed she was, to have Drake in her life. What more could she ask than to spend the rest of her life with this incredible man?

What more, indeed, but a life as long as his. She stirred restlessly. She would not think of that now. She was still young. Old age was far in the future, yet she grew older every day. She had rarely given much thought to death. It was, after all, a fact of life. Unless you were a vampire. Tears stung her eyes. The day would come when her youth would be gone, and her health with it. What would become of them then?

"What troubles you now, wife?"

"Nothing," she lied.

Sitting up, he used the pads of his thumbs to wipe the tears from her eyes. "Since when does nothing make you weep?"

"I'm pregnant," she said, sniffling. "I'm always weepy these days."

"I can feel your sadness." His gaze searched her face. He could see it clearly, even in the dark. "Do I need to read your mind to find out what is bothering you?"

"I'd rather you didn't."

"Then tell me."

"What's going to happen to us when I start to get old and you don't? Will you still love me then? Will you still want me?"

With a sigh, he turned on the bedside lamp, then drew her up beside him, his arm circling her shoulders. Fool that he was, he had put the future out of his mind, content to live in the present with the woman he loved.

Fighting back her tears, she eased out of his embrace.

"Elena . . ."

She shook her head. "You don't have to say anything." Did she really expect him to stay with her, be content to be with her, when she was seventy or eighty and looked it, and he was still a virile male with the face and body of a thirty-year-old?

"It does not have to be like that," he said quietly. "There are ways . . ."

Eyes widening in horror, she scooted backward. "I don't want to be a vampire."

"You cannot become what I am. As I told you before, I was not made a vampire. It is what I am. But there are ways to prolong your life. Your youth. You are young yet. We have years before you need to decide."

"What ways?" she asked, curiosity mingling with revulsion.

"If you drink from me, it will slow the aging process, so that with the passing of each year, your body will only age one day."

"How often would I have to drink your blood?"

"Every night for the first year, then every week, then every month, then only once a year for as long as you wish."

"And when I stop drinking?"

"You will begin to age normally again. But, as I said, you needn't worry about it now." Reaching out, he took her back into his arms, aligning her body with his. "Whatever you decide, I will never leave you. Do you understand? Never. If you choose to live a normal span of years, I will be at your side. The last face you see will be mine, I swear it."

It was a lot to expect of any man, Elena thought, but Drake was not really a man.

"So, wife, have I set your mind at ease?"

"Yes, I guess so." The thought of drinking blood was

repulsive, but to age only one day for each year she lived . . . The idea was mind-boggling. Could it be true?

"It is a carefully guarded secret," Drake said. "You must never tell anyone."

She nodded. If people knew there was a way to live practically forever, they would be hunting vampires relentlessly for their blood. Greedy men would make a fortune selling it. People would kill for it.

"So, no one else—no other human I mean—knows about it?"

"None living."

"But others have done it?"

"Yes."

"What happened to them?"

"There have only been five that I know of. One grew weary of living and reverted to being human. Three died in accidents. One was killed when she decided to share her knowledge with the world. When her vampire mate discovered her intent, she was destroyed."

Elena nodded. "But the blood . . ." She shuddered in revulsion.

"It is a small price to pay for immortality, is it not?"

Elena thought about what Drake had said the next morning while doing the laundry. What would it be like, to live virtually forever? She had asked Drake a similar question once before. His reply had been that it could be challenging after a few hundred years because, by then, one had seen everything and done everything.

She tossed a load of damp clothes into the dryer, piled another load into the washer, added soap and fabric softener as she considered something else Drake had said when she'd asked him about living so long. He had told her that vampires sometimes buried themselves in the ground. To rest. Buried alive, she thought with a shudder.

Still, it would be nice to be virtually indestructible, she mused. If she was a vampire, she could do all the things she was afraid to do, like scuba diving and skydiving and rock climbing. But she couldn't become a true vampire. Not that she really wanted to be one, of course.

But living for centuries, that was within her grasp, if she could just overcome her disgust at drinking blood. She sighed. Maybe it wouldn't be so bad if it was Drake's blood. . . .

She shook her head. It would still be disgusting, she thought. If she didn't have to drink it directly from Drake, maybe she could mix it with a little wine to make it more palatable. But, palatable or not, it would be worth it if it meant a longer life with the man she loved.

Going upstairs to the main hall, she opened the door and peered outside. It was snowing again.

She stood at the door a moment, watching the tiny white flakes settle on the trees and the ground. She had been cooped up inside for days. She was wondering if she dared go outside, just for a few minutes, when a movement to her right caught her eye. Before she could register what she was seeing, a hand clamped a rag over her nose and mouth, stifling her startled scream. Her nostrils filled with a sickly sweet smell, and then everything went blank.

Chapter 35

Elena awoke, not knowing what had happened or where she was, only that she was cold. A quick glance at her surroundings showed that she was in a wooden shed of some kind. Pale sunlight filtered through a small, dirty window set high in one wall. A chill wind howled outside, rattling the door, creeping through the cracks in the old building, making her shiver.

A shiver born of fear rather than the cold slithered down her spine when she realized her hands were tied behind her, and that the brown lump in the corner was moving, standing.

As Elena's vision cleared, a scream rose in her throat, but no sound emerged.

Hatred mingled with lust in Tavian Dinescu's sunken eyes. And then he slapped her. "You little whore," he said with a sneer, and struck her again, harder this time.

Elena's head snapped back, her ears ringing from the force of the blows.

She stared up at him, fear turning to raw terror when she looked into his eyes—his crazy mad eyes. He was going to rape her, here and now, she thought. And then he was going to kill her.

"My baby . . . please . . . don't . . ."

"Shut up!" Grabbing the cuffs of her maternity jeans, he jerked her pants down over her hips, leaving them bunched around her ankles. Her panties followed.

She was sobbing now, alarm for her unborn baby clawing at her mind as Dinescu shoved her down on the floor. Her bound hands dug into her back, but she was hardly aware of the discomfort. She rolled onto her side in a vain effort to crawl away, but it was impossible with her hands tied. Impossible because there was nowhere to go.

She cried out when his fist slammed into her side and then he was flipping her onto her back again, his lips pulled back in a leer. He hit her again, his enjoyment plain on his face as she screamed.

He was going to rape her. *I will have you.* His threat, issued not long ago, echoed in the back of her mind. Whatever he did, she had to endure it, she thought, had to survive for the sake of her baby. And even as the thought crossed her mind, she knew the baby would likely die from her uncle's brutal assault. If that happened . . . She thrust the thought from her mind. She had to survive, for her baby. For Drake.

She squeezed her eyes shut when Dinescu shrugged out of the bulky coat and began unfastening his trousers.

This couldn't be happening, she thought desperately. It had to be a nightmare. She would wake up soon to find Drake beside her.

She cried out when her uncle lowered his bulk over her. *Please*, she prayed fervently, *please spare my baby*.

Tears leaked from her eyes as her uncle's hands moved over her, his touch repulsive, each stroke making her feel dirty, defiled.

She tried to dislodge him, tried to avoid his slobbery kisses, but he was too heavy, too determined, and with her hands tied behind her back, she was helpless. His foul breath made her sick to her stomach, his touch revolted her. Hot, bitter bile burned the back of her throat, and spewed between her lips when his mouth covered hers.

With a harsh cry of dismay, Dinescu reeled back.

Elena turned her head to the side, gasping for breath. Out of the corner of her eye, she saw Dinescu raise his fists to strike her again. Abandoning all hope, she closed her eyes and prayed for mercy.

But the blow didn't fall.

She heard a hoarse cry, a sharp crack, like a bone breaking. Curious, she opened her eyes a little, squinting to see what was happening.

Relief washed through her when she saw Drake. He was here. She was safe. A flood of tears released the tension in her body as he reached for her.

"He will never hurt you again," Drake said, lifting her to her feet, gathering her in his arms. "On my life, I swear no one will ever hurt you again." He quickly untied her hands. Swinging her into his arms, he held her close. Keeping her face turned away from the body sprawled on the floor, he carried her out of the shed, then transported them into the castle. He would go back later to dispose of the body.

He kept a tight rein on his anger as he gently lowered Elena onto the sofa in front of the fireplace, covered her with the afghan, then started a fire in the hearth. He stood there a moment, gazing into the flames, his hands clenched at his sides. Dinescu would never know how lucky he had been, Drake thought. If not for his concern over Elena and what she might think if she knew what he was capable of, he would have torn the man limb from limb and taken pleasure in his anguished screams.

"Drake?"

Wiping his face clean of emotion, he turned to look at her, his gut twisting at the sight of her face, swollen and black-and-blue where Dinescu had hit her. "Do you need something? Aspirin? A cool cloth? Something to drink?"

She shook her head. "How did you find me?"

"I woke up and knew you were gone. I could sense your fear. I followed it to where you were."

"But it's daytime."

"I was never outside." He had transported himself from the castle to the shed. But he would have come after her even if he'd had to cross a desert at midday to find her. Would have walked through the hottest fires of hell itself to bring her home. Kneeling on the floor in front of the sofa, he took her hands in his. "Are you all right?"

"I think so. The baby . . ."

Eyes narrowed in concentration, he pressed one hand over her womb.

"Is she . . . ?" Elena bit down on her lower lip.

"All is well. Her heartbeat is strong and steady."

Fresh tears welled in Elena's eyes. "If you hadn't come in time . . . if . . ." Her tears turned to sobs as the full horror of what had happened, what *could* have happened, set in.

Sitting on the sofa, Drake gathered her into his arms, blanket and all, and rocked her back and forth. "It is over," he said, his voice low, soothing. "He is dead. Our daughter is unharmed." He spoke the last words, hoping they were true.

Elena nodded, her body trembling uncontrollably.

"Elena, beloved, look at me."

Capturing her gaze with his, he spoke to her mind, his

voice quietly calming her as he assured her that he loved her, that she was safe, until she fell asleep in his arms.

Elena awoke with a groan. Her body ached, her face felt swollen where Dinescu had hit her, but those weren't the pains that had roused her from sleep. She pressed a hand to her stomach. Was she having contractions? A gasp of alarm speared through her. It was too soon for the baby to come.

"Elena?" Awakened by the sharp intake of her breath, Drake sat up.

"The baby, I think she's coming."

He glanced at the hearth, igniting a fire to warm her.

"Drake!" She clutched at his hand. "It's too soon."

He swore softly. Had the trauma she'd experienced at her uncle's hands caused this?

She bent over, her arms wrapped around her middle. "You need a doctor," he said. And the best one he knew was one of the drones at the Fortress. A look smothered the fire in the hearth.

Gathering Elena into his arms, he kissed her cheek, then transported the two of them to his apartment at the Fortress. After tucking her into bed, he opened his senses, then summoned the doctor to his room.

The drone, known as Doctor Samuels, arrived moments later, medical bag in hand. A word released the drone from the thrall that bound him.

"My wife appears to be in labor," Drake said, gesturing toward Elena. "See to her."

With a nod, the doctor went into the bathroom and washed his hands, then returned to the bedside. He took Elena's vitals, asked a few pertinent questions, then drew back the covers to examine her.

Drake stood beside the bed, his arms crossed over his

chest. He had not prayed often in his life, but he prayed now, prayed fervently for a miracle.

The doctor was still examining Elena when someone knocked at the door. Before Drake could open it, Liliana stepped into the room. She didn't say a word, merely moved to stand on the other side of the bed.

The doctor pulled the covers over Elena, then looked at Drake. "She's in the early stages of labor," he confirmed. "I will need some hot water and several clean sheets."

"I will get them," Liliana said, and left the room.

"You may want to help her into a clean nightgown," the doctor said.

Drake nodded. "Wait outside."

After the doctor left, Drake pulled the covers from the bed, then undressed Elena.

She looked up at him, her eyes wide. "I'm scared."

"I know." He found a clean gown in one of the dresser drawers and slipped it over her head, then covered her with one of the blankets. "Samuels is one of the best doctors in the world."

She grimaced at the onset of another contraction. "Why didn't you free the drones when you freed the sheep?"

"I honestly did not think of it."

"You should. It isn't fair to keep them here. Or to keep one of the world's best doctors imprisoned when he could be helping lots of people instead of the few who live in the Fortress."

"Yes, wife."

"But I'm glad he's here now." Elena choked back a groan. "It hurts," she wailed, clutching her stomach. "I didn't think it would hurt so much."

Liliana entered the room just then, with the doctor at her heels. She carried several folded sheets; the doctor carried a basin of hot water.

"Drake," Liliana said, dropping the sheets on the foot of

the bed, "I think you should wait outside. Having a baby is women's work."

"No!" Elena exclaimed, grabbing one of Drake's hands. "Stay with me!"

"Whatever you wish, wife," he said, squeezing her hand.

With a humph, Liliana said, "Then at least get out of the way so the doctor can do his job."

"He can work around me. I'm staying right here."

Liliana glared at him.

Drake looked at the doctor. "Is everything all right?"

"Her labor has accelerated," Samuels said.

Elena moaned as her contractions came harder, faster. She clung to Drake's hand, her nails biting into his palm.

"Push," the doctor said.

Elena squeezed Drake's hand harder, a low groan rising in her throat as she labored to bring their child into the world.

Unable to bear seeing her in pain, Drake wrapped his mind around hers, shielding her from the worst of it with his preternatural power.

"We're almost there," Samuels said. "I see the head."

Elena's body tensed and then, taking a deep breath, she pushed as hard as she could.

"That's right," the doctor said. "Just one more push and you can hold your baby in your arms."

Drake wiped the perspiration from her brow. "You can do it, sweeting," Drake said encouragingly.

Elena stared up at him, her hand clutching his as she expelled the infant from her womb in a rush of water and blood.

"It is a girl," Liliana murmured. "A perfectly beautiful little girl."

Leaning down, Drake kissed Elena on the cheek, then whispered, "I love you, wife."

She smiled up at him. "I want to see her."

"The doctor is cleaning her up. She is beautiful," Drake said, "but not as beautiful as her mother."

Moments later, washed and wearing a clean gown, Elena was sitting up, her daughter cradled in her arms. "She's so tiny." She looked up at the doctor. "Is she all right?"

"She's strong and healthy, her lungs are clear, her heart rate is good. I don't foresee any problems."

"Thank you."

"Doctor." At the sound of Drake's voice, the doctor turned to face him. "You will return to your quarters until you are needed." There was a note of command in Drake's voice.

"Yes, Lord Drake," he said, his voice a monotone. Bowing his head, he left the room.

Elena pressed a kiss to the baby's brow, then smiled up at Drake. "She's beautiful," she murmured, running her fingers lightly over the baby's thick black hair. "I wonder if her eyes will stay blue, like yours." She looked up at Drake's mother, who stood near the bed, a rapt expression on her face as she gazed at the baby. "Would you like to hold her?"

"May I?"

"Of course."

A smile spread over Liliana's face as she took the baby in her arms. It was, Elena thought, the first genuine smile she had ever seen on the other woman's face.

"You beautiful little thing," Liliana crooned. "How I wish your grandfather was here to see you." A single scarlet tear trickled down her cheek. "He would have adored you."

Elena glanced at Drake, astonished by the gentleness in Liliana's voice, the love that shone in her eyes.

"Have you chosen a name for her?" Liliana asked.

"Yes," Elena said, smothering a yawn. "Kaitlyn Liliana, after her grandmothers."

Liliana looked at Elena, astonishment clear on her face, and then she looked at Drake. "You are going to name her . . . after me?"

He was as surprised as his mother, perhaps more so, but he managed to hide it. "You are part of the family, after all."

"Thank you, Drake. Elena." Blinking rapidly, Liliana handed the baby to Drake and vanished from the room.

"What was that all about?" Elena asked. "Why did she leave so suddenly?"

"I am not sure," Drake said, "but I think you may have just found the chink in my mother's armor."

Elena slept most of the rest of the day. Toward evening, Andrei and Katiya came to see Elena and the baby. Elena couldn't help feeling a little guilty that Kaitlyn was strong and healthy when Katiya's son hadn't survived.

"She is lovely," Katiya said with a wistful smile. "May I hold her?"

Elena nodded. "Of course." She noted the sadness in Katiya's eyes, the regret in Andrei's.

Katiya cradled the baby in her arms, but only for a moment. Elena couldn't imagine what she would have done, how she would have felt, if Kaitlyn hadn't survived. Her daughter was only a few hours old, and yet Elena already loved her beyond words, had loved her even before she was born.

Andrei and Katiya didn't stay long. Murmuring that Elena was probably tired, Katiya placed the baby in her arms, then quickly turned away, but not before Elena saw the tears in her eyes.

Andrei paused at the door. "Have you decided when to have the ceremony?" he asked.

"We will let you know," Drake said. "Thank you for coming."

When their visitors had gone, Elena glanced at Drake. "What ceremony?"

"It is customary to hold a naming ceremony a week after a child is born."

"I see." She smiled as she stroked the baby's tiny hand. "Are we supposed to send invitations?"

"No." He sat on the edge of the bed. "We will tell the Council when we decide on a date, and they will spread the word to the others in the Fortress."

"*Everyone* is invited?"

Drake nodded. "There is nothing for you to do," he said, lightly stroking his daughter's downy cheek. "It is a simple ceremony, merely a way of introducing our daughter to the residents of the Fortress."

"How many are there?"

"It varies. There are usually forty or fifty here at any given time." He paused, his expression melancholy. "I would have liked Stefan to be here."

"Isn't there any way for you to get in touch with him?"

"No."

"He's your favorite brother, isn't he?"

Drake nodded. As the oldest, he had always felt duty-bound to look after his little brother. Because Stefan was the youngest, there had been little competition between them.

"Hmm. It seems odd that you can read mortal minds, but not those of your own kind."

"You think so? Would you like to be able to read the minds of your family members? Or have them read yours?"

Elena thought about it a minute, then shook her head. "No, I guess not. But I'd like to be able to read your thoughts."

He grinned at her. "If there is anything you wish to know, wife of my heart, you have only to ask."

"How long are we going to stay here?"

"Until after the naming ceremony."

"I hope Katiya will be all right. She looks so unhappy."

"Her sadness will lessen, in time. They will try again next year."

Elena sighed, wishing that everyone could be as happy as she was. "I miss Stefan," she murmured. He wasn't only Drake's favorite, but hers, as well.

Drake nodded. "Sooner or later, he will come home." It might take years. It might take centuries, but sooner or later, Stefan would have to come home. It was in his blood.

Elena glanced at her daughter, sleeping peacefully in her arms. "Do you think we'll be able to get pregnant again?"

"I do not know," he said, waggling his brows at her, "but I am willing to try as often as you wish."

Chapter 36

In spite of all that Drake had told her, Elena wasn't sure what to expect when they went to the naming ceremony a week later. Drake wore a pair of black slacks, black boots, and a blindingly white shirt. Elena wore a dress of delicate white lace that had been a gift from Liliana. The baby wore a long white silk gown, also a gift from Liliana.

Entering the Council room, Elena saw that the members were all present. Like Drake, the Council members and male guests wore black trousers and white shirts. The women were all dressed in white gowns. What must have been a hundred white candles lit the room with a warm glow.

Katiya smiled reassuringly at Elena.

Drake took his place on the dais, with Elena seated at his right and Liliana at his left.

"We are gathered here to celebrate the birth of my daughter, and to give her a name, that she might be recognized throughout our Coven." Turning, he took the baby from Elena. Lifting his daughter in his arms, he said, "From this day forward, this child shall be known as Kaitlyn Liliana Sherrad, daughter of Drake Sherrad and Elena Knightsbridge Sherrad, granddaughter of Liliana Sherrad." He smiled down at his daughter, who stared up at him through wide blue eyes. "Welcome to our Coven, Kaitlyn Liliana. May your life be long and filled with peace and happiness."

One by one, those in the room came forward and swore to protect Kaitlyn and reaffirmed their allegiance to Drake. And then, one by one, they welcomed Elena to the Fortress. It seemed odd, considering all that had happened before, and yet, their softly spoken words of welcome made her feel as if she did, indeed, belong.

Elena was ready to go back to their apartment when it was over. The birth had been difficult and she still tired easily.

She tucked Kaitlyn into her crib and then, stifling a yawn, Elena climbed into bed.

"What did you think?" Drake asked, drawing the covers over her.

"It was very moving," she replied. "For the first time, I feel like I belong here."

"Of course you belong," he said, kissing her on the forehead. "You will always belong wherever I am. Rest now."

Late that night, after Elena had fallen asleep, Drake left the Fortress. Standing outside on a snow-covered bluff that overlooked the valley below, he lifted his head and for the second time in twenty-four hours, he offered a prayer, this one of thanks that Elena and the baby had survived.

Elena had asked about the possibility of more children, but as far as he was concerned, one was enough. He loved his woman too much to put her life at risk again.

Tomorrow night, he would free the drones. He doubted if any would choose to stay, but now that the sheep had been freed, there was little need for the drones. Releasing them would be the last step in abandoning a way of life that had existed for over a thousand years. But it was time. The world was changing.

He was about to return to the Fortress when the air around him shimmered. A moment later, his mother stood beside him. He studied her from the corner of his eye. She wore unrelieved black. Her face was paler than usual. Her pale blond hair fell like a mantle down her back and over her shoulders.

They stood together in silence for several minutes before she said, "I was not pleased when you defied your father's wishes and rescinded his annulment. I knew you did not love Katiya, but I felt she was right for you and hoped that, in time, you would forget Elena and learn to love one of your own kind." Pausing, she took a deep breath. "I see now that I was wrong. You would never have been happy with anyone else."

Drake stared at his mother. Stunned by her words, he couldn't think of anything to say.

"I envy what you and Elena have," Liliana went on quietly, still not meeting his gaze. "My marriage to your father was arranged, as is the custom among our people."

She stared into the distance and Drake had the feeling she was no longer speaking to him.

"I loved your father from the first time I saw him. He was handsome, as you are, strong and proud and stubborn. I knew he did not love me. I knew he would take other wives. There were times when he was cruel, and yet I stayed at his side. I wish now that I had told him I loved him, but I lacked the courage to say the words out loud. Perhaps because I knew he would not say them back to me." She shrugged. "It does not matter now. He is gone, and he will never know how much I cared for him. And now," she said, speaking so quietly he could scarcely hear her, "before I go, I want you to know that I love you, and that I am proud of you."

Knowing she was about to leave, Drake laid his hand on her arm. "What are you going to do?"

"What do you mean?"

"You know damn well what I mean. That little speech sounded a lot like a last good-bye."

She turned her face away, but said nothing.

"I have lost my sire," Drake said, his hand still holding her arm. "I will not lose you, as well. You have a grand-daughter who will need you, sons and daughters who care for you. I want your promise that you will not destroy yourself."

"And if I refuse to give it?"

"Then I will lock you in the dungeon until you come to your senses."

"You are more like your father than I thought," she retorted, but Drake heard the smile in her tone.

"I will not ask Elena to live in the Fortress," he said. "There are too many bad memories here for both of us. But I promise you we will come to visit often. And you are welcome to visit Wolfram whenever you wish, for as long as you wish."

"Drake . . ."

His hand tightened on her arm, his gaze drilling into hers. "I will have your promise before you go," he insisted.

"You have it," she whispered.

He nodded, and then he did something he had rarely done. He kissed his mother on the cheek. "Thank you."

"Thank you," she replied, her voice thick with unshed tears. "Good night."

He remained outside for several minutes, remembering the past, thinking of the future, and then he returned to his quarters. He had expected to find Elena asleep, but she was sitting up in bed, nursing their daughter.

It was, he thought, the prettiest sight he had ever seen in his life.

Elena smiled when she saw him in the doorway, and Drake knew he would ask nothing more of his existence than to go on loving her for as long as they lived.

When she held out her hand, he heeled off his boots, shrugged out of his shirt, then sat on the edge of the bed.

"How are you feeling?"

"A little sore, that's all."

Drake kissed her, then brushed a feather-light kiss across his daughter's downy cheek.

Elena felt a tug at her heart as she watched Drake kiss their daughter. "I was missing you."

"As I miss you," he murmured, "whenever we are apart."

"Tell me the truth. Do you think our daughter will be like you?"

"Yes. Vampire blood is strong. Our genes are dominant."

"So, they'll completely overshadow her humanity?"

"It's possible, but doubtful. I think her vampire side will prevail, though I doubt if her need to feed will be as compelling. I am guessing now, but I think that, because of her human half, she will always be able to eat mortal food and walk in the sun." He smiled as he ran his fingers through a lock of Elena's hair. "She may be weak in some areas, stronger in others, but I think our daughter will be blessed with the best of both worlds."

Epilogue

Eighteen years later

Glancing at the clock, Elena ran up the stairs. "Kaitlyn, do you know what time it is? If you don't hurry, you'll be late for school!"

"I'm ready, Mom," Kaitlyn said, smiling.

Elena paused in the doorway, momentarily taken aback as she stared at her daughter. Where had the years gone? It seemed only yesterday Kaitlyn had been a little girl, learning to walk, to talk, going to kindergarten for the first time. How had she grown up so fast? She was breathtakingly beautiful, with thick black hair and her father's deep blue eyes.

Elena blinked back her tears. They had been truly blessed. None of the things Elena had worried about had happened. Drake had told Kaitlyn early on about her heritage and the Fortress, and when she had expressed a desire to see it, they had gone there one year for vacation. Kaitlyn had loved the castle and the people in it, and had formed an instant bond with Liliana, a bond that continued to this day, Elena thought, but she wasn't surprised. Everyone who met Kaitlyn loved her.

And now she was about to embark on a journey. Today was her last day of high school. She was graduating tonight; tomorrow she was leaving for college in America. It was a day for celebrating. Andrei and Katiya and their children would be arriving after sundown, along with Liliana and a number of Drake's brothers. She wondered, not for the first time, what Stefan was doing. They hadn't heard from him since he'd left the Fortress so many years ago.

Elena walked her daughter down the stairs, other memories crowding her mind—ice-skating in the winter, swimming in the summer, picnics by the lake, horseback riding through the forest, shopping sprees in the city. She had taught Kaitlyn to cook. Drake had taught her to drive. So many happy recollections. Sometimes she wondered what she had done to have been blessed with such a loving husband and daughter. Kaitlyn had brought them nothing but joy. And now, too soon, she was leaving home.

Drake was waiting for them by the front door. Folding Kaitlyn into his arms, he kissed her cheek. "We will see you later."

"Sure thing," Kaitlyn said. "See if you can cheer Mom up, will you? She's crying again."

"I will take care of her," Drake promised.

Elena hugged Kaitlyn, then stood in the doorway, watching her daughter slide behind the wheel of Drake's new Jag. A cheerful wave, the roar of a powerful engine, and she was speeding away.

Her last day of school, Elena thought, and wondered again where the time had gone.

Drake closed the door, then drew Elena into his arms. "We knew this day would come."

"I know. But I didn't think it would come so quickly."
She looked up at him, sniffing back her tears. "What will
we do without her?" She had wanted more children, would
have loved a dozen, but it was not to be.

Drake had no answer for her. He loved his daughter with
all his heart, but Elena was the light of his life, the reason
for his existence. Though she had wanted more children,
he had been relieved when she failed to conceive again.
The thought of losing her filled him with quiet despair.
Needing her as never before, he kissed her deeply, felt her
willing response.

A thought carried them to their room. He undressed her
quickly, then shed his own clothes. Lifting her onto the
bed, he stretched out beside her, his body yearning for her
touch, his heart aching at the thought of losing her.

Elena clung to him, eager, as always, to be in his
arms. The fire between them burned as hot and bright
as it always had. In his embrace, she forgot everything
else. There was only Drake, his mouth working its familiar magic, his strong hands gentle as he caressed her,
arousing her; his voice deep and husky with desire as he
whispered that he loved her, adored her, couldn't live
without her.

She ran her fingertips over his face, traced the muscles
in his arms, rained kisses on his chest. She knew every
inch of his body as well as she knew her own. The passing
years had had no effect on him. His body was still firm and
well muscled. Without an ounce of fat. Soon, too soon, the
years between them would begin to show.

Elena pushed the unwelcome thought away, her lips
hungrily seeking his. When he whispered her name, she
nodded, and then smiled as she felt the graze of his fangs

against her throat, the sweet sensual pleasure of his bite that made their joining all the more exciting.

Moaning softly, she closed her eyes while waves of ecstasy rolled through her, carrying her away to paradise.

Later, lying in his arms, she smiled at him. "Thankfully, some things never change."

He nodded, his expression solemn as he gazed into her eyes. The years had been kind to her. Though she was almost thirty-nine, she looked ten years younger.

"Stay with me, wife," he said, his voice thick. "Onc lifetime will never be enough." His fingers tangled in her hair, as if to hold her close to him forever. "I cannot bear the thought of living without you."

She knew what he was asking. They had not talked of it since the night he'd told her that it was possible for her to extend her lifespan and then explained how it could be done. All she had to do was drink his blood—every night for the first year, then once a week, then once a month, then once a year. Doing so would slow the aging process, so that she would only age one day for every year.

At the time, with her whole life ahead of her, she had been certain she could never do such a thing. But that had been almost twenty years ago. Mortality weighed more heavily on her now. With each passing year, the thought of leaving him pained her more. Though she would have said it was impossible, her love for Drake had grown stronger, deeper, with every passing day.

"Elena." His voice was raw with emotion.

"You're right," she said, sliding the tips of her fingers back and forth over his lower lip. "One lifetime will never do."

"You mean it?" He drew back, his gaze searching her face.

She nodded, and then sighed. The decision, once made, seemed right.

"Elena!" His arm tightened around her, his dark eyes alight with happiness.

"Tomorrow night, after Kaitlyn leaves," Elena said with a smile. "Although I doubt if even an eternity in your arms will be time enough."

Dear Reader—

I hope you enjoyed Drake and Elena's story. Be sure to look for Kaitlyn's story, BOUND BY BLOOD, available now.

A big thank you to all of you who have taken the time to write or e-mail me. I look forward to hearing from you.

Thanks, also, to Maggie Shayne, for giving me a quote. I love her books.

Amanda
www.amandaashley.net

Don't miss BOUND BY BLOOD,
available now!

Chapter 1

Lake Tahoe, CA

Kaitlyn Sherrad rolled down the window of her baby blue Porsche and stared up at the log cabin set alone in the midst of a cluster of tall pines. As usual, her father had out-done himself. Last month, when he had come to the States for her graduation from college, he had asked her what kind of gift she wanted and she had said, facetiously, *Oh, nothing much, just a little summer place in the mountains.*

After pulling into the driveway and cutting the engine, Kaitlyn grabbed her suitcases from the backseat. Smiling with anticipation, she hurried up the narrow, winding, red brick path that led to the front porch. She quickly skipped up the stairs and unlocked the door.

Knowing her father, she wasn't the least bit surprised to find the living room already furnished. An off-white sofa with a high, curved back and a matching love seat faced each other in front of a rough-hewn stone fireplace. A deep mauve carpet covered the floor, flowered curtains hung at the windows. The tables were walnut, as was the large bookcase—already filled with books by her favorite authors—that took up most of one wall.

Dropping her suitcases beside the sofa, Kaitlyn explored the rest of the house—two large bedrooms with a connecting bathroom; a den, complete with desk, computer and printer, sofa and big-screen TV; a small kitchen with new appliances and a refrigerator filled with her favorites foods; a service porch equipped with a new washer and dryer.

She shook her head, a sting of tears behind her eyes. Being an only child, she had always been spoiled rotten, but this went far beyond the ballet classes and piano lessons her parents had provided when she was in grade school, the new wardrobe they had given her every year, the Porsche her father had surprised her with for her twenty-first birthday last year.

She had hoped her folks would spend the summer with her, but trouble at the Fortress had drawn them home. It wasn't always easy, having a father who was the Master of the Carpathian Coven. Sometimes, as now, his duties could not be ignored. Usually, her uncle Andrei handled things at the Fortress, but whatever the emergency had been, it had required her father's attention, which meant that her mother had gone, as well. To her knowledge, her parents rarely spent more than a few hours apart.

Kaitlyn sighed as she removed her sweater and tossed it over the back of the sofa. Someday, she hoped to find a man who would adore her the way her father adored her mother. A man who would live and die for her. A man she couldn't live without.

Picking up her suitcases, she carried them into the first bedroom and tossed them on the bed. This room was done in varying shades of green, with billowy white lace curtains. The twin windows looked out over a sparkling blue lake.

Kaitlyn shook her head. How was she ever going to express her gratitude for the love and kindness her parents had showered upon her? She had thanked them on numerous occasions in the past, but words seemed woefully inadequate. She knew they hadn't been altogether pleased with her decision to remain in California after she graduated from college, but they had accepted it without argument.

Feeling a little homesick, she opened the larger suitcase and began to unpack. Her folks had always treated her like a princess, but then, maybe that was natural, since she had been raised in an old stone castle in the heart of Romania.

She smiled as she hung her clothes in the closet.

All she needed now was a prince.

Chapter 2

Zackary Ravenscroft strolled through the main floor of the casino, stopping now and then to chat with one of the customers, pausing to answer a question here, to address a complaint there. He loved owning a nightclub, loved the excitement that filled the air, the rush of adrenaline that fired the blood of the patrons, the fact that no two nights were ever the same.

Zack had built the casino ten years ago, simply because he was bored and thought it would be a nice distraction. It was one of the best decisions he had made in the last six hundred years. Not only did the casino provide a hefty income, but the constant change in customers assured a steady supply of women. And Zack loved women—all women. Old or young, ugly or pretty, smart or not so smart, black, white, red, brown, yellow—it made no difference. He loved them all. And they loved him in every way imaginable.

Leaving the gaming tables behind, he strolled up and down the aisles of slot machines. He stopped a moment to watch an elderly woman playing one of the old dollar slots. From her shabby appearance, she appeared to be down on her luck and most likely using the last of her money in a desperate hope of hitting it big. He had seen it all before. Usually, he had no sympathy for those who plunked down their last five bucks in hopes of winning a fortune on the turn of a card. Sure, it happened from time to time, but no matter what the game, the odds were always with the house.

The old lady was muttering under her breath.

It took Zack a minute to realize she wasn't cursing but praying.

He frowned as he listened to the urgency of her words, heard the unshed tears in her voice as she sent a desperate plea toward Heaven.

Zack grunted softly. Her husband was sick. He needed an operation, and medication they could no longer afford. She had lost her job. They couldn't pay the rent.

She needed a miracle.

Murmuring a breathless, "Amen," she shoved her remaining three dollars into the machine, then clasped her hands to her breast.

With a bemused shake of his head, Zack concentrated on the wheels of the slot machine.

One gold bar.

Two.

Three.

Smiling, Zack moved on as the machine lit up and bells and whistles went off, signaling that a player had hit the ten-thousand-dollar jackpot. So, he had lost ten grand, he thought, but it wasn't much to pay for a miracle.

He was still smiling when he stepped outside. It was a beautiful night. Cool and crisp. A few scattered clouds drifted across the face of the full moon.

Feeling suddenly restless, he wandered away from the casino, crossed the parking lot, and headed for the wooded hillside that began just beyond the blacktop.

He moved soundlessly through the underbrush, his keen senses aware of the tiny night creatures that scented a predator and quickly scurried out of his way. He caught the scent of a skunk and farther on, that of a deer.

Nearing one of the cabins, he came across a black bear scavenging through a trash can. The bear reared up on its hind legs and sniffed the wind. Apparently recognizing Zack as a threat, the animal dropped back down on all fours and lumbered into the trees.

Grinning, Zack continued on until he came to the solitary cabin at the top of the hill. He paused, surprised to see there were lights on in the house. A plume of gray smoke rose from the chimney. The cabin had been vacant for the last two years. He had, in fact, been thinking of buying the place for a rental.

Ah, well, too late now.

He was turning away when he caught the scent of prey. Glancing back, he saw a young woman looking out the front window. He whistled softly. He had seen a lot of beautiful women in his day, but this one—he shook his head. She was beyond beautiful. Her skin was smooth and unblemished, her eyes a deep dark blue. Hair the color of a raven's wing tumbled over her shoulders.

He frowned when her gaze found his, and then shook his head. She couldn't see him, of course. He was hidden by the darkness. And yet he couldn't shake the feeling that she knew he was there, that she was staring at him, as he was staring at her.

Curious to see her reaction, he stepped out of the darkness into a shaft of bright moonlight.

He had expected her to gasp in surprise, call 911, or hastily move away from the window and close the curtains. Instead, she tilted her head to the side, her gaze moving over him from head to heel, much the way he studied a woman he was considering as prey.

Zack was contemplating what to do next when she moved

away from the window. Moments later, she was standing on the front porch, her arms folded under her breasts.

"What are you doing here?" she demanded.

Her voice was low, soft, and yet he detected a fine layer of steel underneath. He grunted softly. Most women would have been frightened if they looked out their window at midnight and found a stranger standing in the yard. But she wasn't the least bit afraid.

He had to admire that. Inclining his head, he murmured, "Good evening."

She lifted one delicate brow. "I repeat, what are you doing here?"

"Merely enjoying the night air," he replied with a smile. "And I repeat, good evening." He frowned, mystified by his inability to read her mind. It was a skill that had never failed him before and left him wondering if she was deliberately blocking him, and if so, how?

She huffed a sigh of exasperation. "Same to you."

"You're new in the area," he said.

Kaitlyn nodded. He must be a longtime resident, she thought, else he wouldn't be aware of that.

"It's a lovely house," he remarked. "I had intended to buy it myself."

"Sorry."

"No need to be sorry. Our town can always use another pretty face." He took a step forward, extending his hand. "Zackary Ravenscroft," he said. "But my friends call me Zack."

She descended the stairs. "Do you think we're going to be friends?" she murmured, taking his hand.

"I hope so."

"I'm Kaitlyn Sherrad."

He gave her hand a slight squeeze. "Kaitlyn."

She didn't know if it was the sound of her name on his lips, or the touch of his hand on hers that sent a shiver of excitement racing down her spine. Startled, she jerked her hand from his and took a step backward. Who was this guy? She had never experienced a reaction like that with any other man. Stranger still was the bewildering fact that she couldn't divine his thoughts. She supposed there were bound to be a few people whose minds she couldn't read; still, it was disconcerting. Was there something wrong with him, she wondered, or was the problem hers? She would have to ask her father about it the next time he called.

Needing time to ponder her odd reaction to Zackary Ravenscroft and her failure to read his thoughts, Kaitlyn bid him a quick good night and hurried up the stairs and into the house. She closed and locked the door, then stood there, her back pressed against the wood. Who was that guy?

Zack stared after her for several moments before he turned and headed back down the trail toward the casino.

Kaitlyn Sherrad was a puzzle, he mused, and he hated puzzles.